S0-ADT-088

TWO OF A KIND
Lori Copeland
Author of More Than Six Million Books in Print!

"I want you to keep your wild-haired mother away from my father!" Graham said.

"Really," Courtney replied coolly. "Would you care to clue me in on who your father happens to be?"

"Clyde Merrill."

"Oh, brother!" Courtney groaned, and rolled her eyes upward. "I should have known."

"I don't know what that's supposed to mean, but I demand that you prevent Bonnie from seeing Clyde again. Those two make a ridiculous pair, and it seems that it's going to be up to me to put a stop to it!"

"Up to you? Your father's seventy years old. Don't you think he has a mind of his own?"

"Ohhh, yes! He definitely does," the angry young man agreed. "I plan to stop some of his nonsense, starting with your mother! Now, if you're ready to discuss this logically, we might be able to come up with some solution. You surely aren't any happier about the situation than I am, are you?"

"As a matter of fact, I'm not, but it isn't *my* mother who's the problem. Your father has corrupted her!"

LORI COPELAND

TWO OF A KIND

LOVE SPELL NEW YORK CITY

LOVE SPELL®

August 1993

Published by

Dorchester Publishing Co., Inc.
276 Fifth Avenue
New York, NY 10001

Printed in the United States of America.

To every romance reader, ranging in ages May thru December—I offer this book to you with love, hoping in some small way it will express my gratitude for the letters, phone calls, and overwhelming support you have given my writing.

TWO OF A KIND

CHAPTER ONE

"Hot diggity! Am I ever glad that Clyde Merrill lives in this town!" Bonita Spenser's bright blue eyes glowed with an inner light this morning as she sat back and sipped her cup of coffee leisurely.

Courtney lowered the morning paper she was reading and glanced over at her mother disapprovingly. For a woman who would soon be sixty-eight years old, her mother showed no signs of slowing down. On the contrary; she wasn't even breathing hard yet!

"What time did you get in last night?" Courtney asked, her eyes drifting back to the women's section of the newspaper.

"Umm . . . two . . . three . . . I didn't look at the clock. Why?"

"You know that when you went for your check-up last month Dr. Raymond said you had to watch your blood pressure. You're supposed to be home by midnight," Courtney reminded her curtly. "You need your rest and here you are out carousing to all hours—"

"Carousing!" Bonita's indignant voice interrupted her. "Clyde and I were not out carousing! We had two drinks all evening." She thought for a moment, then added, "And that was between us!"

"You are fully aware of my feelings concerning Clyde," Courtney said tensely, flipping through the pages of her paper noisily. "Ever since you two 'found' each other again, you have completely disregarded anything that I have said . . . not to mention Dr. Raymond's warnings!"

"Oh, poo! Dr. Raymond's warnings can go hang. He's a stuffy old fuddy-duddy who hasn't had fun in years!" Bonita sniffed primly.

"Regardless, he is *still* your doctor and you should listen to what he says!"

"When it's time to check out, I'll go. Until then, I plan on living life to its fullest. Now stop buggin' me." The older woman picked up her coffee cup and took another sip.

"I'm not bugging you." Courtney tried to keep her temper under control. It seemed to her that their roles had been reversed the last few years, with Courtney trying to keep her mother under control instead of just the opposite. "I'm only reminding you that you have stayed out to all hours, you've missed your doses of medicine with amazing regularity . . ."

"That's the only regularity I've had in years," Bonita quipped with a twinkle in her eye.

". . . you've eaten pizza, tacos, barbeque ribs." Her daughter's voice droned on, ignoring her comment. "You've discoed, roller-skated, ridden on the back of that ludicrous motorcycle of Clyde's—which, I might add, he drives like a lunatic—" Courtney's voice broke off in exasperation. She looked at her mother helplessly, wondering what in the world she was going to do with a sixty-eight-year-old *delinquent!*

Bonita sat sipping her coffee, listening to her daughter's chastising voice and looking very much like a lawless child. Courtney's tone softened as she reached over and took her mother's hand.

"Mom, now look. I don't want to spoil your fun, but I'm afraid you're going to *kill* yourself. Or, rather, Clyde's going to do the job for you!"

A smile broke through Bonita's petulant features. "Isn't he a hoot!"

"Yeah, a real hoot," Courtney agreed glumly.

"Well, what do you want me to do?" the older woman asked disagreeably.

"I want you to act your age," Courtney said simply.

"Act sixty-eight years old?!" Her mouth flew open. "No way, José!"

"Mother!" Courtney's voice became angry. "You are going to stop this running around with that . . . that man! Clyde's too wild for you." She pleaded hopelessly. "You even said so yourself, now, didn't you?"

"I did?"

"Sure you did. You said when he was eighteen, he was the wildest boy in your town."

Bonita looked back at her daughter in annoyance. "That was over fifty-two years ago, Courtney!"

"Well, it doesn't look to me like he's changed one bit," her daughter defended.

Her mother sighed wistfully. "Oh, yes, he has. He's slowed down some."

Courtney stared at her in disbelief. "I'd certainly hope so! How old is he anyway!"

"Seventy."

"Seventy years old, and he acts like he's twenty!"

"Oh, for heaven's sake, Courtney! Why don't you go out and get a boyfriend of your own and stop worrying about me." Bonita shoved her empty cup away in annoyance.

"I don't want a boyfriend of my own!" Courtney returned sharply. "And we're not talking about me."

"Well, we should be. After all, you're nearly thirty years old yourself, dear, and it's way past the time that you should be settling down with a nice young man—"

"Let's not get into *that* discussion again, Mother! I'm perfectly happy with my life the way it is. I don't understand why you don't feel the same way about me. Why would you want one around cluttering up your life? Daddy's been dead over seven years now and you've been contented until that . . . that . . ."

"Clyde, dear. His name's Clyde. And who says I'm going to want anything but a mad fling with him?"

"Mad fling!" Courtney snorted disgustedly.

"I'm only in my sixties, Courtney . . . I'm not dead."

"You're going to be." Courtney shook her finger at her mother sternly. "You're both going to crash and burn on the motorcycle he drives!"

"He's a good driver," Bonita protested. "Why, just the other day we outran the fuzz on the freeway. You should have . . ." Her voice trailed off meekly at the frown of annoyance on Courtney's face.

"I can't believe you!"

"You're too serious, dear. I always told your father, 'Courtney's too serious about things, Frank.' You never did let yourself go and just have fun." She shook her head thoughtfully. "I don't know . . . maybe it was because we had you so late in life. As an only child you never really got to be with other children, and I think it's made you old before your time," she mused sadly.

"Just because I'm happy without a man in my life makes me *old* before my time? I don't want a man, Mother! I don't need one."

Bonita shook her head again. "Now I'm beginning to think that you're not only old, you're becoming addlebrained too! Don't you remember that nice boy—Mark— that you used to date? You two had a lot of fun together."

"I didn't like him," Courtney announced flatly.

"What about that nice man named Robert?"

"I didn't like him."

"Ted?"

"Ditto."

"Well, for goodness sake, why not?"

12

"He gritted his teeth. All the time, he gritted his teeth! Would you want to spend your life with a man who gritted his teeth all the time, Mother?"

Bonita thought for a moment. "All the time?"

Courtney nodded dismally.

"What about Jim?"

Courtney shoved back from the table and stood up. "He had a lisp when he talked. I felt like I was dating Daffy Duck."

"Oh, he did not! I met Jim on several occasions and he was a nice, rising executive. You're just too picky. Life's going to pass you by, and one day you're going to wake up and be an old woman," Bonita warned grimly.

Courtney turned accusing eyes in her mother's direction. "If I can manage to age at the rate you do, I've got at least a hundred more years to think about it."

"Go ahead, make fun, but one of these days some man's going to come along and make you enjoy life whether you want to or not. Mark my words."

"I would enjoy life, if you'd just let me! I spend half my time worrying about you."

"Well, you shouldn't. I was taking care of myself long before you ever came into the picture. Snazz yourself up a little bit and start looking for a husband," Bonita advised firmly.

"What's wrong with the way I look?"

"Oh, I don't know. You always look too prim and proper. You need to get you some flashy clothes, get your hair cut in one of the new, sexy styles . . ."

"There's nothing wrong with my hair!" Courtney's hand went up to the tight chignon she always wore her blond hair in.

". . . burn your bra. . . ."

Courtney groaned.

"Use more eyeshadow to make the blue of your eyes stand out. You're a pretty girl. Quit trying to hide it!"

13

"How did we get on this discussion!" Courtney exploded heatedly. "I thought we were talking about you."

Bonita looked instantly contrite. "I'm sorry, dear. It's just such a shame to see a lovely girl like you going to waste."

"Don't concern yourself about me wasting away, Mother!" Courtney washed her coffee cup out and set it on the drainer next to the sink. "Are you going to ride to work with me this morning?" she asked, changing the subject.

Bonita's face flooded with guilt. "There probably won't be enough business to keep us both busy this morning. Think it's okay if I come in late?" she asked hesitantly.

"Why?"

"Well"—Bonita grinned sheepishly—"I'm a little tired this morning, so if you don't mind, I think I'll go back to bed for a while. Clyde is coming by this afternoon to take me to lunch, so I'll try to be at work by eleven." She stretched and yawned sleepily.

"I hope Clyde realizes this is the third time this week he's taken you to lunch." Courtney wiped the table off, then pitched the sponge back in the sink impatiently. "Your lunch *hour* tends to run into *hours* lately."

"Too serious. You're much too serious," Bonita warned again as she pushed back from the table and stood up. "I'll see you later this morning, dear." She placed an affectionate kiss on her daughter's cheek as she walked past her.

Courtney shook her head tolerantly and returned the kiss. "You know you really don't have to come in at all today if you don't want to. I'm sure I can handle the shop alone." She loved her mother very much and felt bad sometimes when she had to scold her.

Scooping up her purse and lunch, Courtney let herself out the back door. The early-morning air seemed hot and muggy. Even the breeze off the ocean did little to relieve the sticky feeling she had as she got into her small used car and started the engine. Backing out of the driveway,

14

she headed the car in the direction of the small gift shop she and her mother had opened a year ago when they had moved from Indiana to the small tourist town in Florida. They had visited the small, sleepy town one year while they were on vacation and had immediately fallen in love with it. It faced the Gulf of Mexico, and its old buildings were steeped in history. When Frank Spenser had passed away seven years ago, it had taken Bonita some time to decide she wanted to pull up roots and move somewhere where the climate was warmer. This town had been her first choice when she finally made up her mind, and since Courtney had grown tired of her job as a beauty operator, she welcomed the chance to open a gift shop with her mother. For the last few years, life had been peaceful and serene, although Bonita had always seemed to have ten times the energy Courtney possessed. And, lately, since Clyde Merrill had appeared on the scene, life had taken on a quickening pace. Of all times for Bonita Spenser to run into an old flame, this had been the poorest of timing and the most unfortunate coincidence. Bonita had begun to be restless the last few months, looking for something more out of life than a quiet job and Saturday evening senior citizens' parties. Clyde was the last person in the world Courtney would have chosen as a companion for her. The mere mention of his name grated sharply on Courtney's nerves. And the fact that he insisted on calling Bonita "Bonnie" sent her into near fits! What gave him the right to take such a lovely, refined name and shorten it to his satisfaction! And his actions were certainly not those befitting a seventy-year-old man! Of course, apparently Clyde Merrill didn't consider himself seventy. On the contrary. In Courtney's opinion, he didn't even suspect it! He lived his life at a breakneck pace that made Courtney stand back with her mouth gaping in amazement. Bonita, who had always been a follower, let him lead her into all kinds of hair-raising activities. If he didn't break both of their necks, it wasn't for lack of trying! He was fast becoming a constant source of irritation to Courtney, and she didn't know what to do about it. If she had had any inkling that Clyde Merrill had moved here from Indiana, she would have avoided this town like the plague. The tales her mother had told her over the years of what the two of them used to do when they dated during their high-school days back in Indiana made Courtney shudder, although she had dismissed it at the time as only silly teenage stunts. Little did she know that neither one of them had changed one iota. Putting them together was tantamount to one monstrous headache!

Courtney pulled her car into the parking space in back of her shop and braked to a halt. Within a few minutes, she was inserting the key in the front lock and waving hello to one of the men who worked in the surf shop next door.

"Good morning, Rob!"

Rob Hanson glanced up from the surfboard he was working on and grinned flirtatiously. "Hi, Courtney. How's it going this morning?"

"Fine. It's kind of hot, isn't it?" she called back as she pushed the door open.

"It sure is. Nice day to be out on the beach. Are we going to try to work in some sun later on this afternoon?" His teeth flashed white against the dark tan of his face.

"I'll try, but it will depend on Mother." She waved once more and closed the door to the shop quickly. Rob thought he was God's gift to women. *All* women. He usually drove Courtney crazy with his ribald jokes and suggestive innuendoes. Granted, he *was* good-looking, but as far as Courtney was concerned, he was a definite bore.

The cool air of the air-conditioned shop washed over her as she put her purse away and slipped the carton of yogurt she had brought with her for lunch in the small refrigerator in the back room. It was stocked full of cold drinks, cheese, and fruit. Very rarely did Courtney or her mother leave the shop for lunch. That is, not until "Clyde."

Her eyes fell on the large cardboard box of shells that needed unpacking. Courtney sighed, then tied a colorful apron around her waist and started to work. For the next hour she worked steadily, pausing only long enough to wait on the few customers who drifted into the shop.

The bell above the door tinkled once more just as Courtney dropped one of the shell windchimes she had been trying to hang behind the counter. Crawling on her hands and knees, she pushed her way under a shelf, unconsciously presenting the new arrival with a startling view of her attractive backside.

"Be right with you," she called in a muffled voice as her fingers searched hurriedly around on the floor for the clasp on the windchime. When she heard no immediate reply, she tried again, thinking that the customer hadn't heard her greeting. "Just look around all you want. I'm sure something will catch your eye!"

She muttered irritably under her breath as she shoved deeper behind the counter, searching fruitlessly for her intended object. The customer still didn't make a sound. Assuming that he was taking her advice and looking through the merchandise, Courtney continued her search. Her bottom was sticking straight up in the air by this time and her temper was growing shorter by the minute.

"See anything you like?" she called again in a friendly voice, hoping the potential buyer would be patient.

"Possibly," replied a man's deep baritone voice.

"Well, just put it on the counter. I'll be through here in just a moment." A strained silence followed her words; the man was obviously intent on looking at the wares she was offering.

He cleared his throat. "Is Courtney Spenser in?"

"I'm Courtney. What can I do for you?" Since she was

17

already under the counter, she was determined to find the elusive object.

"Well, for starters, do you think I might talk with you . . . uh . . . face to face?" His voice sounded a little tight.

Courtney frowned, then her eyes widened knowingly as she realized the position she was crouched in. A faint touch of pink rushed to her cheeks as she slowly pushed herself back out from under the shelf and got to her feet. Her gaze encountered the bluest pair of eyes she had ever seen.

"I-I'm sorry," she stammered in embarrassment, wiping her hands on her slacks—something she rarely did. She extended a clean hand to the tall stranger. "May I help you?"

"Are you Bonnie Spenser's daughter?" he asked rudely, ignoring her outstretched hand.

"Yes, I'm *Bonita's* daughter." Courtney's hand fell down limply to her side. "What about it?" He had put her immediately on the defensive by his superior attitude. "And, I repeat, my mother's name is *Bonita, not 'Bonnie'!*"

"I want you to keep your wild-haired mother away from my father," the man stated emphatically.

Courtney's mouth dropped open. "What!"

"I said," he began again tensely, "I *want* you to keep your mother away from my father!"

"Really," Courtney replied coolly. "Would you care to clue me in on *who* your father happens to be?"

"Clyde Merrill."

"Oh, brother!" Courtney groaned and rolled her eyes upward. "I should have known."

"I don't know what that's supposed to mean, but I demand that you prevent Bonnie from seeing Clyde again." The blue of his eyes flashed angrily at her as she stood staring back at him wordlessly. "Those two make a

18

ridiculous pair, and it seems that it's going to be up to me to put a stop to it!"

"Up to you?" Courtney finally found her voice. "Your father's seventy years old! Don't you think he has a mind of his own?"

"Ohhh, yes! He definitely has a mind of his own," the angry man agreed. "It does anything it desires at the present, but I plan on putting a stop to some of his nonsense, starting with *your* mother!"

"Look, Mister . . ." she searched for a name.

"Graham Merrill, and don't take that hoity-toity tone of voice with me! I'm taking valuable time to come by here and talk to you this morning and I don't plan on argu—" He stopped in midword. "What do you think you're doing!" he demanded.

Courtney had dropped back down on her knees and crawled back under the counter. If that pompous ass thought she was going to stand there and listen to his ultimatums, he had another think coming!

"Hey! You! Get back up here!" he ordered in a gruff tone.

"Sorry, I have a business to run, Mr. Merrill. If you can't control your own father, then I'm sure I can't! I have enough problems of my own without taking on any of yours," Courtney told him in a muted voice as she resumed her search. She would go on the theory that if she ignored him, he would go away.

The feel of a large hand grasping her around the ankle and pulling her back out from under the counter made her gasp in angry indignation. "Get your hands off me," she threatened, swatting at his grasping fingers angrily.

"I believe we were having a conversation, *Miss Spenser,* and although your fanny is more pleasant to look at right now than your scowling face, I prefer to look you in the eye when I talk to you," he said firmly as he reached down and grabbed her waist, pulling her to her feet roughly.

"Now, as I was saying," he continued pleasantly as she glared at him disbelievingly, straightening her clothes primly, "I think that you and I should take this matter in hand, and put a stop to it. What do you think we should do?"

"What do *I* think we should do!" Courtney choked out. "Well, how *kind* of you to ask!"

Graham shrugged his broad shoulders indifferently. "I'm a real nice guy. Now, if you're ready to discuss this thing logically, we might be able to come up with some solution." He paused and assessed her flushed face. "Surely you aren't any happier about the situation than I am, are you?"

"As a matter of fact, I'm not, but it isn't *my* mother who's the problem. Your father has corrupted her!"

"I don't doubt that a bit. Nevertheless, together they are a hazard to the community," Graham agreed. "People their age shouldn't . . . well, they should act like senior citizens instead of juvenile delinquents!"

"Well, it just so happens I agree wholeheartedly," she returned swiftly.

"Then what's the problem?" he asked curtly, his blue gaze skimming over the blouse she was wearing.

"It just so happens, I don't like the tone of your voice, Mr. Merrill."

"Tough. This isn't a social call. Now, do you have any suggestions? I'm in a hurry."

"For a start, why don't you take your father's motorcycle away from him?" she suggested tensely.

A frown of irritation crossed Graham's features. "I've tried. I even hid his keys the other day, but he got so mad I thought he was going to have a heart attack, so I had to give them back." For the first time since he had entered the store, Graham seemed to lose some of his confidence.

Courtney's attitude softened somewhat at the boyish look of frustration that came over his face. After all, what he was saying was the absolute truth. Bonita and Clyde *were* far too rowdy for their own good.

"Look . . . everything you've said is true," she relented, "but if you think that I can do anything about it, you're wrong! I've told Mother a thousand times to stay away from Clyde, but she just won't listen."

"Can't you *make* her?" he pleaded hopelessly.

"What do you want me to do, ground her?"

"Ground her, tie her to the bed, hell, I don't care what you do to her. Just keep her away from Dad!" He began to pace the floor, plotting feverishly as he walked. "Now, if we both agree to ride herd on them for the next few weeks, we can probably break this thing off nice and clean. Every time your mother goes out of the house, follow her. Don't let her out of your sight for five minutes."

Courtney placed her hand on her hip and glared at him distrustfully. "And what are *you* going to be doing in the meantime?"

He stopped pacing and placed *his* hand on his hip arrogantly. "What do you mean, what am *I* going to be doing! I'm going to be doggin' the old man's steps. If you think that's going to be an easy job, you're just plain nuts!"

"You're the one who's 'nuts' if you think this preposterous plan will work," Courtney told him tiredly as she turned back to finish unpacking the box of shells. "It just won't work."

"I didn't say it was going to be easy," he reasoned, "but it can work. All we have to do is be sure they're so busy that they'll forget all about each other in a few weeks."

"I don't think so," Courtney repeated in a knowing, singsong fashion.

"Well, aren't you even willing to give it a shot?" he petitioned angrily.

"I'm willing to give it both barrels if it will do any good, but I was merely pointing out to you that *it won't work!*"

"It will . . . I promise you it will," Graham vowed as he resumed his pacing.

Courtney couldn't help but notice that he was undeniably one of the best-looking men she had seen in a long time. If Courtney was guessing, which she wasn't, she would guess him to be in his late thirties. And, if she was interested in the color of his hair, which she wasn't, she would probably agree that it was a very attractive shade of light brown, almost blond. If she liked men with unusual blue eyes, she would have to admit that he had those, all right. Yes, the thought flitted across her mind briefly, *if* she was one of those silly women whose pulses pounded and heart raced at the sight of a tall, muscular man, that would probably be happening right now as she watched Graham Merrill pace back and forth in the small shop. Lucky for her that a man like that held no appeal for her. If he did, she would be in big trouble right now. He had all those things that make women's knees turn to water and cause them to do foolish things. The only imperfection she could see was his nasty disposition!

Once more he paused in his stride and looked at her skeptically. "What are you looking at?"

"Huh . . . uh . . . nothing. Nothing at all." Courtney was mortified that he had caught her staring at him.

Graham glanced down suspiciously at the front of his trousers, then back up to her. "There must be something! You've been staring at me for the last five minutes."

"You have an overactive imagination, Mr. Merrill," Courtney bluffed, turning back to her unpacking. For the first time in her life, she felt disconcerted being with a man. The deep, husky timbre of his voice when he spoke, the way she could see a small patch of curly brown hair peeking up over the top button of his sportshirt . . . all of these things suddenly made her feel very uneasy. "Now if you'll excuse me, Mr. Merrill, I have work to do."

"Fine. Then it's agreed? You'll do your best to keep

your mother busy, and I'll be sure Dad doesn't find time to call her." Graham walked over to stand next to her as she avoided meeting his gaze.

"Now, let me be sure I understand you, Mr. Merrill. I'm supposed to keep my mother away from your father, because *she's* a bad influence on *him*. I'm not to let her out of my sight for more than five minutes, and with a little luck, Bonita Spenser and Clyde Merrill will forget all about each other and act like the senior citizens they are instead of the rebellious teenagers *we* think they are. Right?"

"Right."

"You're a dreamer."

"It will work, I tell you," he said in exasperation.

"It will if we want to be their jailers, but personally, I have better things to do with my time."

"What do you have to do with your time? Dad said you were an old maid," he said bluntly.

"I beg your pardon!" Courtney's eyebrows shot up angrily. How dare he make such a . . . a . . . totally ridiculous statement! She wasn't an "old maid" and very much resented the accusation.

A small grin suddenly began to spread over his features as he turned those startling blue eyes on her and lazily inspected her slight form from top to bottom. There was something about the way he let his gaze rove over her, touching her in an almost intimate manner, that did indeed send her pulse racing. "A prim old maid," he followed up, still grinning devilishly.

Annoyed at the unusual rush of red to her cheeks, Courtney managed to keep her eyes averted from his, nervously piling shell on top of shell as she returned sharply, "I am *not* an old maid!"

"You're not married, are you?" His eyes traveled down the empty third finger of her left hand.

"No. . . ."

"Then, whether you like it or not, Miss Spenser, you *are* an old maid," he pointed out with just a touch of arrogance in his voice.

Courtney continued to pile the shells higher. "Just because I have made it a point to avoid men," she looked at him pointedly, "especially rude, ill-mannered men, and haven't chosen to marry, that certainly doesn't qualify me as an *old maid,* Mr. Merrill."

"Ah . . . now I've gone and made you mad." Graham faked an injured expression. "I'm sorry. I should have realized that a woman your age would not like the idea of being referred to as an old maid."

"A woman of my age?" Courtney knew she should never rise to his bait, but she was powerless to stop herself. "Just how old do you think I am, Mr. Merrill."

Graham met her flashing blue eyes calmly. "Forty-five?"

For the second time that morning, Courtney's mouth dropped open, her outrage preventing her from finding words to tell him just what a . . . a . . . bird brain she thought he was.

Reaching one large hand out, he tapped her chin shut with his fingers. "Did I miss?" he asked innocently.

"*Only* by fifteen years!" Courtney managed to stammer out indignantly.

"Well, shoot, I was close. I would have probably been ten years closer if you didn't wear your hair in that old ma—that style you're wearing it in," he defended with a half grin.

"Now *wait a minute!* What gives you the right—"

"Hey!" Graham threw his hands up in surrender. "I couldn't care less how you wear your hair. All that matters to me is that you do your job and keep your mother under lock and key. You can shave your head in a Mohawk if that pleases you. What are you building? The Empire State Building?" he guessed dryly as they both suddenly became aware of the pile of shells stacked before them.

Courtney's hand paused in midair, then a feeling of absolute disgust washed over her. To think this man could get her so disorganized and make her seem so inefficient made her blood boil! Thrusting the last shell down in extreme annoyance, she turned from Graham and walked swiftly away from him.

The sound of a car horn being tooted impatiently reached both their ears as Graham turned around automatically to follow her. Courtney's gaze wandered out the front window. A stunning blonde was sitting in the front seat of a conservative brown Ford, irritably leaning on the car horn.

Graham peered out the window, then turned back hurriedly to face Courtney. "Look, I have to go now. It's been nice meeting you and I trust you'll hold up your end of the bargain, Miss Spenser." He edged toward the front door, a frown on his features as the sound of the car horn filled the tiny shop once more.

"My, my, we *are* in a big hurry, aren't we?" Courtney heckled, delighted at the look of discomfort on his face.

"Yeah, well, just be sure you keep *her* away from Dad," he instructed again as he opened the door. "We'll have this thing under control in no time."

Courtney's smile was slightly wicked now as she answered rebelliously, "I'll *think* about it, Mr. Merrill."

"Don't think! Do it!"

As he was about to slam the door and hurry out to his impatient blonde Courtney yelled at him. "Hey, Mr. Merrill! I suggest you start your police action today. Clyde has a luncheon date with his wild lady this afternoon!"

With a frustrated nod of his head, he *did* slam the door.

That ill-mannered moron! Courtney sizzled as she watched the brown car pull away from the curb with a screech of the tires. Like father, like son!

Well, it so happens that she *would* keep Bonita away from Clyde Merrill, but *not* because of Graham's idiotic demands, but because she wanted to see this twosome split up herself! If it meant that she would not have to come in contact with Graham Merrill anymore, then this was a job—and granted, it would be one heck of a job—she would diligently work on to bring about the demise of one "Bonnie" and Clyde! She couldn't help smothering a giggle. "Bonnie" and Clyde! How appropriate!

CHAPTER TWO

What was left of the morning passed quietly as Courtney tried to dismiss the image of Graham Merrill from her mind, which was no easy task. Every time she thought of his rude, boorish behavior, she seethed anew. Who did he think he was, coming in here and ordering her around like that!

Bonita had mentioned that Clyde had a son, but Courtney had paid little attention to the fact. And, after meeting his little offspring this morning, she didn't care if she heard the name Graham Merrill ever again.

It was close to eleven thirty before her mother came breezing in the front door of the gift shop. A cloud of overpowering perfume seemed to hover in a thick haze around her as she threw her purse on the counter and gave her daughter a quick peck on the cheek. "Hi, sweetie! What's cookin'?"

Courtney wrinkled her nose in distaste and returned the kiss. "Nothing much. What kind of perfume are you wearing?" she asked, trying to keep from choking.

"I don't know the name of it. Some Frenchy thing. Why?"

"I don't like it, it's too strong," Courtney said disdainfully. She had always preferred a perfume with a light, floral scent.

"Clyde gave it to me. It's his favorite fragrance," Bonita announced proudly, waving her wrists in front of her daughter playfully. "And I happen to know it costs fifty dollars an ounce!"

"There's where two fools met," Courtney grumbled, avoiding her mother's flailing arms. Fifty dollars an ounce! That old geezer! They would have to *pay* Courtney fifty dollars to wear the overpowering stench!

"Clyde been by yet?" Bonita asked, undaunted by Courtney's opinion of her fragrance. She walked over to the mirror and straightened her hair. "The taxi was late picking me up," Bonita explained as she rummaged around in her purse, finally coming up with a tube of lipstick.

"No, I haven't seen him." Courtney watched with fascination as her mother slashed the bright-red lipstick lavishly across her lips. "Why do you wear such a bright color!"

Bonita never blinked an eye as she added more blush to her already rosy cheeks. "Because I like it. Why?"

"It's too loud."

"It's too strong . . . it's too loud . . . I can't ever please you!" Bonita scolded as she threw her makeup back into her purse and snapped the lid shut loudly. "I happen to like the way I look!"

"I didn't say you didn't look good," Courtney defended. "I just think you should dress a little less . . . flamboyantly. . . ."

"Dull. That's what you're really trying to say, isn't it? You want me to dress my age! Just plain dull!"

"No, Mother. Maybe just a little more conservative, for heaven's sake! After all, you are—"

"Don't say it!" Bonita threw up a protective hand. "I *know* how old I am!" Walking over to the glass window that faced the street, she peered out anxiously. "I wonder what's keeping Clyde. He was supposed to be here by one o'clock."

It was on the tip of Courtney's tongue to tell her mother that Clyde's ill-mannered son was what was most likely

28

"keeping" him, but she had enough common sense to realize that if this plan was going to work, Bonita had better never find out about her daughter's conversation with Graham this morning!

"Maybe he had a flat on his motorcycle," Courtney offered helpfully.

"Ummm . . . maybe," Bonita replied absently, "but that wouldn't hold him up for very long. He'd have a flat changed in a few minutes."

"Maybe he just didn't feel like coming over today," Courtney tried again. "After all, Mother, he's seventy years old! The man's bound to have a few off days!"

"Well, he does have a little prostate trouble," her mother agreed reluctantly.

"Mother! For goodness' sake! Do you discuss things that . . . that . . . personal with him?" Courtney was shocked.

"What? His prostate trouble? Well, of course! What's wrong with that?"

"Good grief! You shouldn't be discussing things like that with a man!" Courtney exclaimed.

Bonita dismissed her daughter's concern away with a wave of her hand. "If that bothers you, I'm not *about* to tell you what we discussed last night," she said pertly.

"Oh, brother! *What* am I going to do with you?" Courtney groaned.

"Why do you keep insisting on doing *anything* with me?" the older woman protested. "I think I'll give Clyde a call and see what's keeping—"

Courtney lunged for the phone, clamping her hand over Bonita's hurriedly. *"No!"*

Bonita jumped back in surprise, jerking her hand away sharply. "Why not?"

"Uh . . . you just can't. I've been having trouble with the phone this morning. You can't call out," Courtney

29

fabricated. "The phone company can't get it fixed until late this afternoon."

"Oh." Bonita's face fell in disappointment. "Well, maybe I'll just run next door and call him." She started toward the front door and was nearly knocked off her feet as Courtney rushed past her, falling across the front door protectively. "That's not a good idea either. All the phones are out . . . all over the block." She grinned guiltily. "Sorry." If she let Bonita out of her sight, Courtney would be taking the chance that her mother would be able to reach Clyde, even though Graham was supposed to be in control of his father. She was going to have to play it very safe and not let her mother out of her sight for a moment.

"All the phones?" Bonita asked incredulously.

"Every cotton-pickin' one of them!" Courtney's grin widened and became decidedly more sheepish.

Bonita eyed her daughter suspiciously. "You're acting rather strange this morning, dear. Is there something wrong?"

"No! Nothing!" Courtney replied swiftly. "Look, Mother, obviously Clyde isn't going to make it this morning. Why don't you run on down to the post office and get some stamps?" The post office was only a block down the street, and Courtney knew she could easily walk out on the sidewalk in front of the shop and watch every move her mother made.

"But he might just be running a little late," Bonita fretted, determined not to give up hope. "What if he comes when I'm gone?"

"If he comes while you're gone, I'll tell him you'll be right back," Courtney soothed, giving her mother a gentle push in the direction of the front door. "And while you're down that way, why don't you stop in and talk to that nice Mr. Curtis who runs the meat market," she encouraged.

"I don't like that man," Bonita said defensively as she found herself out on the street. "He's a groper!"

30

"He's a nice man, Mother! And I know for a fact he'd like to take you out sometime. He hints around about you every time I go in."

"Over my dead body! Going out with him would be like spending an evening with a masher. I may not be young and innocent," she admitted, "but I still like my men to at least be polite and respectful, Courtney!"

"It's only polite to stop in and say hello," Courtney persisted. Her mother could be *so* stubborn at times! "Pick up some shrimp for dinner and I'll make a big salad to go with it."

Bonita's face did indeed look very stubborn as she straightened her back and began to trudge off toward the post office. "All right, I *will* pick up the shrimp for dinner, but I'm leaving the other 'shrimp' alone!"

Courtney smothered a smile as she watched her mother flounce down the sidewalk, muttering under her breath about the fact that Harold Curtis was *at least* four inches shorter than she was.

Breathing a sigh of relief, Courtney leaned against the door and watched Bonita make her way toward the post office. How she was ever going to keep her mother's mind off of Clyde Merrill the next several weeks, she didn't know. She was simply going to have to take one day at a time and hope that tomorrow would unfailingly take care of itself. Within a few minutes, her mother disappeared into a small building at the end of the block. Courtney watched for a few more minutes to make sure Bonita was safely at her destination, then went back into the shop out of the hot sun. It would take a little while for her mother to make her purchases and return to the shop.

The hands of the clock had crept steadily toward the noon hour as Courtney's stomach reminded her that breakfast had been hours ago. Deciding to eat her lunch while there was a break in customers, she went to the refrigerator and removed the carton of yogurt. Perched on a tall stool behind the cash register, she sat eating her lunch, savoring the creamy, cold goodness of the low-fat milk and mixed berries, idly rearranging a display of souvenirs in her mind. She wished it was five o'clock and time to go home. She was tired already and tonight held only the promise of running the vacuum and rinsing out a few pieces of lingerie. With a resigned sigh, she scraped up the last of the yogurt and pitched the empty carton in the wastecan. Maybe her mother was right. Maybe it *was* time for her to think seriously about finding someone to share her life with. Before, there had never been a need to consider anyone permanent, but lately the thought of having someone to come home to at night other than her mother had began to take on appeal. Not that she needed a man to lean on, because she didn't, not the way some of her friends seemed to! Too many times she had watched her friends run in and out of love affairs, blindly searching for . . . who knows what? And way too many times they had failed miserably. Courtney used to sit back and watch them, wondering why in the world they would ever want to try again, after the disastrous time they had just come through. But before she would know it, the friend would become involved in another torrid adventure, vowing that this time things would be different! Of course, that affair would fall through eventually, and Courtney would be faced with another period of time where she would try to convince the friend that there *really* was a reason to go on living!

Courtney had decided a long time ago that *her* life didn't need all those ups and downs . . . that she was perfectly content with the way she lived without the complications of a man. She hadn't met a man yet whom she would throw herself off a ten-story building for, and she seriously doubted that she ever would.

Her mind deviously conjured up a picture of Graham Merrill. Now *there* was a man who probably had every woman in town jumping out of windows! Not necessarily in pursuit of him, but as in her case, to get away from him. The nerve of that man barging in here like he did this morning and demanding that . . . Her thoughts broke off abruptly and she glanced up at the clock guiltily. Bonita had been gone over twenty minutes now!

Hoping that her mother had taken her advice for a drastic change and stopped in the fish market to visit with Mr. Curtis instead of madly rushing in and purchasing the shrimp then madly rushing out again, Courtney hurriedly hung the small "Out to Lunch" sign in the window and scurried toward the post office.

The hot noonday sun beat down on the sidewalk as Courtney hastened down the block, peeking in the different shop windows to see if her mother had decided to do some shopping on the way back to the gift store. When she reached the post office, she peered in the front window anxiously, her heart sinking when she saw that the room was empty. Only Harve Gibson, the postal clerk, was standing behind the counter, sorting through some letters. Harve looked up and smiled.

"Afternoon, Ms. Courtney. Sure is hot today, isn't it?"

"Sure is, Mr. Gibson," she agreed hurriedly. "Have you seen Mom today?"

"She was in here a little bit ago. Bought some stamps and—"

"Did you happen to see where she went when she left?" Courtney interrupted worriedly.

"Sure did," Harve acquiesced helpfully, leaning over to spit a stream of tobacco juice in a green-bean can he kept under the counter. "That feller she's been dating came by on that motorcycle he rides and they took off together like greased lightnin'."

"Oh, rats." Courtney slumped against the doorjamb, the heat of the warm July day making her clothes cling

33

like a second skin. "How long ago?" Bonita had given her the slip! Now what was she going to do?

"Not over five minutes ago. You just missed them."

"Five minutes!" What rotten timing. She mentally chastized herself for not walking her to the post office personally. When Mr. High-and-Mighty found out that she let her mother go off with Clyde, he would come storming back, and . . . wait a minute! Why was she so worried? *She* wasn't the one at fault. Apparently Clyde had given his son the old sliperroo. *Graham* had not been watching his father closely enough. Courtney had distinctly warned him that Bonita and Clyde had a luncheon date today, and he should have been on guard for this very occurrence!

Whirling around, she left Mr. Gibson talking to thin air as she stalked back off down the street, slamming loudly back into the gift shop. If Graham Merrill thought he was going to put the blame for this on her, he had better think again! She jerked up the phone book and started thumbing through the M's, rehearsing in her mind exactly what she was going to firmly, but diplomatically, tell him. *She* planned on being a bit more suave in the handling of this matter than *he* had been.

Running her finger down the long column of names, she read outloud, "Merlo, Merrell, Merrick, Merrifield, Merril, Merrill . . . D.D., Dorothy, Ernest, Graham. That's it, Graham Merrill, DDS." A dentist. It figures, she thought as she picked up the receiver and angrily punched out the number. From the moment she had met him, she knew he would be a pain in the . . . "Hello, may I speak to Dr. Merrill, please."

"I'm sorry, the doctor isn't in this afternoon. Would you like to leave a message?"

Would she like to leave a message? Boy, would she. But she didn't think that the receptionist would pass it on to her employer!

"It is imperative that I speak with Dr. Merrill immediately." Courtney used her most professional voice, hoping to bluff the woman. It was soon apparent, however, that the woman would not bluff easily.

"Is this an emergency?" the receptionist asked in a cool tone.

What was there about some people that made you feel ashamed of yourself for calling to bother them? "You might say that. It concerns *his* father."

"When you say *his,* I assume you're referring to *Dr.* Merrill?"

"That's *right.*" He must pick his office help on the basis of their mentality in comparison with his.

"If you'll kindly leave your number, I'll see if the doctor can be reached. This *is* his afternoon off. Dr. Willard is taking his calls."

"This is not a professional call," Courtney told her tensely. "I need to speak to Dr. *Merrill* personally."

"Very well. What is your number?"

"Tell him he can reach me at this number." Courtney rattled off a set of digets rapidly. "Got that?" She hoped she hadn't.

"I got it," the receptionist answered smugly.

"Can I expect to hear from the doctor soon?" Courtney strummed her fingers on the counter agitatedly. By now Bonita and Clyde could be in Georgia shelling peanuts!

"I will try to reach the doctor . . . Miss?"

"Just tell him Bonita's daughter called. That will light a fire under his Bunsen burner." Courtney slammed the phone down irritably. It would be easier to reach Ronald Reagan by phone than Graham Merrill!

Glancing down at her sticky blouse, Courtney frowned and pulled the material away from her skin, fanning some air down the front of it. Rarely would anyone catch Courtney Spenser looking so wilted. This day was turning out to be one in which she wished she'd never gotten up, and she attributed all her woes at the moment to a certain blue-eyed dentist.

The phone rang shrilly, making her lose her train of thought. Jerking up the receiver, she said curtly, "Yes?"

"What do you want?" an equally curt masculine voice responded.

Well, well, Courtney thought. If it isn't Mr. Personality here to spread his charm once more. "Why, Dr. Merrill. How nice of you to call. How's your father?"

"Are you serious? What in the hell is your game, lady?"

"Game? Why, whatever do you mean, Dr. Merrill? You seemed so concerned over *my* mother this morning, I simply thought it only courteous to return the favor. By the way, where *is* your father?" she asked sweetly.

"He went to pick up a carton of milk."

"Really? Well, he picked up a 'Bonnie' on the way." The sweetness had gone sour in her tone now.

"What!"

"That's right," she snapped. "Now, correct me if I'm wrong, but my understanding was that *you* were going to watch Clyde, eve-r-r-r-y little minute of the day. What happened, Dr. Merrill? Were you struck blind?"

"He what! He told me he was just going around the corner to the grocery store!" Graham bellowed. Courtney could hear some loud background noise over the phone. It sounded like there was a swimming party going on. "Why in the devil weren't you watching your mother?!"

"I was!" Courtney yelled. "And don't you *dare* take that tone of voice with me, you . . . you . . ."

"You're going to have to go after them," Graham shouted above the din of the party. "I'm tied up right now."

"Think again, mister. You're the one who insisted on this arrangement. If I have to go after them, you're coming too!"

"Hey, look, can't you handle this . . . ?" His voice broke

off momentarily and Courtney heard a high feminine squeal and Graham ordering people on his end of the line to quiet down. "I'm going to have to get off. I can't hear a word you're saying," he broke back in hurriedly.

"Well, I hope you can hear this!" Courtney practically screamed in the receiver. "You better get your duff over here . . . *now* . . . or as far as I'm concerned, the deal's off!" This man was the most infuriating person she had met in her entire life. No one had ever made her lose her cool as rapidly as he seemed to be able to!

"Cut the hysterics! I can hear you. I'll be over as soon as I can get away!" He slammed the phone down abruptly. Courtney winced as a loud pop came across the wire. Following his rude example, she slammed her receiver back in place, her face turning a bright red as she glanced up to see Rob Hanson standing before her, open-mouthed. By the look of confusion on his face, he must have heard the whole conversation! Graham Merrill was beginning to lower her to his repulsive level and she didn't like it one bit.

"Pesky salesman," Courtney excused lamely with a weak smile.

"Holy cow, Courtney, I heard you while I was still out on the street! What was the guy selling?" Rob gazed at her in bewilderment.

"A bunch of bull . . . manure," Courtney answered angrily.

"They're calling on the phone nowadays to sell bull manure?" Rob asked incredulously.

Courtney gave a fatalistic shrug of her shoulders. "What's going on, Rob?"

"Oh, nothing. I just thought you might be able to get away for a couple of hours and soak up some rays." His handsome face indicated he was not convinced the conversation he had overheard between Courtney and the "bull manure salesman" had actually taken place.

"I'm sorry, Rob, but I can't. Mom's not here right now to watch the shop," Courtney excused, her mind traveling back to the phone conversation. If Graham Merrill didn't get himself over here pronto then she was going to wash her hands of the whole mess.

"Can't you close the shop? There's very little business stirrin' right now," Rob persisted, coming around to prop himself down on the stool next to Courtney. He grinned persuasively. "It's terribly hot out there this afternoon, and the cool of the ocean would feel mighty good."

"Sorry, Rob, but I really can't. Something else has come up and I may have to close the shop anyway. Maybe another time."

"Are you sure?" He reached one long finger out and teasingly followed the outline of her nose. "I'm sure you would enjoy the break." His eyes were sending her a silent message that he would personally see to it that she did.

"I'm sure I would, but I'll have to pass," she said firmly as she brushed his finger aside. "Business first," she added with a bright smile. Brother, that's all she needed now. To spend the afternoon with Rob pawing her!

"I'm going to hold you to your word, Court. Another time?" His gray eyes pinned her seriously.

"Sure, another time." She was busily rearranging a stack of invoices, trying to avoid his penetrating gaze. Some women would be beside themselves if Rob would merely glance their way. Why couldn't she feel that way? Why couldn't she go all mushy inside when a man looked at her the way Rob was doing right now?

"Say." Rob stood up and reached for one of the several coffee cups that were kept under the counter. "What do you think about ol' man Stewart's remodeling ideas?" He walked over and poured himself a cup of coffee.

"I think they sound very expensive. I'm sure he'll have to raise the rent on every one of his tenants after he's through with the renovation project he has in mind."

Courtney watched as Rob stirred cream and sugar into his cup, wishing that he would go back to his own shop. She didn't want him there *if* Graham Merrill happened to show up.

"Yeah, but these old buildings could use some sprucing up. It will help business." He sat back down on the stool and sipped at the hot liquid. "Boy, this is strong. I hope you cook better than you make coffee," he teased lightly.

"That coffee was made early this morning," Courtney reminded him, trying to work around his bulky form. "And I'm not a bad cook." She stopped sorting the papers and grinned. "But then, I'm not a good one either."

"Who cares? The last thing a man would have on his mind if he was in the kitchen with you would be your cooking." Rob smiled back at her lazily, his eyes lingering on the swell of her breast against the fabric of her blouse.

"Don't you have work to do?" Courtney asked uneasily as she pushed past him.

Rob reached out one arm and brought her up close to his broad chest, trapping her between his powerful muscled legs. "Hey, where you going?"

"Let go, Rob. I have things to do." Courtney pushed ineffectively against his strong hold. It seemed to her that Rob was forever using his brawn instead of his brain.

"What's your hurry?" His tone had taken on a seducing quality as his hands ran exploringly down her back. "I was thinking about stealing a kiss from one of the prettiest girls on the block," he informed her in a soft husky voice.

"Rob, I have told you . . ." Her voice became muffled as Rob's mouth swooped down to capture hers. His kiss was far from unpleasant, but still Courtney tried to push away. The last thing she wanted to do was encourage him. He shouldn't be wasting all this charm and masculine superiority on her. He should save it for some woman who would really appreciate it!

After unsuccessfully trying to dislodge Rob's mouth

from hers, she resigned herself to the fact that he was intent upon kissing her and allowed herself to relax in his arms.

She was barely aware of the sound of the bell over the door as her arms involuntarily found their way up around Rob's neck.

"Well, well, well."

Courtney froze in Rob's arms as the deep timbre of a man's voice filled the small room. Oh, rats! Graham Merrill! And he couldn't have come at a more inopportune time. Courtney and Rob broke away at the same time, with Courtney feeling like an absolute fool.

"I hate to break this up, but I believe you summoned me, Miss Spenser." Graham's blue eyes held a hint of a twinkle as he surveyed Courtney's flushed and slightly confused face.

"Dr. Merrill . . . I . . . this is Rob Hanson. He works next door," she stammered lamely. "He just came over for coffee."

"Coffee? My, what a unique way of serving it." Graham extended his hand to Rob. "Graham Merrill."

"Graham." Rob took the extended hand and they shook graciously. "Did I hear Court call you doctor?"

"Yes, I'm a dentist."

"Ugh." Rob grinned boyishly. "Nothing personal, but . . ."

"I know. Everyone hates a dentist," Graham supplied helpfully.

"Honestly? Well, that makes me feel better," Rob said with a relieved laugh. "I get paranoid when I enter one of you guy's offices."

"Dread the chair?"

"No, dread the bill!"

Graham turned to Courtney, who was primly trying to straighten the few errant strands of hair that had come loose in Rob's amorous embrace.

"Heard anything from the gypsies?" he asked.

"No, nothing." She fidgeted nervously with the decorative comb she had fastened in the back of her hair.

"Why don't you forget about getting your hair back up in that tight knot and let it hang down like it seems to want to?" Graham suggested irritably.

"Why don't you mind your own business and keep your nose out of mine?" she shot back rudely.

"Hey, you wouldn't happen to be the bull manure salesman, would you?" Rob asked Graham with a smirk.

"What?"

"Oh, nothing." Rob stood up and started for the front door. "Just a joke. I've gotta run, Court. See you later."

"Yes, see you later," Courtney called as the bell sounded once more with Rob's exit.

"Who's the lover boy?" Graham asked in a disinterested tone as he walked over to examine one of the shell windchimes.

"His name's Romeo. I'm sure you've heard of him," Courtney said snidely. The minute Graham walked into a room, he seemed to put her on guard.

"He must be lost. I don't see Juliet standing around anywhere," he observed blandly.

"I'm sure you wouldn't recognize her if she fell in your lap. I imagine your taste in women runs more on the seamy side."

"Seamy?" He paused and thought for a moment. "No. You don't attract me at all, Miss Spenser."

Courtney's lower lip jutted out a fraction. "Very cute. But I'm surprised I don't. It seems like I always manage to attract the creeps."

"Well, you better grab one next time. That way you won't be an old maid all your life." Graham grinned.

"I really wish you wouldn't worry about my state of matrimony, Dr. Merrill. I don't!" she assured him readily.

"Obviously not."

Courtney walked over to face him stormily. "And what is that supposed to mean?"

"Look, lady, did you call me over here to pick a fight?" Graham turned cold blue eyes on her. "If you did, you have poor timing."

"Why?" Courtney smiled sweetly up at him, remembering the blonde in his car earlier that day and the sound of feminine laughter when she had talked to him on the phone. "Were you having a good time?"

"A hell of a lot better time than I'm having right now." His gaze locked obstinately with hers.

"What a shame. I'm so sorry to bother you."

"I can see that written all over your face," he responded dryly.

"If *you* had been doing your job, I wouldn't have had to bother you," she reminded happily.

"I was. Bonnie probably tracked Dad down at the milk counter."

Courtney gasped indignantly. "She did not! She was on her way home from the post office when he . . . accosted her!"

"Accos . . . ! Get your fanny out the front door, woman! I haven't got time to stand here and listen to your inane jibberish." He pushed her none too gently in the direction of the front door.

"You get your hands off me, you . . . you . . . fool! Where are we going?" she demanded as he snatched the "Out to Lunch" sign off the wall and hung it carelessly in the window.

"I believe you suggested earlier that *we* were going to look for the notorious Bonnie and Clyde," he told her, slamming the door to the gift shop loudly.

"Just look at that sign!" she exploded. "That's disgraceful hanging there all lopsided like that."

"Knock off the mouthin' and just get on." He stopped at the curb still clutching tightly to her arm.

42

"What is this?" Courtney eyed the contraption sitting at the curb haughtily.

"What the hell does it look like? It's a motorcycle," Graham said tightly, throwing his leg over the leather seat and pushing a button on the handlebar. The cycle roared into action with a deafening blast.

"A motorcycle! I'm not riding on any motorcycle! You're as wild as that crazy father of yours," she railed above the loud roar of the engine.

Graham gunned the motor a couple of times, completely ignoring her tirade. "Hop on!" he ordered roughly.

"Not on your life!" She crossed her arms defiantly.

Graham glared at her angrily, then calmly put the kickstand down. With the motor still running, he got off the cycle swiftly and scooped Courtney up in his arms, throwing her on the back of the cycle in a most ungentlemanly manner. He mashed a blue helmet on her head and then put one on his.

"How dare you!" she yelled, her arms still crossed in Indian fashion.

"You'd better shut up and grab hold of something, *Miss* Spenser," he warned grimly as he slid back on the cycle and kicked the stand back up.

"This is an outrage! Where's your car?" she shouted, grasping him tightly around his waist as he gunned the cycle a couple more times, then popped the clutch, sending them into motion.

"At home in the garage. Sit back and relax. You're going to love this," he yelled, grinning wickedly at the sound of rubber squealing on hot pavement.

"Oh, dear Lord," she muttered, burying her face in the broadness of his back and holding on for life. "You're going to kill us!"

"I'm going to kill someone if she doesn't get her fingernails out of my ribs!" he threatened gruffly as they literally flew down the street. "Ouch!" he exclaimed heatedly as

Courtney maliciously pinched him hard before she reluctantly loosened her clutch.

"Are you sure you know how to drive this thing?" she questioned fearfully, cringing against his masculine form as they weaved in and out of traffic. Her hands again gripped the lean tautness of his stomach. She could smell the faint aroma of his aftershave clinging to the fabric of his shirt. He smelled so good! And she was sure she must smell like a sweatbox! What a perfectly miserable, rotten day this was. There she was, flying along on the back of a motorcycle with some strange man, a crazy one at that, looking for her mother and the wild person she was dating! To think, when she got up this morning, Courtney Spenser's world had been sane and orderly. In a matter of hours, Dr. Graham Merrill had managed to turn it into a shambles!

She let out a scream and buried her face back in his shirt as they skidded to the right and barely missed a city bus, her fingernails nearly drawing blood this time. Well, she wasn't going to apologize to the ape! If they both managed to come out of this harrowing ride with only a fingernail scratch, she was going to get down on her knees and kiss the ground! Right now, as best as she could tell, her only major problem was going to be just that. Survive the ride!

CHAPTER THREE

The rush of the wind stung Courtney's face and made her eyes water as Graham barreled along the outer road that ran by the ocean. The beach was crowded with hundreds of surfers and swimmers playing in the refreshing depths of the cool water.

Courtney didn't have the slightest idea where they were going or, for that matter, what they were going to do when they got there. Unless Graham knew more about their parents' habits than she did, they were going on a wild goose chase!

"Where are we going?" she shouted, knowing that conversation at the rate of speed they were traveling was going to be close to impossible.

"This is one of the routes Dad usually takes on his cycle," Graham hollered back. "Are you comfortable?"

"Are you crazy! No, I'm not comfortable!" The wind whipped the words back in her face.

"What's the matter? Don't you like to be out in the fresh air? This is really living." He beat on his chest with one fist, inhaling deeply of the fresh salt air blowing in from the ocean.

"Keep both hands on the handlebars, you idiot!" she cried out as he darted out around a truck and passed a long line of traffic. He was driving as if he was the only one on the road!

"Are all old maids as nervous on a motorcycle as you

are, Miss Spenser?" he taunted as he swerved back smoothly into the line of traffic.

Courtney gave another vicious punch to his ribs, causing him to come up off his seat swiftly.

"Cut that out!" he yelled at her.

"You stop calling me an old maid!" she warned.

He tried to push her hands away, and with a defiant movement, she slammed her hands around his middle, missing her mark by a good five inches. A feeling of nausea welled up in her throat as she became aware of where her hands were now gripping! Courtney felt Graham's body tense as he squirmed in his seat, trying to shake off her intruding hands. Turning just enough on the seat that his eyes were level with hers, he glared at her pointedly. Her hands weakly climbed back up to safer ground as she met his hostile stare.

"Keep your eyes on the road!" she spat out nastily.

"*You* keep your *hands* to yourself!" he returned sharply, his eyes going back to the traffic before him.

Courtney could have died! Surely he didn't think she'd done that on purpose!

"Do you have any idea where they might have gone?" she called out nervously, trying to break the strained silence between them. She arranged her hands very quietly and very loosely around his waist.

"None whatsoever. I'm just taking a wild guess that maybe Dad took Bonnie on a scenic ride along this route."

"Have you ever stopped to think what we're going to say if we do happen to find them?" Although Bonita was well aware that Courtney did not approve of her seeing Clyde Merrill, Courtney was sure that her mother's mouth would drop wide open when she saw her daughter come riding up on the back of Graham Merrill's motorcycle, tracking her down like some runaway child!

"We'll figure that out *if* and when we find them," Graham said, gunning his way around another car.

46

For the time being, Courtney gave up all pretense of conversation and decided to concentrate on just hanging on to the muscular form seated before her. She could worry about her mother later. Right now she was going to worry about herself!

Hours later, she was sure she would never walk again. Her legs were aching from straddling a motorcycle seat, her lips were dry and cracked from the assailing wind, and she was sure that her nose was as red as a beet from the glaring sun. And she had always heard that cycling was fun!

Graham had said barely three words to her the last fifty miles. He had kept his eyes fixed on any passing cycle riders, dedicated to their joint purpose.

"Can't we stop for a minute and get something cold to drink?" Courtney pleaded. "I don't think we're going to find them." She hated to complain, but she couldn't take much more of this.

"Yeah, in a minute," he grunted. Courtney groaned as they took off on a dirt road, bumping along painfully until he finally stopped the cycle under a large tree.

Courtney willed her legs to move as she rolled stiffly off the bike and fell down on a clump of grass. She lay for a moment staring up at the cloudless blue sky, waiting for any type of feeling to return to her numb limbs, then wishing it hadn't.

"Why didn't you stop at that last gas station?" she moaned between parched lips. "I told you I was dying of thirst."

"You're a real panty waist, do you know that?" he grumbled as he wearily removed his helmet and stretched out beside her. "Damn, it's hot!"

Courtney reached up and unbuckled her helmet, taking it off her sweatsoaked hair. Running her fingers through the damp locks, she reached up and unpinned the bun, letting the silken mass flow down over her shoulders. Raising the thick hair up with her hands, she let what small breeze there was play over the back of her neck.

Graham turned over on his side and watched the trickle of breeze catch the blond strands of her hair and toss them gently about.

"You have beautiful hair," he observed quietly, reaching out to catch a piece of the spun gold between his fingers. "Why *do* you wear it up like that?"

"Because I like it that way," Courtney replied, feeling her pulse accelerate slightly at his touch.

"It's prettier when you let it down like this." His fingers gently toyed with the strand of hair, rubbing it languidly, the blue of his eyes growing deeper. "It feels like silk." He lifted a piece and brought it up to his nose. "And it smells like—"

"Wet chicken feathers," Courtney supplied helpfully, snatching her hair away from his fingers.

"No, I was going to say it smells like wildflowers. But if you say it smells like wet chicken feathers, then I'll take your word for it." He yawned. "I'm too beat to argue."

"It couldn't smell like wildflowers after the day I've put in," Courtney snapped, feeling very irritable at the way her senses seemed to suddenly remind her of the fact that she was in the presence of a very attractive man.

They were both quiet for a few moments, relaxing in the shade of the overhanging branches of the massive oak tree they were under.

"Why don't you hop on the cycle and go back up to that gas station we passed a few minutes ago and get us something to drink?" Graham suggested. He was lying with his eyes closed, one arm thrown up over his forehead, his tall form relaxed.

"Me? I don't know how to ride a motorcycle. I've never been on one in my life until a few hours ago," Courtney scoffed. The lazy drone of a fly filled the silence as she swatted it away from her face.

"All you have to do is—"

"Look! Forget it! I wouldn't ride that motorcycle if it meant I was going to die of thirst."

There was the faintest trace of a grin on Graham's features as he opened one eye and looked at her. "Do you want to wait here while I go back up and get us something?"

"I'll have to. I don't think I *could* get back on that thing right now," she admitted.

"Okay. You wait here while I ride back down to the station," he relented, rolling to his feet. "Any preference?"

"Wet, and lots of it," she muttered, lying back in the grass and shutting her eyes against the fading sun.

In a few minutes, she heard the cycle roar into life and Graham ride off. As she lay basking in the coolness of the shade, her thoughts turned back to her mother. Was she as hot and miserable as her daughter was? She smiled to herself. It would serve Bonita right if she was! After what she had put Courtney through that day, she deserved to suffer a little. She closed her eyes for a moment, weariness creeping over every part of her body. The thought of a cool shower, a shampoo, and clean clothes danced through her mind. Graham must think she looked a sight! She checked her thoughts hurriedly. What Graham Merrill thought was the least of her concerns. His only thoughts were probably centered on finding his father and ridding himself of the "old maid" he had toted around all day so he could get back to the blonde he was with this morning. Old maid indeed! That was the first time she had ever heard herself referred to as that! He certainly had a very warped view of a liberated woman. His wife . . . her thoughts skidded to a halt. Good heavens! I wonder if he's married? Maybe the blonde was his wife! Her face flamed anew as she thought about where her hands had landed earlier and the undeniable feel of his maleness. Well, what did she care whether he was married or not! That was the blonde's problem, not hers. And it suddenly made her very uneasy that her heart would lurch in such a silly way when she thought about Graham Merrill being married.

She brushed angrily once more at the pesky fly buzzing around her nose. For the life of her, she couldn't understand why he made her feel so . . . different. She brushed at the fly again, too tired to open her eyes. He had done nothing but get under her skin from the moment she had met him, so why was she so aware of his masculinity? Other men had never affected her in the same manner. What was so unusual about Graham Merrill? The fly tickled across her nose again and she slapped out at it, losing all patience.

A deep chuckle made her eyes fly open, and she frowned sternly as her gaze came in contact with a clear azure one. Graham was bent over her, running a piece of tall grass across her nose playfully.

"Stop that!" she snapped in embarrassment, rolling away from him. "I didn't hear you ride up!" She couldn't believe that she had been so deep in thought that she hadn't even heard the roar of the motorcycle!

"Well, I see your rest hasn't helped your disposition any," he observed, dropping down beside her and opening a large brown paper bag he was holding. "Are you hungry?"

Courtney sat up and peered over his shoulder into the sack. "What have you got?"

"I picked up some lunchmeat, pork and beans, potato chips . . . you name it, I've got it." He drew out a loaf of bread and pitched it at her. "Here, you make the sandwiches."

"What kind of lunchmeat did you get?" she asked as she untied the piece of plastic on the bread sack. "And what do we wash our hands with?"

Graham tossed her a package wrapped in white paper. "You'll have to wipe your hands on your pants. This isn't the Waldorf Astoria, you know."

"Oh, good grief! I feel like I've picked cotton all day. Didn't you even think to buy anything to wash our hands with?" She peered at him hopefully.

His concern for cleanliness was appalling, she observed, as he took his pocket knife out and began unconcernedly to spread mustard on the piece of bread she had just handed him.

"Nope. You want mustard on yours?" He held up a slice of bread temptingly.

"I can't eat without washing my hands first! Gad!" Courtney glared at him in disgust. "You're a dentist and you're this lax about cleanliness!?"

"Hey, look, I'm just eating a pickleloaf sandwich, I'm not doing surgery. Now make up your mind. Do you want mustard or not?"

"What have you been doing with that knife?" she asked suspiciously.

"Autopsies."

Courtney dug in the bread sack for a new slice of bread. "I'll take mine plain, thank you." Looking down at the pile of lunchmeat before her, she wrinkled her nose. "Is pickleloaf the only kind you bought?"

Graham was hungrily devouring his sandwich, totally ignoring the fact that she hadn't even started eating yet. "I didn't go to a delicatessen, Miss Spenser. It was just a little hole-in-the-wall service station that happened to carry a few groceries. What's the matter with pickleloaf?"

"I hate pickleloaf."

"That doesn't surprise me. Why don't you force yourself to try some? It tastes fine to me," he told her as he reached for another slice of bread and the jar of mustard.

"If you'll push yourself away from the trough long

51

enough to hand me my drink, Dr. Merrill, I think I'll start on that. *If* you don't mind."

With an obliging shrug of his shoulders, he handed her a can of soda. "As long as we're having dinner together, why don't we call each other by our first names," he suggested as he made himself another sandwich.

Courtney snapped the tab off her drink and took a long swallow. Her mouth felt like she had been chewing sawdust all afternoon.

"Now tell me, Courtney"—Graham leaned back and munched on his third sandwich—"what *does* an old maid like to eat?"

Taking another long drink of her soda, she ignored his taunting words.

"Filet mignon?" he guessed.

Reaching for a slice of bread, she folded it in two and bit into it, glaring at him silently.

"Aren't you going to come over here and poke me in the ribs for calling you an old maid?" Graham unbuttoned his shirt and opened the front of it to reveal a broad chest covered with a mat of light-brown hair. He looked down, examining the various scratches she had made with her fingernails every time he passed a car this afternoon. "Hell. I look like I've been in a fight with a cat!" he exclaimed, painfully rubbing his wounds.

Courtney valiantly fought to avoid staring at his naked chest, but failed miserably as her gaze fastened on the scratches. Once again her pulse had that funny fluttering feeling as she noticed the way the hair on his chest disappeared in a thin line down the front of his jeans.

"Did I do all that?" she asked shakily, her bread trembling slightly in her hand now.

"That . . . and I think I've probably got two or three fractured ribs. You can poke harder than any woman I've ever met."

Courtney tore her eyes away from his virile physique

52

and tried to swallow the wad of bread she had in her mouth that suddenly tasted like paste. "That will be hard to explain to your wife," she challenged.

"What wife?" Graham reached for a handful of potato chips.

"I assume the impatient blonde you had in your car this morning was your wife."

"Nope. She's not my wife. I'm not married."

There went her fluttering pulse again!

"You want some of these beans?" He held up a small can that he had just peeled the tab off of. "I'm sure they're clean," he said as he offered her a plastic spoon.

"No, thank you. This bread is fine."

"Well, Courtney, I've been thinking. When we find Bonnie and Clyde, we're going to have to lay down the law to them. I've tried diplomacy with Dad, now I'm going to have to get tough." He spooned some beans in his mouth and chewed thoughtfully. "We are going to have to forbid them from seeing each other again after today."

"Just like that. You think all we have to do is say, 'Mom, Dad, I know you're not going to like this, but you are not to see Bonita/Clyde ever again.' Then I suppose you think they'll simply roll over like trained dogs and obey." Courtney wadded up another bite of bread and stuck it in her mouth heatedly.

"I didn't say they were going to like it," he agreed, spooning the last of the beans in his mouth, "but, for their own good, we're going to have to make them accept it. I can't spend my afternoons running around the countryside trying to chase them down."

"No, I suppose you're too busy having swimming parties to waste your time chasing—"

"Hold it," he interrupted. "In the first place, it's none of *your* business what I do with my afternoons, and in the second place, I only have two afternoons a week to waste, so I'm pretty picky on *who* and *where* I waste them."

"Why *aren't* you married?" Courtney asked in a rather resentful tone. She didn't know why that subject seemed to interest her so, but she supposed that she would feel a lot more at ease with this man if he were . . . someone else's problem.

Graham glanced up in surprise, his hand pausing in the process of stuffing chips in his mouth. "I've never really had time for a wife. Why do you care?"

"No reason. It just seems strange a man your age would still be single."

"I don't think it any more strange than a woman *your* age still being single," he returned in an easy tone.

"I've had opportunities to marry. I just haven't found a man I would want to spend the rest of my life with," Courtney protested, motioning for him to hand her the bag of chips. "It just so happens I like my life the way it is."

"To each his own," Graham dismissed. "Now, I think it would be smart if one of us could get either Bonnie or Clyde out of town for a few weeks. With the way my office hours are set up, it *is* going to be awfully hard to keep an eye on Dad all the time."

"You should delegate that job to your receptionist," Courtney remarked dryly. "I bet *she* would get the job done. And stop referring to Mom as 'Bonnie'!"

Graham grinned. "I see you've met my nurse, Schultzie."

"No, thank goodness, I only spoke with her on the phone. Where did you find her . . . in a prison guard tower?"

Taking one last swallow of his drink, Graham flipped the empty can back in the brown paper sack, then stretched his long frame back out on the cool patch of grass. "Old Schultzie's tough, but since I have my office in my home, she has to be."

"Is she . . . uh . . . young?" Courtney pretended to be busy cleaning up the remains of her lunch.

Graham closed his eyes, a look of amusement stealing across his face. "Yeah, she's around . . . oh, I don't know. And her measurements are . . . oh, brother, I wouldn't even want to guess. She has big blue eyes and her hair . . . well, you'd just have to see her to believe her."

"It sounds like it's rather hard for you to keep your mind on business," Courtney snapped.

"Well, I will have to admit that doing a root canal pales to insignificance when she's standing there beside me," he murmured in a dreamy tone, a lazy grin spreading across his face.

"What does your blonde think about your infatuation with your office nurse?" Courtney asked lightly, then could have bitten her tongue off. Why couldn't she get her mind off *his* love life!

"You know, I have the strangest feeling we're off the subject of Bonnie and Clyde again and on the subject of my personal . . . uh . . . habits. Why is that, Miss Spenser?"

"Oh . . . well, I . . ." Courtney's face flamed bright red. "I'm sorry. I was only making conversation. Your lov . . . your personal habits . . . are certainly no concern of mine!" she stammered. She felt as flustered as a shy young teenage girl would if the captain of the football team had smiled at her!

"Why, I do believe you're blushing, Miss Spenser," Graham drawled in a sleepy tone. "Did I embarrass you?"

"No, of course not. Now, as you were saying about Mom . . ."

"No, now wait a minute." Graham reached out and caught her hand in a teasing manner. "This is beginning to get interesting. How come you're so interested in Schultzie, and the blonde, and Annie, and—"

"Annie?" Courtney cocked one perfectly arched brow.

"Haven't I mentioned Annie?"

"I don't believe you did," Courtney replied coolly, feigning indifference. Her fingers tingled where he touched them.

With deliberate slowness, he began to pull her toward him. "I didn't, huh? Well, we'll discuss her another time. Right now let's discuss something more important."

"Okay," Courtney said nervously as she drew closer and closer to his broad chest. "Who do you think the next President of the United States will be?"

"No, not *that* important," he interrupted. The deep blue of his eyes caught the lighter blue of hers. "Tell me, Miss Spenser, how would you like to be kissed? I mean really kissed by a man?"

"Please, Dr. Merrill . . ." Courtney pulled back hesitantly from his ever-tightening embrace. "I really think you're overstepping your bounds . . ."

"Graham . . . call me Graham." His hold was persuasive and firm as he drew her into the harbor of his arms. "You know, you're really very pretty," he observed in a rather indifferent manner as he reached out to lightly smooth errant strands of hair away from her face. For some strange reason, Courtney was finding it very hard to breathe. Their faces were only inches apart now as he continued to talk in a quiet, suggestive tone. "Now, if you haven't been kissed by a man—I mean really kissed the way a woman like you was meant to be kissed—then I think you should give strong consideration to letting me show you how good a kiss can really be."

Courtney thought he surely must be putting her on, but his tone sounded serious.

"You see, it's all in the shape of the mouth. I've studied all about those important things in college . . . in depth, I might add." One large hand ran undemandingly along her ribcage as he talked, causing tiny shivers to race up and down her spine. "If two people's mouths don't fit right together, the kiss will probably be a very disappointing occurrence."

"I'm sure you're an expert in your field," Courtney agreed uneasily, still trying to back away from his embrace. Wouldn't that be a fine kettle of fish! After all the complaining she had done to Bonita about dating Clyde Merrill, that she, herself, would become involved with *his* son!

"Yes, I am," he acceded readily. "Now, of course, one kiss doesn't *always* prove that two people couldn't practice a little and learn to fit their mouths together right, but if it works right the first time, it saves a lot of time and trouble," he encouraged, making no move to bring her any closer, yet making her very aware of their closeness.

"You must remember, Dr. Merrill—"

His finger came out to lightly touch her lips in correction. "Graham."

"Yes . . . well . . . Graham, you must remember," Courtney replied, trying to keep her voice steady and ignore the tantalizing scent of his aftershave, "that you're assuming that I've never been kissed by a man. Surely you don't think I've been locked away in a cellar for thirty years. I hate to disappoint you, but I *have* been kissed. You know, morals are just not what they used to be," she added dryly.

"Yeah, I know." He grinned. "It's hard to find a good, virtuous woman nowadays."

"I'm sure it is, especially with men like you running loose." She smiled back sincerely.

"I still say, I think I could teach you the fine art of kissing. Of course, I would only agree to do it because you've been such a good sport about helping me find Dad today." His hand was becoming a little more aggressive now, running smoothly along the curve of her breast, but not stopping to linger. "And you would have to promise me you wouldn't get any crazy ideas about you and me.

Not only do old maids make me nervous—I feel like I have to be completely honest with you, Miss Spenser . . ."

"Courtney," she murmured as his lips gently brushed hers. He tasted salty, like the chips he had been eating. Potato chips had always been one of her weaknesses.

"Courtney." Their mouths met a little more firmly this time. He played with her lips in a tempting series of short brushes, turning her insides into a quivering mass of flutters. For a moment, she completely forgot who she was, where she was, and who she was committing this nonsense with as she leaned against the broadness of his chest and offered him easy access to her mouth. He was right about one thing. He was one heck of a kisser! Their mouths *did* seem to fit together in a most enjoyable way, and the way he was playfully nibbling at her lips between snatches of kisses could easily make any woman turn to putty in his hands.

"You said something about wanting to be honest with me," Courtney reminded him breathlessly as his mouth took possession of her ear, sending goosebumps over her skin as he kissed the white lobe, then tugged at it with his strong white teeth.

"Ummm . . . I did?" His mouth ran down her neck, kissing the slender column hungrily.

"Yes, you did. You said old maids made you nervous, and . . ."

"Oh." His mouth caught hers again, kissing her with serious intent this time.

Her emotions seemed to have gone berserk as she wrapped her arms around his neck and returned his kiss with fervor. His hands were buried in the thickness of her hair and her senses reeled. It was very disconcerting to Courtney to realize that for the first time in her life, being in a man's arms was an exciting, stimulating experience.

As if he too suddenly became aware of the intensity of

the kiss, Graham broke away, the blue of his eyes turning a dark cobalt. "What I was going to say," he whispered huskily, "was that old maids made me nervous, and I could never fall for a woman who didn't like pickleloaf."

"Didn't like what?" Courtney asked, still slightly dazed by the power of his kiss.

Graham grinned wickedly. "You heard me."

Courtney finally recovered her wits about her and shoved back from his embrace irritably. "Well, set your mind to rest, Dr. Merrill. *I* wouldn't ever take anything you said *or* did seriously. And, furthermore, I don't appreciate your taking advantage of me like this." Courtney's face was confused, ashamed, and angry. Angry at herself for succumbing to his . . . his . . . blatant masculine charms! He obviously thought he was giving an "old maid" a thrill by kissing her!

"Taking advantage of you! Now, just a minute! I didn't see you protesting the kiss!" Graham got to his feet, picked up his helmet, and shoved it on his head. "Why is it every time a woman's kissed, she acts like the idea had never occurred to her? Don't tell me you didn't want me to kiss you, because you did. I saw it in your eyes."

"Really. Well, tell me, Dr. Graham, what do you see in my eyes now?" Courtney asked in a tight voice.

"The urge to kill, *but* that wasn't what was there ten minutes ago!" he added quickly.

"But it *is* there now, so I suggest we forget all about this unfortunate incident and you take me home. From now on, if we have any business together, you can call me on the phone. Otherwise, *you* and *your* despicable motorcycle better stay away from me!"

"Gladly. No wonder you're an old maid!"

Courtney's foot shot out and kicked him soundly in the shin, then she was instantly appalled at her actions. She had never done a thing like that in her life, not even when she was a small child!

"Damn it!" Graham grabbed his leg and hopped around irritably. "That beats all I've ever seen! The day I have to put up with a woman like you will be the day I resign as a man, *Miss* Spenser! You may find this hard to believe, but you're the *first* woman in my life who hasn't welcomed my kiss!" He raised his voice to talk above the sudden noise of flock of birds flying over head. "You won't have an opportunity to turn your snooty nose up again. . ." His voice trailed off as they both heard a telltale plop.

Courtney's mouth dropped open as her eyes focused on the timely deposit one of the flying birds had made on Graham's helmet.

"I hate to shatter your illusion, but there's apparently one other in the world who has the same opinion of your kiss *and* your philosophy of women as I do, Dr. Merrill," she said triumphantly, trying to smother a giggle.

"Hell . . . is that what I think it is?" Graham reached up hesitantly to feel his helmet.

"I wouldn't do that if I were you," Courtney warned, bursting out in laughter in spite of herself.

"Miss Spenser, I fail to find this humorous," he said with as much dignity as he could muster under the circumstances. "Would you kindly place your tush back on that motorcycle and allow me to rid myself of you as soon as humanly possible."

Courtney swept grandly by him, projecting an air of superiority. "I'd be most happy to, Dr. Merrill."

She bit her lip to keep from falling over the motorcycle in a fit of giggles.

It was his turn to smile when he heard her let out a painful groan as she once again straddled the leather seat. Placing the helmet back on her head, she looked up at him and burst into laughter once more. "You look ridiculous with that bird poop on your helmet."

"Oh, really? Would you like to trade helmets with me?"

He reached up and tightened his chin strap, then took his seat on the cycle in front of her.

"No, thanks. I look terrible in that color."

"I can't say that it does anything for me either," he replied dryly as he started the engine. "Where do you want to go? To your house or back to the shop?"

"Back to the shop. I left my purse there." She settled down on the seat more securely and wrapped her arms around his waist.

"Let's just watch the hands this time," he warned, giving her a knowing look. "Remind me to show you how to make a pass at a man using just a little more discretion, Courtney ol' girl."

Giving him a jab in his already bruised ribs, she squeezed her arms tighter. "You just drive this thing in a more sane manner and I promise to keep my hands under control. Besides, men with bird manure on their helmets have no appeal to me whatsoever," she assured him loftily.

With a broad grin, he gave her a sexy wink, then tore out of the shady resting place with the zeal of a wild man.

It was nearly dark by the time they rode up in front of the gift shop, and as Courtney had suspected, the ride back had been as harrowing as the previous one.

"You missed your calling in life," Courtney grumbled as she slid off the motorcycle, every bone in her body smarting. "You would have made an excellent ambulance driver."

"As I said earlier, you're a real pansy." Graham unbuckled his stained helmet and slipped it off his head. Surveying the evidence of the bird's ill-timed missile, he grimaced, then propped the helmet up on the handlebars. The faint sound of a phone ringing filtered through the air as Courtney removed her own helmet and unsuccessfully tried to straighten her ravaged hair.

"Is that your phone?" Graham asked, glancing toward the door of the gift shop.

61

Courtney listened intently as the phone rang once more. "Yes, I think it is. It must be a wrong number. Most people know the shop is closed at this hour." As if the phone were confirming her statement, it promptly fell silent.

"I hope I can find that extra key to the shop," she murmured thoughtfully to herself. Graham had ushered her out of the shop so hurriedly this afternoon that she had forgotten to grab her purse with the shop's keys in it and the door had locked automatically. "There's no reason for you to wait, Graham. I think I have an extra set of keys to the shop in the glove compartment of my car."

"You go see if you do. I'm in no hurry," he replied calmly, still staring at his helmet. "Just make it snappy."

Courtney turned around and glared at him impatiently. "I thought you just said you weren't in any hurry!"

"I'm not. But that doesn't mean I want to hang around here all evening either."

"Schultzie or the blonde?" She couldn't help but ask.

"Wrong on both counts. Liza." He gave her a brutish grin.

Courtney gave him a glare, then marched around the back of the shop where her car was parked. Luckily she never locked her car and the glove compartment was also open. It took her a few minutes to find the extra set of keys and come back around to the front. "I have them. You can go now," she said curtly.

"The phone's been ringing again," he observed. He was stretched out nearly full length on the motorcycle, his arms propped behind his head and his boots propped on the handlebars.

"Again?" That did seem strange. It must be getting close to nine by now and the shop was always closed by five. "I wonder who it could be."

"Beats me," he murmured disinterestedly.

I would love to, she thought snidely, as she surveyed his

62

careless reclining position. She was so tired she was about to drop and there he lay, like some pompous king on his throne, biding his time until he was free to join one of his little playmates!

As she walked by him on the way to unlock the front door, she deliberately bumped the cycle, sending the king scrambling for his balance.

"Ooops. Pardon me. I must be getting clumsy," she apologized insincerely. Before he could make an angry retort, the phone sounded shrilly once more. "I wonder who in the world that is!" Courtney inserted the key in the lock and pushed the door open. The ringing persisted as she made her way across the dark room, feeling for the light switch. She stubbed her toe and sucked in her breath in pain. Hopping over to the receiver she snatched it up and gasped out a weak, "Hello."

"Courtney! Where have you been!?" Bonita's voice sounded as agitated as Courtney felt.

"Where have *I* been? Mother! Where in the world are *you?* We've been running around this town all afternoon looking for you and Clyde!"

"Who's we, dear?"

"We! Graham Merrill and me!"

"Graham's there with you now?" Bonita asked hurriedly. "I didn't know you two even knew each other."

"Yes, I think he's still out there. Where are you?" Courtney demanded once more.

"Oh, good, Clyde's been trying to reach him all afternoon too." Bonita's voice sounded relieved. "Just a minute, dear. I want to tell Clyde that I found you." Courtney heard Bonita cover the receiver with her hand and speak to someone. In a few moments she came back on the line. "Clyde wants to talk to Graham, Courtney. Can you call him to the phone?"

"Yes, but Mother—"

"Don't argue, dear. Just do as I say. We haven't got but

a few minutes to make this call." Bonita was using her stern motherly tone, one she didn't use unless absolutely necessary.

Courtney laid down the phone and turned around to summon Graham just as a man's voice nearly startled her out of her wits.

"Who is it?"

Gad! Courtney clutched at her chest and sank weakly against the counter, her heart pounding like a jackhammer. "Why don't you warn someone when you sneak up on them like that!" she gasped.

Graham looked at her as if she were nuts. "Sneak up on you! I've been standing here for the last five minutes!"

"Well, I didn't know it! Couldn't you have breathed harder?"

"*If* there was anything in the vicinity to *make* me breathe harder, I could."

"I can do without your obscene remarks," she said coldly, reaching for the light switch. "You're wanted on the telephone."

"Oh, good! I hope it's Beth," he taunted, his blue eyes twinkling.

"Wrong."

"Liza?"

"Try one of the *few* males you know," she coaxed with a saccharine smile.

A look of pure disgust flooded his handsome features. "*Now* who's being obscene!"

"It's your *father!* Now hurry up and answer it!"

"Dad? How in the dickens did he know I was over here?" Graham picked up the phone hurriedly. "Dad?"

Deciding to stick close, Courtney leaned tightly against Graham's broad frame and tried to listen to the conversation.

"What?" Graham exclaimed.

"What?" Courtney whispered as she poked him on the shoulder, anxious to find out their parents' whereabouts.

"What!" Graham exclaimed again, more incredulously this time.

"What? What are they saying?" Courtney persisted, pressing in closer.

Graham glanced at her irritably and inched away from her clinging form, trying to shrug away from her and carry on a conversation at the same time.

When the third "What!" came out of his mouth, she lost all patience. Grabbing his arm hostilely, she mouthed the word tensely. *"What!"*

"They're in *jail!*" he mouthed back impatiently.

"What!"

He covered the receiver with his hand and glared at her angrily. "Miss Spenser! Would you kindly stop giving me your impression of a damn light bulb and let me get on with this conversation!"

She was annoyed at his tone but too upset about her mother to interrupt his conversation. In jail! Her own mother was in jail! How disgusting! And it was all Clyde Merrill's fault. Courtney's scowl deepened as she stood watching the man before her talk rapidly to his father. Her life had been turned upside down by the Merrill men and she didn't appreciate it one little bit!

Graham slammed the phone down angrily, then turned to Courtney. "They were caught speeding out on the freeway. You better go down and bail your mother out."

"What about your father?" Courtney asked hurriedly, still finding it hard to believe her mother would embarrass her like that.

"Not me. I'm going to let him spend the night in the tank. Maybe by morning he'll be in a more receptive mood when I discuss *your* mother with him!" Graham snapped testily.

"*My* mother! *She* wasn't the one driving!"

"Maybe not, but this is the first time *he's* ever been in jail, and I can only attribute the company he's keeping lately with some of his juvenile actions!"

"You wouldn't dare let your own father stay in jail overnight," Courtney growled threateningly.

"You want to bet? I have an informal date I've just decided to keep, Miss Spenser. If you'll excuse me." His voice was coolly polite as he started backing out the front door of the gift shop.

Courtney stood watching him go, her temper seething. Was he serious! "You come back here!" she yelled above the explosive roar of the cycle springing into action. "You're not going to leave me to face this all alone!"

"I hate to repeat myself, but . . . wanna bet?" He popped the clutch and sped noisily away into the night.

Courtney watched until the taillights of the cycle dimmed out of view. He was serious. That asinine fool *was* serious. Well, if he thought he was going to leave her mother in the "tank" all night, he was loco! He could do whatever he wanted to about his father, but she was going after her mother and putting a stop to this nonsense once and for all!

CHAPTER FOUR

"I have never been so humiliated in all my life, Mother!" Courtney angrily snapped the cap back on her ballpoint pen.

"But Clyde thought we could outrun—"

"I don't want to hear about it," Courtney warned between clenched teeth. "I've about had it up to here with you and Clyde!" She made a slash across her forehead to indicate how far she had "had it."

"Did you bail Clyde out too?" Bonita asked meekly, as she hurriedly followed her daughter down the deserted halls of the police station. "He'll want to see about getting his cycle."

"I did not bail Clyde out!" Courtney snapped, fighting to keep her temper under some reasonable sense of control. "Even his own son isn't going to bail him out! He can rot in the 'tank' for all I care!"

"Oh, my . . . Courtney, dear . . . I know you're upset, but we can't let poor Clyde stay in here all night! He lost his wallet during the chase and he has no money. We can't leave him here. The coppers might decided to rough him up a bit."

"Oh, good Lord, Mother," Courtney said disgustedly, "You've got to stop watching all those old Edward G. Robinson movies! Why in the world would the police want to rough up a seventy-year-old man?"

"Well, I think that one named Ralph would love to

punch Clyde out," Bonita said indignantly as she scurried along behind her daughter breathlessly. "This is the second time Clyde's tried to outrun him on the freeway and I could tell by the look in Ralph's beady eye—you see, he has these little black, beady eyes—"

"Look. I don't want to hear about Ralph's beady eyes! I don't want to hear another word about that ridiculous motorcycle, and most of all, I don't want to hear another word about Clyde Merrill! Do you understand, Mother? *Not one more word!* He has a son, granted not a very bright one, but, nonetheless, he does have one who should take the responsibility of his own father. I am not putting out one cent on your . . . your . . . senile playmate!" Every bone in Courtney's body was screaming for a hot tub of water to soak in, and the mere thought of a Merrill set her nerves on edge. Personally, she hoped they locked Clyde *and* his son up and threw away the key.

The night air felt hot and muggy as mother and daughter walked out the front door of the police station, Bonita still protesting the fact that Clyde would have to spend the night behind bars.

"I'll pay you back," she offered worriedly as Courtney paused on the steps and took a deep breath of fresh air, trying to calm her shattered nerves. "If you'll lend me whatever it takes to pay Clyde's fine . . ."

"No. N-O," Courtney replied heartlessly.

"Ten dollars? All I need is another ten dollars."

"No."

Bonita's face fell. "Well, horsefeathers, Courtney! What's poor Clyde gonna do?"

" 'Poor' Clyde should have thought of that before he gunned his way down the freeway so carelessly," Courtney pointed out unsympathetically. "Let his son worry about him."

"Where *is* Graham?" Bonita perked up at the prospect of help for Clyde. "Of course, his own son wouldn't let him spend the night in jail!" Her face brightened considerably.

"Mother! You haven't been listening to a word I've said! I told you Graham refuses to bail Clyde out. If you're counting on that horse's—" Her words were cut short as she ran smack into a broad wall of a man's chest. "Why don't you watch were you're going!" Courtey sputtered heatedly as she tried to regain her balance.

"Why don't you move it out of my way, lady!"

"Well, well." Courtney smiled insincerely, "if it isn't Mr. Majestic . . . Florida's answer to Charles Bronson."

"Yes. Fancy meeting you here, Miss Spenser. Is this what an old maid does with her spare time? Hang around on the steps of the local police station and watch the eligible men walk by?" Graham asked.

"Yes, but I'm usually not as disappointed as I am this time. Most eligible men have been worth the wait, but of course, there's always an exception to every rule." She surveyed him haughtily.

He looked back at her aloofly.

"I don't believe you've met my mother." Courtney finally eased the strained silence.

"I don't believe I've had the honor," he replied in a polite but definitely disinterested tone.

"Mother, this is Graham Merrill. Graham, my mother, Bonita Spenser."

Graham stepped forward and took Bonita's hand. He was mildly surprised. He didn't know exactly what he had expected in the form of one "Bonnie" Spenser, but it certainly wasn't the lovely lady standing before him, smiling radiantly. "My pleasure, Mrs. Spenser. I've heard a lot about you from Dad."

"And I've heard a lot about you, Graham. Clyde is so proud of you!" Graham looked a bit uncomfortable as Bonita shook his hand exuberantly. "Such a fine-looking man you are. Just like your father." She turned to Courtney and motioned with her eyes for her to take a closer look at the fine, eligible, good-looking man standing right at her doorstep.

Courtney's gaze shot upward in mute exasperation.

"Have you come to spring Clyde?" Bonita looked at Graham expectantly.

"Yes—"

"Oh, good, I'll go give him the happy news." Bonita spun around and was gone before either Courtney or Graham could protest.

"Now, Miss Spenser, where were we?" Graham turned back to face Courtney. "Oh, yes, you were telling me how you usually went about meeting the men you date—"

"You're very funny, Mr. Merrill. You should have been a comedian," Courtney said as she pushed her way around him.

"That's funny. A lot of my patients have said the same thing when they get my bill." Graham stepped back in her path to deliberately annoy her.

"Get out of my way." Her eyes met his hostilely.

"Am I in your way?" he asked innocently, refusing to budge an inch.

"Yes, you are," Courtney replied. She was determined to not let him get under her skin. "Move."

"Please?" he coaxed with an infuriating, tiny grin.

"*Move it, Mr. Merrill!*" she ordered between clenched teeth.

"Doctor. It's *Dr.* Merrill, darlin'," he drawled sweetly.

Her temper gave way as she jerked the strap of her purse up roughly on her shoulder and started around him. They both let out a gasp as the heavy purse swung out and hit Graham in a very inopportune place.

"Damn!" Graham jumped back and glared at her angrily, putting a protective hand to the injured area.

Courtney had the decency to blush, but she felt very little remorse about what had just occurred. "Gee. I'm

70

sorry, *Dr.* Merrill," she said insincerely as an angelic smile spread across her face. "Did my mean old purse hit you?"

"Have you got something against the tone of my voice, lady?" he demanded crossly. "I've noticed you've been trying to raise it a pitch or two all day!"

Courtney's face did turn beet red now as she recalled this was the second time today she had pounced on his most sensitive area. "Oh . . . I'm sorry," she mumbled in embarrassment, nervously adjusting the strap on her purse. "Well"—she took a deep breath and grinned—"what are you doing here? I thought you were going to let your father spend the night in jail." She mentally crossed her fingers hoping that she had successfully changed the subject.

Still eyeing her suspiciously, Graham straightened up and tucked his shirttail into the pair of jeans he was wearing. "I *should* let him sweat it out here for a *week,* but . . ."

"But you decided it wouldn't look good for *Dr.* Merrill to let his seventy-year-old father sweat it out in the 'tank,' " Courtney finished.

"Something like that," he grumbled.

"Good thinking. Well, I'm taking the other half of the three-ring circus home and putting her to bed." Courtney started down the steps once more. "Tell Mother I'm waiting for her in the car."

"Wait a minute." Graham's voice stopped her. "I think while we have them *both* together, this is the time to have a little talk with them."

Courtney paused, then sighed tiredly. "Can't it wait? I think I've about handled all of this . . . this fiasco I can for one day. I'm tired, sore—"

" *You're* sore!" Graham glanced at her in annoyance, his body still aching. "My heart bleeds for you, lady, but I think this is the best time to break this little relationship up."

71

"Oh, all right! Where do you want to talk to them?" Courtney was too tired to argue. This had been the longest day of her life.

"Let me bail him out, then we'll meet you and your mother back over at your house," Graham suggested absently. "They're not going to like it, but I'm going to have to lay the law down to them, once and for all."

"Well, I agree with you on one thing," Courtney admonished quietly as she sat down wearily on the step to wait for her mother.

"Really? What might that be, Miss Spenser?"

"They are definitely *not* going to like it!"

"Now, see here, Buddy, I think that's a crock of manure!" The years had been unusually kind to Clyde Merrill. At the age of seventy, he still was a dynamic figure of a man. It was easy for Courtney to see where Graham got his good looks.

"Buddy?" Courtney glanced up from the chair she had slumped into upon entering the house, meeting Graham's determined face.

"He always calls me Buddy," he dismissed curtly.

"Well, that's what your name *should* be," Clyde said, pacing the floor agitatedly. "I told your mother when you were born I wanted your name to be *Bud Clyde Merrill!* But no! She had to go get all fancy and name you Graham!" He spit the name out like it left a bad taste in his mouth. "Always makes me think of crackers!"

Graham looked at Courtney and rolled his eyes upward. They had all gone back to Courtney and Bonita's home straight from jail.

"What is your full name?" Courtney asked, smothering a smile at the look of distress on Graham's face.

"Just never mind!" Graham dismissed snappishly. He turned back to his irate father. "Now, look here, Dad, we're not discussing my name! We were talking about you

72

and—" He paused and glanced respectfully at Courtney's mother. "We were discussing you and Mrs. Spenser."

"Bonita, dear. Just call me Bonita." She patted Graham on the shoulder in a motherly fashion.

Graham edged away uneasily, his blue eyes surveying her suspiciously. "Yes. Well, as I was saying . . ."

"I know what you were saying and the answer is *no.*" Clyde picked up the fractured conversation. "Bonnie and I are perfectly old enough to do what we want to. Hang it all, boy! When you reach our age, there's not that much left *to* do! Why do you want to go spoil all our fun?"

"All I'm asking is that you give up that blasted motorcycle before you kill yourself and whoever happens to be riding with you at the time . . . and stop seeing Mrs. Spencer quite so often!" Graham fired back angrily. He had laid the law down several times since they had gotten home, and several times Clyde had picked it up and thrown it back at him.

"I'm not planning on killing anyone," his father scoffed. "I was riding a motorcycle long before you ever came on the scene," Clyde reminded sharply.

Courtney swung her foot back and forth from her relaxed position and idly watched the two men exchange heated words. There was very little that she could say that would add anything. After all, she had told her mother the same thing for the last two weeks and gotten the same reception. Well, perhaps she had gotten a little *quieter* response than Graham was getting.

"Graham, dear, your father is a very good driver," Bonita tried to interject. "This is the first time anything like this has ever happened."

"Please, Mrs. Spenser, just keep out of this." Graham was polite but firm.

"Don't you talk to my mother that way!" Courtney was out of her chair and on her feet in a flash.

"Then tell her to refuse to go out with Dad when he asks!" Graham shouted.

"I will not! It's your father who's causing all of this to begin with and, if you think—"

"Children, children," Bonita broke in soothingly. "There is no need for all of this!"

Graham and Courtney were facing each other like two boxers in a ring, both sets of blue eyes flashing angrily.

"Now all three of you listen to me!" Graham shouted furiously. "I'm going to tell all of you *exactly* how it's going to be and *that's final!* I'm laying down the law! *You* and Bonnie are not to see each other again! You're going to park that motorcycle, and you're going to start going to those local bingo games instead of riding around town like a wild man! Is that understood?" He looked his father straight in the eye, the way a man should.

"The hell I am," Clyde responded flatly, stalking over to the sofa and planting himself down firmly. "You have anything to drink, Bonnie?"

You could have heard a pin drop as the two women in the room glanced at each other nervously.

Graham glared daggers at his father, then let out a defeated sigh. "Will you at least slow down on your cycle?" he pleaded in a small boy's tone.

"Nope. But I'll tell you what, Buddy. I promise that I won't try to outrun old Ralph on the freeway any more. I can tell he's getting a little testy about that," Clyde bargained shrewdly.

"Is that a promise?" Graham perked up.

"That's a promise, boy. Now, where's that drink, Bonnie?" Clyde rose from the couch and took Bonita's hand. "Come on, I'll help you make it." They walked off toward the kitchen, arm in arm, laughing about something that Clyde had whispered in her ear.

Graham sank down on the sofa wearily. "Well, at least I made him promise to slow down."

"Yes, I noticed how effective you were in laying down the law." Courtney sat down beside him. "Well, now what?"

Graham was staring up at the ceiling in remorse. "I don't know. I've got to think on this."

Courtney stared at the ceiling in quiet companionship with him. He gave a long sigh. "Damn, this has been one hell of a long day."

For one brief moment, Courtney felt a rush of tenderness toward the man slumped tiredly next to her. It *had* been a long day, and the lines of weariness etched around Graham's tanned features testified to that fact. Without thinking, Courtney reached over and gently soothed the tight lines around his eyes. "I know. All I want is a hot bath and something cold to drink. Would you like something?" she asked, suddenly remembering her manners.

His eyes opened slowly, meeting her clear, honest gaze. "What are you doing?" he asked abruptly.

"What?"

"I said, what are you doing?" He motioned with his eyes toward her fingers.

Courtney's hand dropped away rapidly. He must think her very forward! "I asked if you wanted anything to drink," she said easily, totally ignoring his puzzled gaze.

"Yeah . . . I'd take something cold." He was still watching her like a hawk watches a snake.

"I'll get us some iced tea," she replied demurely, rising from the sofa gracefully.

"Oh, Miss Spenser."

"Yes?" She cocked her head toward him.

"You weren't getting ready to make another move on me . . . were you?" He grinned wickedly, his eyes motioning to another area of his body this time.

Courtney's face clouded up and he barely had time to duck as a pillow came sailing by his head, followed by another one, and yet another one.

Some women could *never* take a joke!

It was very late when Courtney finally locked the door and turned the porch lights out. She stretched tiredly, grimacing anew at the newly found soreness each bone seemed determined to produce. The hot bath she had taken earlier had done little to relieve the tenderness of her thighs. If she hadn't known better, she would have sworn she had been straddling a boxcar all day!

Bonita walked into the room, lavishly spreading hand lotion on. "You look very tired tonight, dear. Have you had a bad day?"

Bad day? Ha! Courtney thought. That was the understatement of the year! "I am a little tired, Mother. I think I'll go straight to bed."

"You never did tell me how you met Graham," the older woman reminded, her eyes growing tender as she gazed at her daughter's lovely, but tired, features.

"Oh, he stopped by the shop this morning and . . . introduced himself." Had it only been this morning? It seemed months ago!

"Wasn't that nice of him!" Bonita exclaimed warmly.

"Simply super!" Courtney couldn't quite hide the sarcasm in her voice.

Bonita looked up in surprise. "Don't you like him?"

"No, Mother, I don't like him," she said honestly.

"For goodness' sakes! Why not? From what I hear, he has every woman in town trying to snag him! Not only is he nice looking, he has a thriving business, a lovely home . . . why, Courtney dear, he's *the* most eligible bachelor in town!" Bonita was clearly puzzled over her daughter's lack of interest.

"And you want me in there digging for the 'prize' with all those . . . those other lunatics running after him! No, thanks. And stop trying to marry me off! The last thing in the world I'd marry is some manic dentist who rides a motorcycle!"

"He doesn't ride a motorcycle all the time, dear. He has a nice brown Ford he dri—"

"Mother! I don't care if he drives a Rolls-Royce! Now, let's change the subject!" Courtney had clearly lost patience with the discussion.

The room grew silent as her mother gave her a petulant look, then reached for the evening paper. Courtney picked up a nailfile and irritably went to work on a nail she had broken trying to buckle her motorcycle helmet. It had taken her a month to grow it to the length she liked, and then it had taken exactly ten seconds to break it nearly to the quick!

"The beauty shop over on Palm Drive is having a special on haircuts and permanents," Bonita read aloud. "I'll give you the money to go over and have yours fixed if you want to."

Courtney glanced up from her filing. "Are we back on my hair again?"

"No, I just thought I'd mention it. You don't have to get so touchy, dear," she said innocently. "Even though your hair would look better shorter, it's up to you how you wear it."

Obstinate blue eyes locked with Bonita's. "I happen to like my hair this way. Do you mind?"

"Not at all, dear. I just thought if that nice Graham happened to ask you out, you'd want your hair to look nice."

Courtney threw the nailfile down on the coffee table irritably. "I wouldn't go out with that nice 'Graham' if he offered to take me to the Bahamas, Mother! One Merrill man is all I can deal with. And while we are on the subject . . ."

"Oh, no!" Bonita groaned, laying the paper down hurriedly. "Here we go! Now, before you start in on me again, *I* am going to bed."

"No, you're not!" Courtney blocked her path. "Not until you promise me you'll at *least* date a few other men."

"I am not going out with Harold Curtis, the butcher, and that's that!"

"Who said anything about Mr. Curtis, for heaven's sake! There *are* other men your age, Mother."

"I *like* Clyde," Bonita said flatly.

"All right, so you *like* Clyde. But what would it hurt to go out with someone else for a change? I'm not asking you to *marry* anyone, just go to the movies with another man *one* night." Courtney was desperate to find someone who could take Bonita's mind off Clyde Merrill. Preferably someone who was sane!

"Who?" Bonita snapped curtly.

"I don't know. . . ." Courtney searched her brain for a likely candidate. Mr. Curtis was strictly taboo. Obviously her mother would rather go out with an African head-hunter before spending an evening with Harold Curtis. Suddenly Courtney's eyes lighted. "How about Walter Jarmen?"

"Who?"

"Walter Jarmen! You know! The man down at the used car lot!"

"Ohhhh, deliver me!" Bonita groaned, slapping her hand to her forehead. "That man's so feeble, he can't hardly blow his own nose! Surely you wouldn't do a thing like that to your own mother, Courtney!"

"Well, *I* don't see anything wrong with him!" Courtney protested.

"Then *you* go out with him. I'm certainly not!"

"Mother! He's eighty-five years old. Why would I want to go out with him?" she exclaimed with exasperation.

"Exactly. So, why would I?"

"Okay, okay. Let me think for a minute," Courtney

relented. Walter *was* a bit slow for her mother's taste. In a few minutes she slapped her hands together in glee. "I've got it! Francis Mercer!"

Bonita looked at her distastefully. "The man who owns Mercer Wall Coverings?"

"Right! What's wrong with him?"

"Have you got an hour?"

"Mother! Now who's being picky? Francis is a dignified, very well to do business man. Just last week he was asking about you. It would be a snap to arrange an evening out between you and him. How about it?"

Bonita mulled the unpleasant thought around in her head for a moment, then replied, "Very well, dear. On one condition."

"What's that?" *Anything* to get this deal squared away!

"You go out with his son, Fredrick."

Anything but that! "You must be joking." Courtney's smile wilted from her face.

"No, I'm not. If I have to be miserable, you do too," her mother said in a no-nonsense tone.

"Mother, Fredrick is about as exciting as a wet noodle."

"Really?" Bonita raised an unsympathetic brow. "Then he *must* take after his father."

"Okay, if that's your terms, then I'll meet them." Courtney was between a rock and a hard place. She could surely stand Freddy Mercer for one lousy evening. That would give her mother a chance to see that there were other men in this world—men who would treat her with the dignity and respect a lady of her age should expect.

"Oh, brother. You really are desperate, aren't you?" Bonita moaned.

"Not desperate. Don't look at it that way, Mother. Look at it as a perfect opportunity to enlarge your social life!"

She sniffed disdainfully. "When do I have to face this cruel and inhuman punishment?"

"I'll set it up as soon as possible. I'm sure Francis Mercer will be delighted at the prospect of an evening with Bonita Spenser!" Courtney encouraged brightly.

"Oh, I'm sure he will," the older woman replied glumly. "I just bet old Freddy will be chafing at the bit, too, when he finds out Bonita Spenser's daughter will be along!"

Courtney frowned. She had forgotten that little piece of bad news. Old Freddy "Hands Mercer" was worse than being out with an octopus, but she'd manage. "Well, don't worry, I'll take care of everything. As I said, I'm sure the Mercer men will be delighted."

The Mercer men were more than delighted. They slurped up the unexpected invitation like a cat laps up spilled milk.

It was decided that after an early dinner, Courtney and Bonita would meet Francis and Fredrick at the movies. Courtney had decided to be merciful and make it a simple evening. They were to go to the movies, then coffee afterward.

"Now, I want you to be on your best behavior, Mother," Courtney warned as they emerged from the small restaurant two nights later and started walking down the street to the movie theater.

"Do I have to go through with this, dear?" Bonita fretted. "Clyde wanted to go roller-skating tonight!"

"It's too late to back out now," Courtney hissed under her breath, taking her mother's hand and dragging her along beside her. "Now, smile!"

They both pasted weak smiles on their faces as they approached the two men standing in front of the theater.

"Hello, Francis! Freddy." Courtney made her voice sound bright and cheerful. "I hope we're not late."

"Not at all. Hello, Bonita!" Francis reached out and took Bonita's hand in his and pumped vigorously. Courtney appraised his still-manly physique. His shoulders were broad, and he had a head full of snowy-white hair. He wasn't all that bad, she thought defensively. As her eyes quickly surveyed the triple bifocals he was wearing, along with the blue suit and red tie, she had to amend her thoughts swiftly. Then again, he wasn't all that good. But then again, his son was nothing to write home about either. Freddy Mercer was in his early thirties and had already been through two marriages. Of average build, his mouse-brown hair matched his mouse-brown eyes perfectly. The strong smell of a man's cologne filled the air as Freddy slipped a breath mint in his mouth and stepped to Courtney's side.

"Good evening, Courtney. You look lovely as usual."

"Thank you, Freddy," Courtney murmured, avoiding the hand that reached for hers. "Well. It's been hot, hasn't it?" She tried to start the ball rolling.

"It certainly has," Francis acknowledged heartily. "A nice cool night at the movies will be a welcome change."

"What's playing?" Courtney had left the choice of the movie they would see up to her mother. She glanced up at the billboard and her mouth fell open involuntarily.

"I thought the men might enjoy a nice western, dear," Bonita said helpfully.

Courtney swallowed hard. Good Lord! Her mother had brought them to see *Midnight Cowboy* ! *Midnight Cowboy* was anything but a "nice western"!

"Well, ladies, I think we better get in line. The movie starts in ten minutes," Francis urged, guiding Bonita toward the ticket window.

Within minutes they were in the dark, cool interior of the theater. Most of the seats were taken, and it took a few minutes to locate four in a row. Naturally the four were directly in the middle of the theater, causing a disruption to the entire twelfth row as the two couples murmured apologies and tromped over feet, purses, and tried their best to avoid spilling drinks on the occupants of the other seats.

The minute they were seated, an unwanted arm snaked out and pulled Courtney close. "My, isn't this nice?" Freddie asked in a whisper. "Are you comfy?"

"Yes, thank you." She shrugged uneasily out of his embrace and turned her attention to the movie. She had dated Freddy Mercer once before and it had been the biggest mistake she had ever made in her life.

"Have you seen this movie?" Freddy whispered wickedly.

"Yes." Courtney kept her eyes glued to the screen.

"I just love 'westerns,' don't you?" he persisted with a smirk.

"Some of them." His arm snaked back up around her chair.

"Freddy," Courtney asked a few minutes later, "would you mind getting us some popcorn?" It was apparent that Freddy needed something to keep his wandering hands busy!

"So soon? The movie's barely started!"

"I know. Get me a package of Milk Duds too, will you?" She planned on keeping her mouth stuffed all night so ol' Freddy wouldn't be able to make use of that gross of breath mints he had been bolting down for the last fifteen minutes.

Freddy mumbled under his breath, but obligingly leaned over and whispered something to his father. They both rose and fought their way back up the aisle, the foursome fast becoming a nuisance to row twelve.

Courtney leaned over and smiled encouragingly to her mother. "Are you having fun?" she whispered.

"No," Bonita quietly mouthed back.

Courtney shrugged, then settled back down to watch the movie. She had to give Bonita a little time. She would have fun. . . .

In a few minutes, half the people in the row were forced to stand up and let the Mercer men back in with the drinks and popcorn. One lady three seats down hissed sharply as Freddy accidentally stepped on her foot, setting up a loud chorus of *shhhh!* It took another few minutes for everyone to get settled back down again and the row to return to order.

The theater was so dark that Courtney had to strain her eyes to find her popcorn. For a few minutes she munched contentedly along, watching the show and wishing fervently that *she* had been the one to select the movie.

It wasn't long before Freddy's hands were on the move again. At first Courtney discreetly kept moving them. When the circumstances called for more forceful action, she plucked his hand off her thigh and laid it back down on the arm of the seat. Minutes later it was back on her thigh once more. This guy definitely could not take a hint! Once again she removed it gently. Once again it came back.

Courtney endured another five minutes of cat and mouse before her patience came to an abrupt halt. With one angry jerk, she threw Freddy's arm off her shoulder, sending her box of popcorn flying into the lap of the man sitting on the left side of her. With an embarrassed gasp, she lunged for the box, hearing a sharp intake of breath as her hand jammed into what was undoubtedly a man's more tender area.

"Excu-u-se me!" She whispered in a horrified tone. That *had* to have hurt like blue blazes!

The man leaned over and groaned painfully in her ear. "Have you ever tried yelling 'Hey you' or something like that to get my attention, Miss Spenser? It would be a heck of a lot easier on me if you would, you know."

"Graham!"

"Not any more, honey. Gertrude is more fitting," he returned with a grimace.

83

"I didn't know you were sitting here!" she exclaimed in surprise.

"I'm amazed I still am. Any other man would be stretched out on the floor passed out cold by now."

Their loud whispering was causing a disturbance in row twelve *and* thirteen now.

"Is that man bothering you?" Freddy whispered from her right side.

"No . . . er . . . I know him," she returned quietly.

She tried to make out who was sitting on the other side of Graham. It was a woman. A very pretty woman. An unusual surge of jealousy shot through her as she tried to concentrate once more on the movie.

It was no use! Suddenly she was acutely aware of Graham's large frame sitting next to her. Strange. A few minutes earlier she hadn't even noticed who was beside her. But now she could catch the faint whiff of his sexy aftershave and almost feel the heat off his tanned, muscular arms as they barely brushed her bare ones now. Was it her imagination, or had he scooted closer? It was impossible to keep her mind on the screen. Without being obvious, she tried her best to get a better glimpse of the woman he was with. *I wonder if that's Liza, Schultzie, the blonde. . . .* She fumed silently. Obviously he had a different lady for each night!

He leaned just a fraction closer and whispered out of the corner of his mouth, "Who's the wimp you're with?"

"None of your business," she returned tightly, keeping her eyes glued to the movie. She couldn't have told anyone what was happening if her life depended on it.

"Oh, come on. What's his name?" he persisted smoothly.

"Would the monkey you're with like a banana?" she taunted back.

"I don't think so. I just bought her some popcorn on the

way in. Now, what's the wimp's name?" He shifted a little closer, his mouth barely brushing her ear now.

Courtney felt her knees turn weak and her stomach develop a case of unruly butterflies. Suddenly the world consisted of two people: Graham Merrill and Courtney Spenser. For the moment, all else seemed to be nonexistent.

"His name's Freddy Mercer," she answered in a quiet murmur. For some unexplained reason, she was mesmerized by the touch of his lips on her ear.

He wasn't kissing her ear, he was merely leaning over until his mouth gently brushed against the white lobe. "That's not the same man who was kissing you the other day, is it?"

Graham's voice was barely a low husky whisper now. The "wimp" and the "monkey" didn't seem to notice that Graham and Courtney were conversing.

"No." She thought for a moment, then added, "That was Rob." Courtney swallowed hard and closed her eyes, savoring the musky male scent of him and the way he was making tiny shivers race wildly up and down her spine.

This time the hand that took hers in the dark was welcomed. Gently he caressed the palm with his thumb in slow, lazy circles. "Anything serious between the wimp *or* Rob and you, Miss Spenser?" he asked conversationally.

"Again, none of your business, Dr. Merrill."

There was the brief sound of a low male chuckle in her ear. "Surely an old maid can do better than bring a wimp to the movies with her. Look at him. All he wants to do is eat popcorn," he pointed out politely.

"Ha! That 'wimp' has more hands than Carter has Little Liver Pills," she scoffed in a low tone.

"Wouldn't you rather be brought to the movies and kissed than watch your date eat?" His soft words sent the stomach butterflies working overtime as his hands kept hers tightly imprisoned in his.

She turned slightly in her seat until her mouth was close to his ear now. "Maybe," she breathed in a sexy breathlessness, "but don't you think you'd better turn your attention back to your *own* date, Dr. Merrill, and let me worry about mine?"

Graham peered over at the woman next to him, who was deeply concentrating on the movie. "Naw. She's watching the movie."

"Are *you* serious about her?" Courtney couldn't resist asking.

"Miss Spenser. Does it appear to you I'm serious about her?"

"How should I know?" Courtney feigned indifference. For all she knew, he might take one girl to the movies and hold another one's hand all the time!

"Well, I'm not," he whispered back. "This was a spur-of-the-moment idea."

"You're not interested in her?" Courtney's heart lurched. Was it possible that one woman out of a million would escape his interest? Not that it made her any difference, but still it didn't keep her heart from thudding almost painfully in her chest.

"Who? Myrna? Now, what would she have that you think I'd be interested in?"

"How should I know?" Courtney replied crossly.

"I'll bet you think I like the way she's built." He whistled suggestively through his teeth. "Or all that gorgeous red hair and those big blue eyes. Or maybe the size of her . . ." He whistled through his teeth again.

"I suppose you don't?"

"Naw. I don't think so," he scoffed.

"Why not?"

"I don't like the dress she's wearing."

Freddy leaned over and peered at Courtney in the darkness. "What are you and that fellow talking about!" he demanded in a low growl.

86

"Uh . . . nothing really." Courtney smiled guiltily and scooted away from Graham hurriedly. "Just idle chit-chat."

Although she had moved away from Graham, her hand still rested firmly in his. Out of the corner of her eye, she saw the beginning of the tiniest grin at the corners of his mouth. A totally smug male grin.

Leaning back in her seat, she let his smile seep over onto her lips. Let him sit there and think she enjoyed him secretly holding her hand! He was so arrogant she would never make him believe that she didn't. But then again, she was no fool. She might make *him* believe that his touch didn't stir her, that the feel of his hand holding hers didn't thrill her, that the way his mouth had brushed against her ear didn't make her long for the touch of his lips on hers . . . feelings no man had ever really brought alive in her. At that moment, in that dark theater, for the first time in Courtney Spenser's thirty years, she knew what it felt like to actually desire a man. Whether she liked it or not, she was beginning to desire Dr. Graham Merrill in all the ways that would understandably feed his colossal ego! *Fool, fool, fool!* a small voice inside her shouted, but Courtney barely heard it as she grasped his hand tighter and smiled contentedly into the darkness.

The heat still held the city captive as the Mercers and Spensers emerged from the movie two hours later. Courtney watched almost resentfully as Graham and his date walked past the foursome standing outside the theater.

"Graham, dear!" Bonita called amiably. "Why, I didn't realize that you were here!"

"Good evening, Mrs. Spenser." Graham paused, glancing over at Courtney with that smug grin still on his face.

"Bonita. You *must* call me Bonita, dear," she urged, taking his arm and pulling him over to introduce him to Francis and Fredrick.

After the round of introductions were completed, Graham politely introduced Myrna.

"How do you do," Courtney murmured, her enthusiasm for the meeting sadly lacking.

"Where's your father tonight, dear?" Bonita asked Graham timidly.

"I'm not sure, Mrs—Bonita. I think he went roller-skating."

Bonita's lower lip sagged and she shot Courtney an accusing glare. "Oh."

"Well, Mother, I'm sure Dr. Merrill and Myrna want to be on their way," Courtney intervened brightly. She still was shaken by the fact that she had actually sat in that dark movie theater and held hands with that man all evening. She had no idea what had gotten into her!

"Oh. Well, tell Clyde I said hi." Bonita looked at Graham pitifully.

"I will. Nice seeing you." Graham took Myrna's arm and steered her off in the direction of the parking area.

Courtney watched his strong, manly stride as they disappeared down the street, her mind wandering back to the kiss he had given her the first day they met. He would probably be "teaching" Myrna how to kiss before the evening was over! For the second time that evening, painful stabs of jealousy shot through her.

Straightening her shoulders, Courtney forced her thoughts back to the present. That kiss hadn't mattered. Any man could kiss her and make her feel the same way.

"Shall we go for coffee now?" Freddy asked, breaking the silence.

Courtney glanced up and met his admiring gaze. For a moment she had forgotten he was around.

"Sounds great." She smiled, but her heart wasn't in it. Any man kiss her? she thought again. Hardly. No, Graham's kiss had been different and that realization didn't improve her evening one iota!

CHAPTER FIVE

For seven long days, Bonita had not mentioned Clyde Merrill's name. She seemed to have settled down, and peace reigned over the Spenser household once more.

As Bonita sat fanning herself with the small cardboard fan she had picked up at the last county fair, she sniffed the air appreciably. Although she couldn't actually see the ocean, she could smell it. It had been another scorcher that day, and she had decided to sit out in the yard for a while that evening to enjoy what breezes the ocean could carry inland.

The backyard was alive with the sounds of nature. The lush green trees and plants were a comfort to Bonita. She had always loved to work in her yard when Frank was alive. . . . She paused, and her eyes misted. Frank. The thought of her husband of over thirty years tugged painfully at her heartstrings. Frank had been gone for seven years now, but somehow the ache of loneliness was just as sharp that night as it had been the first year she was left alone. Thirty years. A long time to spend with a man. At first, all Bonita could remember were the good times she and Frank had spent together. All the little quarrels, disagreements and sometimes outright shouting matches seemed to have been blotted out of her memory forever. Frank Spenser had been such a vitally alive man, and when he died, a part of Bonita had gone with him. Only the part of himself that he left behind, his daughter, Courtney, made the last few years bearable.

Every day Bonita drank in the sight of Frank as she saw his blue eyes staring back at her when she looked at her daughter. And the way Courtney's chin would jut out stubbornly—just as Frank's would when things didn't go to suit him. Courtney's nose was her mother's, but the shape of her face was Frank's.

Bonita sighed as she shifted around in her lawn chair, trying to force away thoughts of Frank. It had taken her a long time to resign herself to Frank's death, but over the last few months she had finally decided that no matter how hard she fought against it, Frank Spenser *was* gone. No longer would he pull into the drive at night, or kiss her good-bye in the morning. No longer would he be there for her to lean on, take over all the thousand and one little things a man did to keep a house running. She could no longer curl up in his arms at night and feel like she was safe and protected against the world. He wouldn't be there for her to tell all her monumental problems to and have him turn them into molehills.

Bonita knew all these things—yet it still hurt so very, very much. Courtney had been a comfort to her in the past years, but Courtney was still young and had her own life to live. That was the one thing she was determined would not happen. She did not *ever* want to be a burden to her daughter. Too many times she had seen her friends make their children's lives miserable by demanding time and attention. Bonita Spenser would never impose that problem on Courtney. She didn't want to live her life through her child. She wanted a life of her own, not to mention the fact she'd like to see Courtney happily married and settled down.

A tiny, radiant smile crossed her wrinkled features. She had had Courtney late in life. She had been three years younger than Courtney was now when she first met Frank.

One year later, she married him. They had had to wait ten long years before Courtney was born, despairing at times of ever having a family, but when Courtney finally arrived, Bonita felt life had given her more than her share of happiness.

Heaving another wistful sigh, Bonita fanned faster. She did wish that Courtney would get on the ball and find herself a nice, solid husband! For the life of her, she didn't know how her daughter had escaped some sort of serious involvement all these years. A lot of willing candidates had been around, but Courtney had politely turned them down and made her way alone. Bonita was honestly beginning to wonder if Courtney would ever fall in love.

"Pssst!"

Her fan slowed as she cocked an ear. "Did someone call?"

"Pssst, over here!" The hushed whisper came from behind some tall shrubs in the back corner of the yard.

She got up and walked hesitantly toward the voice, her eyes peering into the darkness. "Is that you, Clyde?"

"Yes. Come over here." He sounded worried.

Bonita made her way through the thick bushes, then stopped abruptly as she ran into the tall form of Clyde Merrill.

"Why, Clyde! What are you doing out here in the bushes?" she exclaimed happily.

"Now, fifty years ago, I would have had an appropriate remark to make at this point, but I'm afraid my age really *is* catching up with me." He winked playfully.

Bonita blushed and reached out to take his hand. "Your age will never catch up with you, Clyde Merrill. But, really, why are you out here like this?"

"I was afraid to let your daughter see me," Clyde admitted sheepishly.

Bonita glanced back at the house hurriedly. "I don't

think she did. She was going to take a shower and wash her hair."

"Good. Maybe we can sit out here and talk for a while," he answered in a relieved tone.

"Here?" She glanced around once more at the rather weedy area, thinking about all the little crawly things that might be lurking in the brush.

"Sure, why not?" Clyde sat down and patted a place beside him. "I had to sneak away from Buddy. That boy's been watching me like a hawk! This will be the first place he comes looking for me, and I don't want him finding me tonight."

"I know," Bonita agreed, settling herself down on the grass next to him. "Courtney's been the same way. I'm surprised she lets me go to the bathroom by myself lately."

"Those two are bound and determined to keep us apart, and I don't like it one bit." Clyde patted her hand affectionately. "I've missed you this week, Bonnie Spenser." His eyes twinkled merrily in the darkness as he smiled down on her.

"I've missed you too, Clyde Merrill."

"You know, we shouldn't let those two pipsqueaks tell us what we can do, don't you?" he scolded in a grumpy tone. "Darn it, if that boy wasn't so old, I'd turn him over my knee and show him who's boss!"

"They're just concerned about us, dear," she excused in a pacifying voice. "Although I know exactly how you feel."

Clyde turned to her with an incriminating glare. "How was the movie the other night?"

"Oh—interesting," she replied weakly. "How did you know about that?"

"My little 'blessing' let me know about it as soon as he hit the door that night. Said he had seen you and Francis Mercer there."

92

"Yes, he did," Bonita admitted, "but I didn't want to be! Courtney made me go."

"Well, I didn't like it one bit," Clyde grumbled, his hand tightening on hers, "but I know what you have to put up with. Buddy made me take that dippy Mildred Mosely to that stupid bingo game last night! Boy, that was a crock of manure if I ever saw one!"

"You took Mildred Mosely to the bingo game?" Her heart fell. Now Mildred would be bragging all over town that she had been out with Clyde!

"Yeah, I took her. Spent the whole night listening to her complain about her aches and pains," he said glumly.

Bonita smiled at him sweetly. "You can't fault her for that, Clyde! My goodness, I have a lot of aches and pains myself."

"Yes, but you don't sit around and gripe about them all night," he protested grimly. "I don't exactly feel like I'm twenty-one myself, but I try not to make everyone else around me miserable!"

Her spirits lifted at the compliment. That's one of the things she liked most about Clyde. He wasn't a complainer.

They sat together in the darkness, neither one speaking for a while. The sounds of the summer night encased them as they held hands, enjoying each other's presence.

"Did you go skating the other night?" Bonita asked pleasantly.

"I went for a little while. It wasn't much fun without you," he replied quietly.

"I thought about you all that evening," she confessed. "I would much rather have been with you than Francis."

"You would?" His face lit up. "You didn't have a good time with him?"

"Oh, I had a good time . . . I guess. Francis is a very nice man. . . ." Her voice trailed off.

93

"Oh." Clyde's tone was a bit petulant. "You going out with him again?"

"I hope not. I mean, he hasn't asked again."

"Will Courtney make you if he does?"

"I don't think she'll *make* me," Bonita defended. "I just hate to upset her. She thinks she's looking out for my interests."

Again the silence fell between them. The moon rose higher in the sky, casting its shady beams across the couple. It was so nice to sit there and just talk together, Bonita thought. So nice to once again have a strong shoulder to lean on.

"Clyde, do you ever get lonely? I mean really lonely," she asked softly.

Clyde picked up a blade of grass and leaned back against the privacy fence. His expression grew solemn and thoughtful. "Yes, Bonnie. I get lonely at times."

"How long has your wife been gone?"

"Twelve years. Some days it seems like twelve hundred, then at other times it seems like twelve hours. But one thing that's consistent is the loneliness. It doesn't ever get any easier."

"I was sitting here earlier, thinking about Frank. I miss him so much at times." Her voice sounded almost child-like in the darkness. Small and insecure.

Clyde glanced over and his expression grew tender. "You and Frank had a lot of happy years together. Why shouldn't you miss him?"

Bonita shook her head thoughtfully. "I feel rather embarrassed sometimes when I realize he's been gone for seven years now and I still wake up in the middle of the night crying. People tell me I should snap out of it, that he's been gone long enough for me to adjust . . . and most of the time I have adjusted," she added defensively, "but at other times . . ."

"At other times the pain puts you in your own private

94

corner of hell," Clyde finished. "I know where you're coming from, Bonnie. I've been there many times myself. Don't think that women are the only ones who suffer and feel insecure when they lose their mate. I walked around in a daze for over a year after Emily died. There were times in the first few months after her death, I'd walk through the house at night and see her everywhere I stepped. If I went to the kitchen for a glass of water, she'd be standing at the stove making dinner. In the living room, she'd be sitting in that big old chair she always sat in, knitting or crocheting, or whatever it is you women are always doing." He sighed softly. "That's one of the reasons I finally sold the house. I couldn't sleep in our bedroom for six months after she died. I slept in the guestroom."

"And you still miss her very much," Bonita whispered in complete understanding.

"Yes, I still miss her very much," he agreed. "But life goes on, Bonnie. Neither Frank nor Emily would have wanted us to just sit around and wait for death to snatch us up. What we had with Frank and Emily was warm and wonderful. It can never be replaced. At least not in the same form." He turned to face her in the shimmering moonlight, one large finger gently wiping away the stray tear that fell from her misty eyes. "I may not ever love a woman in the same way that I loved Emily, but I'm not at all sure that I *can't* love another woman. What about you, Bonnie? Can you ever find room in your heart for another man?"

"Yes," she whispered truthfully. "I loved Frank with all my heart, but I think that maybe I'm ready to say good-bye to him now."

As their eyes met, there was a radiant shining of new understanding in each weary pair. There would never be another love like Frank Spenser in Bonita's life, nor would there be another Emily for Clyde. But they both still had a lot of love left to give, and their gaze held the promise of a new future—one free of the past.

Clyde pulled her face closer and his lips brushed hers sweetly. "We both may be old fools, but I want to keep seeing you, Bonnie."

"Oh, I want that too, Clyde. I want that very badly." She accepted his kiss eagerly, feeling alive for the first time in seven years.

"Mother?" Courtney's voice reached them in a hazy fog.

"That's Courtney, dear," she murmured, unwillingly pulling away from his tender embrace.

"Blast it all! Do you think she's seen us?" Clyde grumbled, peeking out through the shrubbery.

"No, she couldn't have. She probably looked out the window and wondered where I'd gone," Bonita soothed.

Clyde groaned painfully as he stood up and rubbed his back. "Darn joints are stiffenin' up on me."

"Next time we'll meet in the park, dear," she offered, helping him rub the sore spots. "We'll be able to sit on one of those nice benches."

"Do we have to keep sneaking around like a couple of damn teenagers?" he asked irritably, shaking her hand away.

"Shhh, Courtney will hear you!" Bonita warned.

"Well, let her hear me! She and Buddy both need to be told who are the parents and who are the children. They seem to have forgotten!"

"Let's not upset them, Clyde. Maybe if we give them a little time, they'll get used to the idea of us seeing each other," she urged quietly. "You know how upset Graham was the other night. I hate the thought of fibbing to them, but I think it's best if we just continue to see each other on the sly. What they don't know won't hurt them."

"I don't like it *one* bit, Bonnie, but if that's what you want, that's the way it will be. I've already told Buddy that he isn't going to run my life! Now it's up to you to get it straight with your daughter," he warned.

"Just give her a little time. She'll come around," Bonita predicted, biting her lip apprehensively. She wasn't at all sure Courtney would come around, but she wanted the peace and tranquillity of the past week to last for a little longer.

Clyde pulled her back to him for one last stolen kiss. "You see that she does," he ordered gruffly, kissing her most soundly. "I'll call you soon!"

By the time Bonita stepped out from behind the shrubbery, her face was flushed and her heart was beating like a jackhammer. Seventy years old or not, Clyde Merrill was still all man!

The next morning at the shop, Courtney was beginning to get downright worried. She had found out long ago that things that seemed too good to be true were just that. Too good to be true!

With a sense of uneasiness, she watched her mother humming happily under her breath as she dusted the shelves, acting for all the world like she didn't have a care. It was hard to believe that Bonita and Clyde would give up so easily on their tenacious relationship. In Courtney's opinion, something was rotten in Denmark!

"You seem awfully happy this morning, Mother. Any particular reason?" Courtney asked pleasantly.

"No, dear." Bonita continued humming along.

It had now been nearly two weeks since the night Graham and Courtney had bailed their parents out of jail, and other than the night of the movie, her mother hadn't mentioned Clyde. Strange. Really strange. Courtney couldn't help but wonder where Bonita had been going the last few evenings when she had said that she was going down to the senior citizens' center, or to the ladies' aid quilting party held once a week at the church . . . or strangest of all, to some nursing home to visit a friend Courtney had never heard of.

Maybe Courtney *was* being a little paranoid when she had accused her mother of having grease on the back of her slacks when she returned home from visiting Bertha Adams at the nursing home, three nights ago, but it had looked mighty suspicious. She decided to fish around.

"How was Mrs. Adams?"

"Who?" Bonita paused and glanced at her daughter.

"Mrs. Adams, the friend you went to see the other night."

"Oh, *that* Mrs. Adams." Bonita smiled angelically. "She's fine." She busied herself dusting again.

"Fine? I thought she fell and broke her hip and two ribs." Courtney watched her mother warily.

"Oh, she did. But she's fine other than that."

The bell over the door tinkled as Rob Hanson breezed in and walked over to where Courtney was busy arranging a new shipment. "What's up, doll?"

"Good morning, Rob." She sincerely hoped he wouldn't think it necessary to spend the next thirty minutes regaling her with his questionable charm.

"Where you been keeping yourself lately?" He reached out and stilled Courtney's flying hand.

"I've been busy." She smiled halfheartedly up into his tanned, handsome features. "Did you want something?"

Rob emitted a low, sexy growl and wiggled his eyebrows suggestively. "Do I want something!"

"Good morning, Robert, dear," Bonita called from atop her perch. "You're looking nice as usual."

"Hi, Bonita." Rob turned his attention away from Courtney and onto her mother. "What are you doing way up there?"

"Dusting the top of all these shelves. Goodness! They haven't been cleaned in months."

"Aren't you afraid you'll fall and hurt yourself?" Rob

watched uneasily as she crawled from shelf to shelf, then turned back to Courtney. "Aren't you afraid she'll fall and break her neck?"

"Yes, and I've told her so umpteen thousand times, but you can plainly see how seriously my opinion is taken," Courtney replied calmly. "Possibly she'll listen to reason when she finds herself lying next to Mrs. Adams in the nursing home with both her legs broken."

Rob flashed a startling white grin in her direction. "Is little Courtney in a bad mood this morning?"

"No. On the contrary, I'm in a good mood." Courtney smiled back. "Want a cup of coffee?"

"Sure. Why not?" He heaved his athletic frame up on the counter and made himself comfortable as Courtney poured his coffee. "How about going out to dinner with me tonight?"

"Sorry, I have to wash my hair tonight," Courtney returned quickly.

"You just washed your hair last night," Bonita reminded her helpfully, in a cloud of fogging dust.

Courtney shot her an irritated glance, then tried again. "The kitchen floor needs to be waxed."

"I did that after you left this morning."

"Mother! Please! Rob and I are having this discussion," Courtney said in exasperation.

"Well, I'm *sorry*, dear. I just thought that you would probably enjoy a nice night out with Robert." Bonita went back to her dusting.

"Yeah. And Robert would enjoy a nice night out with Courtney. How about it?" Rob took another sip of his coffee and grinned at her engagingly.

"I don't think I'd better, Rob. I was going to fix a quiet dinner for Mother and me, then turn in early," Courtney hedged.

"Count me out," Bonita called down brightly. "I'm going out tonight."

"Where?" Courtney whirled around and faced her mother.

"Uh . . . back to see Bertha Adams," she returned swiftly.

"Again? That's three times this week!"

"I know. But I promised her I'd stop by again tonight." For some reason, Bonita's face looked terribly sheepish at the moment.

Courtney's mind shifted back to last night when her mother had mysteriously oiled her roller skates just before going to bed. "Are you sure that's where you're going?" Courtney questioned skeptically, a distrustful gleam growing in her eye.

"Oh, for goodness' sakes, Court, why don't you leave your mom alone and stop making excuses? Will you or will you not go out to dinner with me tonight?" Rob asked impatiently.

Courtney searched her brain to come up with some plausible excuse, but failed. "What time?" she asked in a defeated tone.

"Seven. Put your glad rags on, baby, 'cause we're going to paint the town red!" Rob jumped down off the counter and gave her a squeeze.

Courtney smiled weakly and wondered, not for the first time, why she didn't find Rob attractive. What was it about Graham Merrill that attracted her, when Rob didn't? Graham Merrill. Now what had brought his name to her mind?

"I'll be ready by seven." What else could she say?

By six thirty that evening she had managed to think of at least five more excuses why she shouldn't go out with Rob. She just plain didn't want to was at the head of her list, followed by the fact that she wasn't interested in a man, any man, at the moment. For the life of her, she couldn't understand why she wasn't flattered by Rob's attention. He was certainly nice looking and Rob would probably never think of hauling her around on some ludicrous motorcycle like one certain man had seen fit to do! The mere thought of that incident made her blood boil, as she angrily inserted a tiny gold stud in her ear and secured it. Casting one last appraising glance in the mirror, she marched out of her bedroom into the living room. It was still twenty-five minutes before Rob was due, so she picked up a magazine and leafed through disinterestedly.

Bonita had left for the nursing home nearly an hour ago, using the excuse that she wanted to stop for a hamburger on the way. Courtney had never heard of this Bertha Adams that Bonita was such good friends with until this week, but she was grateful her mother had found someone to take her mind off Clyde Merrill. For just a brief moment, Courtney found herself wondering what his despicable son, Graham, was doing this evening.

The phone rang, making her jump with a start. She picked up the receiver and said hello.

"Hello, is Bonita there?"

"No. She's out for the evening. Is this Grace?"

"Yes, Courtney, this is Grace. Do you know where Bonita is?" Grace Wilder asked in her quiet, pleasant tone.

"She went down to spend the evening with Bertha Adams. Do you want to leave a message?"

There was dead silence on the other end of the line for a moment, then Grace cleared her voice and said, "Surely you're mistaken, dear."

"Mistaken? No, Grace, I don't think so. Mom's been going to see Bertha quite regularly for the last week."

"I don't find that at all funny, Courtney!" Grace said sternly. "Bertha Adams passed away three weeks ago."

"Passed away?" Courtney's voice came out in an audible squeak.

"It was in the paper, dear. Right there in the obituary column."

101

"Dead! Bertha's dead!" Courtney repeated in a strangled tone.

"As a doornail," Grace confirmed.

Why that low-down, conniving . . . Bonita had deliberately lied to her for the past week! But it didn't take a genius to figure out who was responsible for her mother's deplorable actions. It could only be one sneaky, wily, underhanded coyote—Clyde Merrill!

By the time Courtney was able to get rid of Grace on the phone, she was shaking like a leaf. The thought that she had been such a gullible fool left her temper soaring. She would bet her last dime that Clyde and Bonita had been whooping it up for the last week right under their children's unsuspecting noses! Of all the nerve!

She snatched the phone up, then slammed it back down when she realized she didn't know the number she wanted to dial. Rummaging through the small drawer of the phone table, she found the directory and once again looked up the name Dr. Graham Merrill. *Dr.* Merrill was going to hear about this! Apparently he had been neglecting *his* duties and failed to keep a watchful eye on his father.

After dialing his home phone number, she listened with a sinking heart as his answering service came on the line.

Once more she was forced to sit and drum her fingers agitatedly on the table as she waited for his service to reach him. Ten minutes later the phone finally rang.

"This is Dr. Merrill."

"Dr. Merrill. This is Courtney Spenser!"

Graham let out a low groan. "Oh, hell, I didn't recognize the number."

"Listen, Casanova, I do hate to bother you, but are you aware that *your* father and *my* mother might very well be off on his death-trap machine again tonight?" she asked curtly.

"Get out of here," he scoffed. "Dad's at a VFW meeting."

"*You* get out of here! VFW meetings are only on *Thursday* nights."

"Are you serious? He's been going up to the VFW hall for the past week nearly every night," Graham said disbelievingly.

"Just like Mom's been going to quilting circles, senior citizens' meetings, and the biggest farce of all, to visit poor, old, *dead* Bertha Adams!"

"Dead who? Will you stop talking in circles and tell me what's going on? You're interrupting my evening," he said bluntly.

"Oh, I am *so* sorry." Her voice dripped with sarcasm. "Whose turn is it this evening? Liza, Schultzie, the blonde, Myrna the monkey—"

"Wrong. Clarissa the winner. What's the matter, Snow White? Did one of your wimpy dwarfs forget to pick you up tonight?" His voice held as much sarcasm as hers did.

"I did not make this call to listen to your insults," she informed him coolly. "I thought that you might possibly be interested in tracking your father down before he is arrested for speeding and thrown in jail again."

"Are you *sure* Bonnie and Clyde are together?" It was glaringly apparent he wasn't crazy about cutting his evening short.

Courtney had a moment of uneasiness before she answered him. She wasn't *really* that sure that Bonita and Clyde were together.

"Well! Are you sure, Miss Spenser?"

"Well, I'm *fairly* sure, Dr. Merrill!"

"Boy, I can see why you're still an old maid," he said rudely. "You're enough to drive a man nuts."

"If *you* were the man I was driving, it wouldn't be a very long trip," she responded unperturbed. "Now, kiss Clarissa good night and hustle on over here. We have work to do. By the way, pick me up on the corner. I'll explain later." She placed the receiver back in the cradle before he could speak.

Courtney glanced at her watch and noted that Rob would be there in a few minutes. She scurried around the room looking for a pen and paper, mentally berating herself for taking the coward's way out. It was a nasty thing to do to Rob, but she knew if she called or tried to explain in person, he would insist on coming along with her, and the last thing she wanted was to have to put up with *two* asinine men in one evening!

Scribbling a hasty message on the note pad, she ripped off the sheet and secured it to the front door. Feeling for all the world like the dirty rat she was, she bounded down the street in a dead run, irritated yet curiously exhilarated at the thought of seeing Graham Merrill once again.

CHAPTER SIX

A brown Ford sedan shot up to the curb and screeched to an angry halt. The passenger door flew open and a deep male voice gruffly ordered Courtney, "Get in!"

Courtney glared irritably at the occupant of the car. "Why, if it isn't Manners Merrill." She stepped into the car and barely had time to shut the door before the car roared away from the curb. "I see you're no better at driving a car than you are a motorcycle!"

"You are getting to be a real pain in the posterior, Miss Spenser," Graham said in a tightly controlled voice. "Couldn't you have taken care of this without my help?"

"No. You're the brains of this operation. I'm simply carrying out your orders." She smiled at him innocently. "If you remember, I'm supposed to ride shotgun on Mom, while you ride herd on Clyde, which, by the way, you have failed miserably at, I might add."

"He told me he was going to a VFW meeting! How was I to know he was pulling one on me? You wait until I get my hands on him," he muttered impatiently.

"Well, don't feel bad." Courtney sighed. "Mother's pulled an even bigger one on me. She's supposedly been visiting a friend in the nursing home all week and I just found out the woman has been dead for three weeks!"

"This has got to stop!" Graham wheeled around the corner and merged the car onto the freeway. "I spend half my time trying to track those gypsies down and I'm get-

105

ting tired of it. Why can't they stay home whittling and knitting like most ordinary people do at their age?"

"Mother doesn't like to knit," Courtney pointed out.

"Well, get her some yarn and make her!"

"I can't 'make' her do anything, Graham. Good heavens! I'm still the child and she's the mother! You're just upset because I interrupted your date with—"

"Clarissa," he supplied helpfully, "and you're darn right I'm upset! Do you realize it took me a full week to talk her into going out with me?"

"What a pity. My heart really goes out to you," she said sympathetically. "All that hard work down the drain."

He glanced at her coldly out of the corner of his eye. "I can see it really tears you up," he replied dryly.

"Oh, it does." She crossed her hands in her lap primly and grinned. "It really does."

"I don't suppose you would have any idea where they would go, do you?" he asked, changing the subject for the moment.

"Maybe skating . . ."

"No, I saw Dad's skates in the closet as I left earlier."

"What about the amusement park?"

"Possibly, but I think he was out there this weekend. At least he brought home a bunch of goldfish in bowls, about ten of those cheap dishes, and about sixty packages of cigarettes he said he won somewhere."

"Does he smoke?"

"No." Graham looked at her in exasperation. "What difference does that make? You should see his room. It's a real pig sty with all the junk he drags in."

"I know. Mother must have been with him. She has a bunch of stuffed animals and a sack of canned goods she said she won at the country store."

"Maybe they've gone to a movie," Graham offered as he swung the car off the ramp to drive by one of the local movie theaters. They drove down the streets peering anxiously for any sign of Bonita and Clyde.

"Would they be in his car or on his motorcycle?" Courtney asked thoughtfully.

"I don't know. He was still home when I left this evening."

"Then he could have taken his skates after you left," she reminded him. As they slowly passed the theater, it suddenly dawned on Courtney that this definitely was not where her mother would be. It was the same movie they had seen with the Mercer men last week.

"Graham, I don't think they would be here."

Graham glanced over at her, then up to the marquee. Courtney could have sworn he blushed as he read the sign aloud. "*Midnight Cowboy.* Oh, yeah, I forgot."

"Yes, Mom's already seen the . . . movie."

Graham increased his speed once more, moving away from the theater. "You know you should be ashamed of yourself for taking your mother to a movie like that," he scolded curtly.

"Me! I didn't take her. She was the one who selected the movie," Courtney defended.

"Oh, now come on, Courtney!" Graham clearly didn't believe that!

"She did!"

"Your mother wanted to go see that movie about a couple of—"

"She didn't know they were hustlers. She thought it was going to be a western and she thought that Francis and Freddy would enjoy . . ." Courtney felt her face turning red.

"I'll just bet old Freddy enjoyed it."

"I wouldn't know. He didn't say," she returned hurriedly. "Besides, where do you get off telling me I shouldn't be at that movie. I seem to remember you were there." Boy, did she ever remember he was there. Her

107

stomach still lurched when she thought of his touch and the brush of his lips across her ear in the dark movie theater.

He turned and smiled at her wickedly. "Well, it certainly turned out to be more enjoyable than I had planned on."

Courtney knew he was thinking of how he had touched her and kissed her ear, which probably meant about as much to him as his blond date had that evening!

"Really? I don't remember much about the movie," Courtney said coolly.

"The movie?" Graham smile grew broader. "I don't remember much about the movie myself."

Trying to ignore his tormenting manner, Courtney suggested that they try another theater several blocks away. Two hours later they were still searching unsuccessfully for the wandering parents.

"I'm starved," Graham announced in a grumpy voice as they walked into one of the local bowling alleys. "If they're not in here I'm going to take time for a hamburger and a beer."

"What's the matter, didn't Clarissa feed you this evening?" Courtney chided as they entered the smoky building.

Graham winked at her sexily. "Man does not live by bread alone."

Courtney looked at him distastefully and fanned the air with her hand irritably. "Let's just get on with our business and get out of this stuffy place." The air hung thick with blue smoke and the room was very noisy.

"What's the matter, Miss Primmy Britches? Don't you like bowling alleys?"

"I wouldn't know. This is the first time I've ever been in one. I can find more important things to do with my time than throw a ball at a bunch of wooden pins." She looked at him aloofly. "I leave that to people like you." The word "you" came out like a dirty no-no.

"You're no fun at all," he told her matter-of-factly as his eyes scanned the room for Bonita and Clyde. "Do you see them anywhere?"

Courtney squinted into the haze of smoke and bodies. "No, do you?"

"Not at the moment. Let's walk over to the snack bar and get a hamburger. They've got the best burgers and fries in town."

"I'm sure." Courtney's nose turned up in disapproval.

They made their way over to the counter and Graham dropped down on one of the barstools, motioning for Courtney to join him. Reaching for a napkin in its holder, Courtney wiped off the seat before she sat down.

"Are you afraid you'll pick up some kind of disease?" Graham asked as he watched her fold the napkin neatly and lay it in the ashtray.

"This place doesn't look very sanitary to me," she mumbled uneasily.

"This place is clean," he dismissed her objections sharply as he picked up the menu and glanced over it. "I'll take a hamburger and fries. What do you want?"

Courtney bit her lip. She was hungry since she had missed her dinner too, but she really didn't want to eat in a bowling alley!

"Maybe I'll have a cup of coffee." At least the boiling water should kill whatever germs were lurking nearby.

"A cup of coffee." He threw the menu down on the counter and motioned for the waitress. "Two hamburgers, two fries, and two beers."

"I didn't want a hamburger," she protested.

"Cheeseburger?"

"Are you sure they're clean here?" she asked suspiciously.

"Positive. I come in here and clean in my spare time," he whispered secretly.

"Well, maybe I will take a cheeseburger," she relented hesitantly.

"You're just about the bravest woman I've ever met," he complimented mockingly as he winked at the waitress.

When the waitress brought their meal and set it before them, Courtney's nose turned upward once again.

"Now what's wrong?" Graham asked curtly.

"It's the beer."

"What's the matter with it? Not your brand?"

"No, not that. I rarely drink anything and when I do, I certainly don't drink it out of the bottle," she said.

"Well, pardon me. Judy! Bring the princess a crystal goblet to sip from," Graham called out obligingly. He turned back to face her. "How's that?"

"You don't have to make a public spectacle!" She glared at him angrily.

"Sorry, honey, it's just that I'm not used to being with royalty. Tell me. What does a princess do on a date?"

"This 'princess' rarely dates, but when she does, it certainly isn't with a common serf," she returned smoothly.

Graham looked at her, a tiny smile escaping from his stern features. "Oh? Then what does she do with all her time?"

Courtney shrugged her shoulders disinterestedly. "She just sits around the castle all day yelling 'off with their heads, off with their heads'!" She smiled sweetly back at him. "Actually, it's a pretty boring life."

As she tried to keep the grease from running down her arm, she eagerly ate her cheeseburger.

"I have to admit, this is good," she told him as she stuck another french fry in her mouth.

"I told you the food was good," Graham said between mouthfuls. "Want another burger?"

"Are you going to have another one?"

"I'm thinking about it."

"Well, maybe I could eat another one. Tell her to put more catsup on the next one."

Graham motioned for the waitress once more. "Two more cheeseburgers with extra catsup, Judy." He turned to face Courtney. "Did you want extra grease too?"

"No, I think they're overly generous with that." She gave the most ladylike burp Graham had ever heard.

Graham looked back at her and grinned, really grinned at her for the first time. Her heart fluttered at the sparkling flash of his white teeth against the deep tan of his face. "You know, you're not bad when you come down off your high horse, Miss Spenser."

"You better enjoy it while it lasts," she warned with a playful wink. "It will probably go any minute!"

They settled back down to finish their dinner, eating in companionable silence.

Graham was interrupted several times by people stopping by to chat with him. He always introduced Courtney in a courteous manner, making her feel a little less self-conscious than she had been feeling. Contrary to first impressions, Graham Merrill seemed to be every ounce the gentleman when he wasn't trying to irritate her.

"Do you come here often?" Courtney asked as they turned back to their meal after the third interruption.

"I bowl in a league here every week. And a lot of my patients bowl here too," he explained as he ate the last of his fries.

Courtney munched on her second cheeseburger as she watched the group of bowlers closest to her laughing and having what appeared to be a marvelous time. She herself had never bowled. It had always seemed like a man's sport to her. Her dates had been more limited to dinner at the finest restaurants, then dancing afterward. She had never met a man quite like Dr. Graham Merrill, and at the moment she didn't know whether to classify that as a minus or a plus!

"Have you ever bowled?" he inquired.

"Me?" Courtney laughed and wiped her hands on the napkin lying in her lap. "No, I've never tried it," she confessed.

"Would you like to?"

Courtney looked surprised. She had thought he would be eager to return to his interrupted date if at all possible. "Now?"

"Unless you have something else to do. I don't think we're going to find Dad and Bonnie."

"Bonita," Courtney corrected hurriedly, "and I don't have anything else to do, but I thought you might want to get back to Clarissa."

"No, the night's ruined," he admitted defeatedly. "We might as well try to salvage some of it."

The warm, glowing feeling Courtney had begun to experience disappeared rapidly with his tactless words. Obviously he didn't want to spend the evening with her, but he was trying to make the best of a bad situation.

"You would have to show me what to do. I don't know the first thing about bowling," she warned as they slid off the barstools and Graham paid the bill.

"We'll have to rent you a pair of shoes, then we'll get you a ball over there on that rack." He pointed to a long row of bowling balls.

"Rent my shoes?" Courtney's face paled at the thought of wearing shoes that everyone in the world had worn previously.

"They've been sanitized!"

"But, Graham, I don't want to wear other people's shoes." She groaned weakly.

"Oh, hell. You're about as much fun as a soggy cookie. Wait here." He started to walk away from her, then turned and asked curtly, "What size shoe do you wear?"

"Seven and a half . . . but I won't wear those nasty . . ." She found herself talking to thin air as he strode

112

angrily away from her. Five minutes later he returned and put a shoe box in her hand. "Here. Put these on and follow me."

She glanced at the box in her hand and saw that they were a new pair of leather bowling shoes. She watched his retreating form with disbelief. He had bought her a brand-new pair of shoes! How utterly impractical!

"Graham, I can't let you buy these for me," she protested as she hurried to catch up with him. "How much were they? I'll pay you back." She had no idea what she would do with a pair of bowling shoes after that evening, but she certainly wasn't going to be indebted to him in any way.

"Just put them on and go over there and pick out a ball." He was standing at a locker trying to work a combination lock.

"I don't know the first thing about picking out a ball," she said worriedly. "Maybe this isn't such a good idea after all. These shoes are a waste of perfectly good money since I'll never wear them again after tonight—"

Graham slammed the locker door shut, a bowling ball and a pair of shoes in his hands now. "Every red-blooded American should have their own pair of bowling shoes," he dismissed absently as he pushed past her and walked over to the rack of balls. "How heavy a ball do you think you can handle?"

"What do you mean, how heavy?" she fretted. "I told you I don't know the first thing about bowling."

Graham sat his ball down on the floor and studied the selection before him. He turned back around to size up Courtney's small frame, then reached down and selected a ball. "Here, try this one."

Courtney's arm sagged to the floor as she tried to hold the ball he had given her. "My gosh! How much does this weigh?"

"Twelve measly little pounds," he chided.

"I think I'm going to need a few measly little pounds less." She grunted, handing the ball back to him.

"Well, I can go back behind the counter and get you an eight pounder they keep for babies and gnomes," he offered patiently.

"That won't be necessary," she shot back crossly. "I'm sure I can find something that hits a happy medium."

"Fine with me," Graham agreed happily. "I'll go get our score sheet."

It took several tries before Courtney was able to come up with a ball that didn't feel like it weighed a hundred pounds. She carried it over to the bowling area where Graham was sitting, putting on his bowling shoes.

"I see you finally found one," he said irritably. "I thought for a minute we were going to have to have one custom made."

"Very funny." Courtney banged the ball down on the conveyer and reached in her box for her shoes.

Graham picked up the ball she had selected and surveyed it carefully. "I hope you haven't got a good arm on you. As light as this ball is, you'll throw it through the back of the building if you're not careful," he observed.

Ignoring his taunting observations, Courtney stood up and looked down the narrow alley at the row of white pins sitting at the end. It suddenly looked a long way down there to try and throw a ball.

"I really don't think this is going to be very fair," she pointed out. "You apparently do this all the time and I don't even know where to begin."

"I'll spot you pins," he said easily. He stood up and reached for his ball. In another minute the pins had splattered against the back wall in a perfect strike. Looking at her smugly, he motioned for her to step up on the approach.

"Go ahead, take a warm-up shot."

114

Courtney swallowed hard, then reached for her ball. "Where do I stand?"

"See all these arrows?" Graham took her arm and guided her to the center of the approach. "The proper way to bowl is to use the arrows marked on the lanes. Some people prefer to look at the pins themselves, but I always throw on a certain arrow to be sure I hit the pocket each time."

"Pocket?"

"The pocket is the head pin, or number one, and three pin. You want to try to throw the ball where it will break into the head pin at an angle. If you hit the head pin straight on, chances are you're going to come up with a big split that will be impossible to pick up."

"It sounds easy enough," she agreed.

"It's harder than it sounds," he warned. "Now what I want you to do is throw a couple of practice balls to get the feel of it." He stepped back away from her to watch her beginner's approach.

Courtney's eyes were glued on the pins, one and three, sitting at the end of the alley. She surveyed the red arrows worriedly for a moment, then reared back to throw the ball at the arrow in the middle.

Both Courtney and Graham gasped as the ball flew backward out of her hands and barely missed hitting Graham in the area in which she had several times before been guilty of hitting him.

"Miss Spenser!" Graham straightened up and glowered at her soundly. "You are undoubtedly a walking hazard to my future children!"

"I'm sorry." Courtney wanted to cry. She had never been so klutzy in her whole life and especially never around a man.

"Just watch what you're doing!" He stepped back around behind her and his arms closed around her firmly.

115

"Hold on to the ball like this." His hands took hers and placed her fingers in the holes strategically.

"I am sorry," she whimpered, her knees turning to pure jelly as the sexy smell of his aftershave drifted tantalizingly around her. His arms wrapped tighter around her and he unconsciously pulled her up closer to his body to fit her hand into the ball. It suddenly became almost impossible for Courtney to breathe.

"Now, look. All you have to do is hold on to the ball tightly. . . ." He paused and sniffed her neck appreciably. "What kind of perfume are you wearing?" he asked softly.

"I—I think it's called Chloe," she murmured nervously.

His face buried deeper into the side of her neck for a moment, then he whispered huskily, "Darn, it smells good."

"I'm glad you like it," she acknowledged in a shaky voice. She wasn't at all sure her legs were going to support her much longer if he continued to hold her like he was.

"Okay." He seemed to regain control of himself as his embrace loosened and his voice turned businesslike once more. "Now try to throw it between the middle and third arrow."

Courtney held on tightly and carefully threw the ball. It lumbered slowly down the alley, finally reaching its destination and knocking over one pin.

"Not very good, huh?" she asked disappointedly.

"Well, Earl Anthony won't have to lay awake nights worrying about his job, but you'll improve," he said optimistically. "Try again."

After several more tries Courtney was managing to hit the pocket with increasing regularity. When she got her first strike, she jumped up and down in glee, delighted that she had finally accomplished her goal. "Will you just look at that!" she exclaimed happily. "You better call Earl and tell him he can start worrying now!"

Graham grinned and patted her on the head. "I think you're going to be a real natural, Miss Spenser. How about another bottle of that socially unacceptable beer?"

"Oh, I don't know, Graham." Her face clouded with concern. "I don't ever drink and I've already had one this evening."

"I don't think one more beer will put you under the table, but it's your choice."

"Well, what the heck." Courtney was feeling lighthearted and it was extremely warm in the bowling alley. "I'll have just one more."

"Be right back." Graham walked toward the bar as Courtney threw several more balls down the alley. By the time he returned, she was ready to challenge him in a game.

"All right. I'm ready to take you on," she said before she took a long swallow of the cold beer, straight from the bottle. She glanced around uneasily to see if anyone had seen her. Gad! He was beginning to drag her down to his level!

"Sounds good to me. I'll give you an eighty-percent handicap. That ought to be fair."

"How much do you usually bowl a game?" she asked, draining the last of the bottle and setting it down on the desk. She gripped the side of the seat as the world began to tilt crazily. "Whew. I think I drank that too fast."

Graham looked at her flushed face and smiled. "Better slow down if you're not used to drinking," he warned, sipping his beer slowly. "My average is around a hundred ninety-five in my bowling league."

"A hundred ninety-five! What's the highest possible score?"

"Three hundred, but I don't think either one of us will ever have to worry about that." He stood up and reached for his ball. "I'll try to take it easy on you."

Courtney giggled, then slapped her hand over her

mouth in mortification. She wasn't the giggling type! It must be the beer, she decided. She made up her mind to drink no more that evening.

Courtney kept up surprisingly well as the evening progressed. Graham seemed to be having a hard time, complaining that the lanes were too "dry," making his hook ball very ineffective.

"You are nothing but lucky," he accused her as she got her third strike in a row.

"I'm trying my best to take it easy on you." She giggled, draping her arm around his neck. "How about 'nother one of those deli-c-i-ousss cold beers?"

"You've had four. Are you sure you can hold another one?" Graham said dryly as he straightened her back up.

"Certai-n-ll-y, kind sir. I have an unusual thirst tonight. It must have been all those greasy chees-s-bur-gers." She patted his shoulder affectionately. "Don't you want another beer?"

"No, and I don't think you do either. How about a cup of coffee?"

"Coffee!" She fanned her hot, flushed face rapidly. "It's too hot for coffee."

Graham pulled her down on his lap and reached up to push back a stray lock of moist blond hair. "Miss Spenser, I hate to be the one to tell you this, but I think you're fast becoming loaded to the gills."

Courtney gasped indignantly. "I certainly am not! I don't even drink, Mr. Merrill!" She got up off his lap angrily. "It is extremely warm in here tonight, and I am unusually thirsty, that's the only reason I'm drinking beer at all. If you won't go get me another one, I will." She tossed her head in a haughty, perturbed manner.

"I'll be happy to buy you another one, but don't blame me if you wake up with a head as big as a bushel basket tomorrow morning," he warned, rising to his feet and starting toward the bar.

118

"That's ridiculous," she called smugly to his retreating back. "One more beer is not going to make me drunk!"

"I'll agree with you on that," he called back sweetly. "You're already there!"

When he returned, she downed the beer hurriedly and went back to the game. Twenty minutes later she was thirty points ahead of him and thirsty again.

"Just one more," she argued, draping herself around his neck again as he tried to add up the score.

"No way! You've had five too many as it is. Let's finish this game and I'm taking you home," Graham refused firmly.

"But I'm so thirsty!"

"Go get a drink of water."

Courtney looked over to where the water fountain had been earlier and groaned. Someone had moved it. There was nothing over there now except a blurry bunch of objects fastened to the wall.

"It's gone," she whispered in his ear.

"What's gone?"

"The water fountain. Someone stole it!" She giggled and buried her face in his shoulder.

"Oh, my dear Miss Spenser. You are going to hate yourself in the morning," Graham predicted as he stood up and supported her slender frame. "I think it's time to go home."

"No!" She shoved away from and looked down the long fussy alley. "I want to finish my game. I'm beating you and you can't stand it is why you want to go home."

"You have a four-six split. It's the last frame. You're well over thirty pins ahead of me so I'm beat either way I go. Let's go home." He tried to take her arm, but she pushed him away.

"I wanna see if I can knock that split down," she said stubbornly.

Graham sank back down in the chair amusedly. "Okay.

You pick that split up, then we'll go home." He knew she had about as much a chance of picking that split up as a snowball had in hell, but he was willing to let her try.

"If I do, will you buy me another beer?"

"You pick up that four-six split, and I'll buy you a case of beer," he offered magnanimously.

"Oh, a whole case?" Her face lit up expectantly.

"A whole case," he reaffirmed.

"The kind in the little bottles we've been drinking tonight?"

"The same!"

"Oh, good." She picked up her ball and walked to the red arrows. She stood, biting her lip thoughtfully and studying her target intently.

Graham smothered his laugh. If she honestly thought she was going to pick that split up, she was drunker than he thought!

Shutting her eyes, and hoping, she threw the ball as hard as she could. The ball wobbled down the alley for a full ten seconds before it barely brushed by the four pin, tipping it over to slide gently into the six pin.

The pencil dropped out of Graham's hand the same moment his mouth dropped open in disbelief.

Courtney opened her eyes and smiled happily. She had done it! Brushing her hands off in satisfaction, she turned back around to face her skeptical companion. "I'll take the first bottle out of that case right now," she said triumphantly.

Courtney was never sure if he actually did buy her that beer. Everything turned decidedly muddled after that. She did remember him practically carrying her out to his car, mumbling about the incredible odds against her picking up that split. After a fit of uncontrollable giggles at her front door when she couldn't find her key, he had finally picked her up and carried her into the house.

120

"Where's your bedroom?" he asked in a loud whisper. He hoped that her mother was still out for the evening.

"I don't remember!" She broke out in another round of snickers as he went down the hall looking in each room. When he came to one that looked decidedly feminine, he deposited her on the bed and pulled her shoes off.

"Mr. Merrill!" She slapped his hands playfully away from her feet, then doubled up in laughter once more.

"You're screwy, lady," he grumbled, pulling the sheet up over her. "You better sleep this off—" His words were cut short as her arms crept up seductively around his neck and her face sobered.

"I want to thank you for my perfectly lovely bowling shoes," she slurred happily.

"No big deal," he brushed off, his pulse jumping at the intimate way her hands began to thread seductively through his hair. This woman spelled danger to Graham Merrill. His life was nice and uncomplicated, just the way he wanted to keep it. Courtney Spenser was becoming entirely too appealing to him, and that thought made him a bit edgy.

"But they're so-o-o beautiful. I've never had anyone buy me bowling shoes before," she said.

"I'm glad you like them." Graham smiled down at her, their eyes meeting for an instant.

"I think I should kiss you for giving me such a nice gift," Courtney announced matter-of-factly. Graham had been more than accurate when he had predicted earlier that Courtney was going to hate herself in the morning!

"That's not necessary," Graham told her, realizing that he had her at a distinct disadvantage at the moment.

"But I want to!" Courtney jerked his head down roughly, her eyes meeting his obstinately.

"Then be my guest, sweetheart, but just remember, you're the one who suggested it," he warned.

Courtney's eyes grew soft and luminous. "You don't want me to kiss you?" she asked in a hurt voice.

"I didn't say that either," he defended in a shaky whisper. "I just don't happen to take advantage of women when they're in your condition."

"I am not drunk!"

"Whatever you say," he agreed smoothly, waiting for her to take the initiative.

They looked into each's others eyes, saying nothing. Courtney's breath caught as she saw the beautiful clear blue of his gaze. "You are awfully good-looking," she revealed honestly. "You look exactly like Jim Palmer."

"Jim Palmer?" Graham looked at her in surprise. "Are you a baseball fan?"

"No, why?"

"He's a pro-baseball player."

"Oh, really? I thought the gorgeous hunk just modeled underwear," she said in a puzzled voice. Wrapping her arms around his neck more snugly, she sighed wistfully. "I bet you look very lovely in your underwear too."

Graham looked properly embarrassed. "Think so? You're very lovely yourself," he confessed.

"If I had any interest in men whatsoever, I would probably be very attracted to you," she said candidly.

"That's encouraging. And, if I had any interest whatsoever in old maids, I'd have to say that you're one appealing lady," he admitted.

"You sure you don't mind if I kiss you?" she asked again.

"I'll try to live through it," he consented.

"Okay, here goes." She pulled his mouth down to meet hers. The kiss was brief and over in moments. "Thank you very much for my shoes," she said politely.

"That's it?"

"Yes, I kissed you, didn't I?"

"Well, I must admit, I was expecting something a little

more than that little peck." Damn! If she didn't smell so good, he wouldn't be pursuing this like he was.

"Little peck! That wasn't a little peck, Mr. Merrill!"

"Is that how you always kiss a guy?"

"I don't . . . I rarely kiss other men. But, yes, that's how I do it! Is there something wrong with the way I kiss?"

"No. It just seems like you should make it a little more personal, that's all. I had the feeling you'd give the same kiss to your Uncle Harvey!" he said disappointedly.

Courtney looked at him quizzically. "I don't have an Uncle Harvey."

"I meant that as a comparison," he chided gently. "Now look, let me show you how to really kiss a man. Okay?"

"Sure," Courtney brushed off aloofly. "I guess it might come in handy one of these days." She prayed he couldn't hear her heart pounding like a jackhammer!

"You're sure? You won't get mad and have a screaming fit in the morning when you sober up and realize what you've been doing the night before?"

"I am *not* drunk!"

His mouth swooped down to gently touch hers, stilling her useless protests. Courtney's eyes closed as his mouth gently caressed hers. His kiss was heavenly. She could faintly smell his aftershave and he tasted clean and fresh. She sighed as he deepened the kiss, her arms pulling him closer to her.

Their tongues met and plied softly with each other's as she snuggled against him. Somehow she knew he would kiss like this. Even though he had kissed her before, this kiss was new and exciting. As far as she was concerned, he could keep it up all night and she would never raise a voice of protest. All too soon it was over, leaving them both breathing raggedly in the quiet stillness of the bedroom.

"I believe you've been putting me on, Miss Spenser," he

teased softly as his lips brushed hers once more. "You don't need lessons in kissing any more than I do."

"Uh . . . mmm, I think I'm getting to be a natural at it, just like my bowling," she conceded gracefully.

"I think so." They kissed again, longer and deeper this time.

It was with extreme regret that Graham finally pulled away and tucked the sheet back around her neatly. "I think I'd better go before my teaching starts branching out into other areas," he said in a shaky voice.

"Oh." Her voice sounded very disappointed. "Do you have to?"

"I have to," he said firmly, moving away from her. Another few minutes, and he wouldn't be leaving at all!

Courtney was asleep before she had the words out of her mouth. He stood up and looked at the lovely girl lying on the pale-yellow sheets, and he grew very apprehensive. That kiss had had a very disturbing effect on him. In his life he had kissed more than his share of women, but this kiss was different from any other he had experienced. Thank God she wouldn't remember any of this in the morning, and he was sure going to try his darnedest to forget it himself!

CHAPTER SEVEN

"You're *not* dying, dear. You only think you are." Bonita wiped a cold cloth across her daughter's forehead and clucked her tongue in a motherly fashion.

"No, I am, Mommy. I'm dying," Courtney moaned. Her head felt as big as a basketball and there were nine Kareem Abdul-Jabbars trying to make dunk shots with it.

"You know, Courtney, this surprises me. I would think that you would be the last person in the world to overindulge." Bonita ran cold water over the cloth and placed it back on Courtney's head gently.

"Just go away and let me die." She groaned, rolling over on her stomach and placing the pillow over her throbbing head. "This is all your fault in the first place," she accused in a muffled voice.

"Mine? How can you say that!"

"Because if it hadn't been for you, I wouldn't have been in that horrible bowling alley to begin with!"

"You were at a bowling alley last night? Gee, that's funny. I was too."

The pillow came off of Courtney's head in a flash, tumbling her blond hair in wild disarray around her pale face. "Ah-ha! So you were there! What did you and Clyde do, see us coming and hide?"

"No, dear, we didn't see you," she said honestly. "Who were you with?"

125

"I was with that idiot, Graham Merrill, that's who!" Courtney winced painfully at the sound of her own voice.

"You were with Graham! How nice! But what were you doing at the bowling alley?"

Courtney sat up and glared at her mother sternly. "Looking for you! How was dear old Bertha, Mother!"

"Bertha?" Bonita gave a nervous laugh. "Oh, she's resting comfortably. . . ."

"I sincerely hope so. She *died* three weeks ago!"

"Oh . . . you found out about that." Bonita backed away from the bed sheepishly.

"I can't believe you deliberately lied to me. How could you!" Courtney wilted back down on the pillow and pressed the cold cloth against her pulsating head.

"I wouldn't have to if you would stop being so bossy." Bonita sniffed indignantly. "I don't like telling you stories, dear, but you force me into being dishonest."

"Just exactly *where* were you last night?" Courtney demanded irritably.

"Clyde and I were playing pool."

"Pool! Mother," Courtney wailed. "You surely weren't at some . . . some pool hall!"

"We weren't at 'some' pool hall, dear. We were right there at Fun City," Bonita chided in a defensive voice. "It's a very reputable fun center where families go to enjoy an evening out."

"Fun City? That's where we were." Courtney frowned.

"I don't know why we didn't see you. Clyde and I bowled a couple of games then we decided to play pool."

"Have you been seeing Clyde these past couple of weeks?"

"Yes!"

"Don't shout," Courtney pleaded helplessly as she buried her head back in the pillow. "Don't even breathe hard if you can keep from it."

"Oh, poor dear, you're really miserable this morning,

126

aren't you?" Bonita sympathized, walking back to tuck the sheets around the small blond form lying on the bed. "What in the world did you have to drink?"

Courtney's stomach rolled viciously at the mere thought of what she had been drinking the night before. "Beer—and please, I don't want to even think about it!"

Bonita crossed over to the window and glanced outside at the bright sunshiny morning. It was so unlike Courtney to wake up with a hangover. Her daughter had always been the model of temperance. At times, Bonita would have welcomed this small sign of human frailty, feeling that for once Courtney needed to loosen up and have a good time with a member of the opposite sex. But a nagging sense of guilt overrode her feelings this morning. If she had not lied to her daughter, Courtney would never have been in this miserable condition this morning. Feelings of frustration hit Bonita before she was able to shove them away. She had to give Courtney a little longer to accept the fact that although her mother was sixty-eight years old, she was still very much a woman. A woman who had found, in the December years of her life, a man who could make her feel, and laugh, and love once more. Bonita would be patient. She must, because she had no intention of giving Clyde Merrill up. At least not unless she was forced to, and she prayed that would not happen.

"Mother, I'm not going to be able to go to work this morning," Courtney conceded in an agonized tone. "Can you handle the shop alone today?"

"Why, of course, dear. You just stay home and rest." Bonita turned from the window with an understanding smile on her face. "I won't have any trouble handling things."

Courtney spent the rest of the morning in bed, vowing to murder one certain dentist should she ever have the misfortune to meet up with him again. Her face flamed bright red every time she thought of how very little she remembered about last night. She was able to recall just enough to make her groan with mortification each time she thought about draping her arm around his neck and asking for *another* bottle of beer! He was probably having the laugh of his life this morning, thinking about the "old maid" who had gotten plastered while trying to learn to bowl! She shuddered disgustedly. If she was lucky, she would never have to see him again. And the only way to assure that was to try once again to get Bonita away from Clyde.

Rising out of bed slowly, Courtney made her way into the bathroom on shaky legs and took an ice-cold shower. By the time she had dressed and fixed herself a cup of black coffee, she was finally beginning to feel life returning to her aching body. Her head still throbbed, but in a more civilized manner.

The doorbell rang as she finished the last sip of her coffee. With a painful wince, she washed the cup out and laid it in the drainer.

"Mr. Curtis! How nice to see you." Courtney smiled brightly as she opened the door and confronted Harold Curtis, the butcher.

"Good afternoon, Courtney. How are you this fine day?" Harold's smile was most pleasant, and Courtney couldn't help but wonder why Bonita found the thought of spending an evening with him so repugnant.

"Fine." Her head pounded painfully at the bright sunshine, but she didn't think Mr. Curtis would be interested in hearing about her hangover.

"I've brought Bonita by some chops she wanted." Harold handed Courtney a large package wrapped in heavy white paper. "She wanted me to be sure and save her some."

"Thanks. That's very kind of you, Mr. Curtis." Harold Curtis *was* very nice. "Come on in while I get your money."

Harold stepped inside the house while Courtney left the room to get his money. Minutes later she returned and offered him a twenty-dollar bill.

"I hope you have change?"

"Yes, no problem." Harold dug in his back pocket and extracted a large brown wallet. "Is your mother home?" he asked conversationally as he made the change and handed it to her.

"Mom's down at the shop. Did you want to speak to her?" Courtney asked hopefully.

"Oh, I didn't want anything in particular." Harold hung his head shyly.

"Oh? Well, I would be happy to give her any message." Courtney was disappointed. If only Harold would ask Bonita for a date, then maybe something more would develop.

"No, no message." He stuffed his wallet back in his pocket and picked up the basket he had brought the chops in. "I just thought perhaps if she wasn't busy tonight—"

"She's not!" Courtney broke in hurriedly.

"Oh?" Harold's weathered face brightened.

"No. No, she's not!" She smiled encouragingly. "Did you have something in mind?"

"Well." Harold shuffled his foot nervously. "There's the bingo game tonight down at the senior citizens' hall."

"She'd love to!" Courtney accepted speedily. "What time will you pick her up?"

Harold looked up in surprise. "She'll go with me?"

"Sure," Courtney said smoothly, "she'd love to. Bingo is one of her favorite games!"

"It is? I could have sworn she said she didn't like bingo."

"What time do you think you'll be by, Mr. Curtis?" Courtney pursued intently. She had to get this thing nailed down quickly.

"About seven, I guess." Harold paused and looked at

129

Courtney suspiciously. "Are you sure she'll want to go? Maybe I should stop by the shop and ask her myself."

"Oh, no! Don't trouble yourself, Mr. Curtis. She'll go," Courtney assured, pushing him toward the front door hurriedly.

"Well, if you say so." Harold found himself out on the front porch before he could offer any more skepticism.

Courtney gave one last friendly wave as she stepped back in the house and closed the door swiftly. Letting out a long sigh of relief, she leaned against the door and smiled. Now, *all* she had to do was get Bonita to agree to the date!

Graham looked up as his father walked in his office, a disapproving scowl on his face. "Where were you?"

"What do you mean, where was I? Home, why?"

"I mean, where were you last night."

"I told you, Buddy, I went to . . . I went out. Why?" Clyde's features turned as stubborn as his son's.

"To the VFW meeting?"

Clyde shuffled over and took a seat in front of Graham's desk. "Maybe. Maybe not," he hedged. "I'm old enough to go out nights by myself, aren't I?" he grumbled.

Heaving a sigh of defeat, Graham pushed back from his desk and stood up. He stretched his muscular frame and flexed his shoulders tiredly. "You were nowhere near the VFW hall last night and you know it."

"Who finked on me?" Clyde sat up in his chair straighter.

"Miss Courtney Spenser 'finked' on you," Graham said tiredly.

"Why can't she mind her own business," Clyde sputtered, "and let me mind mine?"

"I thought we agreed you were not going to spend as much time with Bonnie as you had been. Now I find out you two have been seeing each other all along." Graham

130

turned to face his father. "What have you got to say for yourself?"

"Not one blessed thing, Buddy. You're the one who decided I wasn't going to see Bonnie, not me. Dad blast it, boy, I like that woman and you're not going to prevent me from seeing her!" Clyde jumped to his feet and pounded on Graham's desk for emphasis.

"Dad," Graham reasoned patiently, "you and Bonnie are not good for each other. Why don't you try to find a nice quiet little lady to date? One who likes to knit, bake apple pies."

"I don't particularly like apple pies, and even if I did, I wouldn't date a woman for that reason alone!" He paused and looked at his son oddly. "Would you?"

Graham looked uncomfortable as he sank back down in his chair and picked up a paperweight to toss idly back and forth in his hands. "We're not talking about me."

"That's the problem with you younger generation," Clyde accused sharply. "You seem to think that just because we've grown older, we're not entitled to the same rights as you. Well, I'm here to tell you, boy, I don't give a damn whether a woman can bake a decent pie any more than you do. You may find this hard to believe, but there *are* other things that attract my attention! The body may be fallin' to pieces, but there's not a darn thing wrong with my mind!"

Graham slumped down in his chair and looked even more uncomfortable. "Come on, Dad, you don't still—" The thought was more than a little disconcerting to him. Surely all *that* had stopped when Graham's mother had died, hadn't it?

Clyde looked at his son and frowned in disgust. "Now, do I ask you personal things like that?"

"No, but this is different."

"No, it isn't." Clyde's face turned softer. "That's what I've been trying to tell you, son. It's not one bit different.

It may not be as easy as it once was," he agreed, "but my feelings are no different from yours when it comes to a nice, soft lovely woman to hold in my arms."

"Look"—Graham tossed the paperweight back down on his desk—"I'm not arguing that fact as much as I'm arguing the point that you and Bonnie Spenser are starting to be a real pain in the rear end, not to mention that daughter of hers! Do you know she fouled up another perfectly good evening for me last night?"

"How?"

"She—" Graham caught himself. If Clyde found that he was the instigator on trying to keep him and Bonnie apart something would hit the fan, and it wouldn't be air! "She needed to speak with her mother about something and she called me to see if I knew where you were. I got the message at Clarissa's. Naturally, like a dum-dum I assumed you were at your VFW meeting. Miss Spenser pointed out that VFW meetings were held only on Thursday nights, so we decided you and Bonnie had snuck off somewhere together."

"So? What's the problem. Couldn't she have looked for her mother on her own?"

"No, I—I offered to help."

Clyde glanced at his son knowingly. "She's not bad for an old maid, is she? She's got one of the cutest little shapes I've seen in a long time."

"I wouldn't know. I haven't noticed," Graham replied indifferently. "She's not my type."

"Oh? Surely you're not blind, Buddy!"

"No, I'm not blind, Dad." Graham leaned back in his chair, propped his feet on the desk, and crossed his arms behind his head. "She's way too soft. She doesn't like a thing I do. Her idea of a good time is an expensive restaurant, dancing, then reading poetry by the fire." He shook his head thoughtfully. "Not my type at all."

"Well, I've never tried to pick your women, and I don't

132

want you to pick mine." Clyde stood up and made ready to leave. "What time will you be ready to eat this evening?"

"Not too late." Graham stood and walked with his father out of the office. "My last appointment is at five."

"Okay, I thought I might fix us a pot of chili," Clyde told him amicably.

"Don't put in any of those green chili peppers," Graham warned. "I was up all night the last time I ate your chili." He paused and smiled at an elderly woman patient sitting in the waiting room. "Hi, Mildred. How are you today?"

"Hello, Dr. Merrill. Not very well, I'm afraid. I woke up this morning with this terrible ache in my back . . ."

"See you later, son." Clyde stuck his ballcap on his head and started out the front door.

"Hey, wait a minute, Dad. You want to say hello to Mildred, don't you?" Graham's arm snaked out and stopped his father's rapid exit. "Mildred, come here and say hi to Dad."

Mildred sprang to her feet, her face wreathed in an expectant smile. "Clyde, how nice!"

"Oh, brother." Clyde groaned under his breath.

"How are you, Clyde? I haven't seen you lately." Mildred batted her eyelashes coyly.

"Been busy." Clyde grunted. "See ya later, Buddy."

"Wait a minute, Dad." Graham stopped him again. "What's your hurry? I bet Mildred would appreciate some company. I have another patient before her." He turned to Mildred and smiled innocently. "Wouldn't you?"

Mildred beamed. "I wouldn't mind at all if your father wanted to stay and chat."

"I can't stay, Buddy," Clyde nervously pleaded. "I have to go start our dinner."

"We can eat out tonight," Graham offered. "Say!" He

slapped his knee thoughtfully. "I've just had a great idea. Why don't you and Mildred go to the bingo game they're having down at the senior citizens' center this evening? We can all go have dinner when I finish up here, then you two can run along and have fun—"

"She can't!" Clyde butted in.

"Why not?" Both Graham and Mildred answered at the same time.

"Well, weren't you going to do something to her teeth? That's it! Mildred won't be able to eat and that would be terrible. I'll just wait and take her when she'll be able to have a good time."

Graham reached over and put his arm around his dad's shoulders reassuringly. "Hey, good news! I'm only going to clean Mildred's teeth today. She can eat anything she wants, isn't that right, Mildred!"

"That's right, and I would love to play bingo tonight even though my arm is killing me!"

"I'm going to get you for this, Buddy," Clyde muttered sickly.

"Don't thank me, Dad. I'm sure Mildred is going to enjoy the evening as much as you do. I'll even drive the two of you over," Graham offered innocently. He knew he would have to drive them over or Clyde would never go! "Now if you'll both excuse me, I have to order a case of beer to send to a lady."

Clyde glared at his son angrily, but realized full well that he was trapped. "A case of beer doesn't sound like anything you would send to a lady!"

"Oh, it's not just any beer. It's the beer that comes in those 'cute little glass bottles.' You know, the kind they serve at the bowling alley?" Graham grinned mischievously.

Clyde grunted and took his cap off defeatedly. "Still doesn't make sense to me."

"It doesn't have to. The lady will understand. I lost a

bet to her. Just make yourself comfortable," he advised Mildred and his dad, "I'll be through before you know it."

Clyde smiled weakly at Mildred, then slumped down in the chair next to her as Graham whistled his way back to his waiting patient.

The senior citizens' center was filled to overflowing as Courtney, Bonita, and Harold Curtis walked through the front entrance. After a somewhat stormy session with Bonita earlier, Courtney had decided it would be best if she accompanied her mother and Harold that night. To say that her mother had been upset would be misleading. Incensed might be the more appropriate word. Courtney was still holding her breath for fear she would flatly refuse to play bingo with Harold, but so far Bonita had gone along peacefully.

"Looks pretty crowded tonight," Harold observed, peering through the haze of smoke that was already filling the large hall. "I think I see some empty chairs over on the west wall."

"Good, Harold. You lead the way and Mother and I will follow." Courtney smiled encouragingly at him. Although Bonita had agreed to come, she hadn't said more than three words to Harold all evening.

"Mother! You have to say something to the poor man," Courtney hissed under her breath as they threaded their way through the crowd. "You can't leave all the conversation up to me!"

" *You* made the date," Bonita reminded curtly. "It sure wasn't my— Oh look! There's Clyde and Graham!" Bonita's face came radiantly alive.

Courtney froze as her eyes encountered Graham Merrill's aloof blue ones. "Oh, good grief! What are they doing here?"

"Playing bingo, I would imagine," Bonita said helpfully. "Oh, poo. Look who's with them! It's that dippy Mil-

135

dred Mosely!" Her voice sounded as disappointed as her face looked.

"Well, so what? You're here with Harold Curtis."

"Do you have to keep bringing that up!"

"Shhh! Harold is going to hear you. Look, he's motioning for us. He must have found some seats." Courtney took Bonita's hand and dragged her through the maze of bodies until they reached Harold.

"Oh, these are nice seats," Courtney complimented, pushing Bonita down next to Harold then taking the seat on the other side of her. "Aren't these nice seats, Mother?"

"Yes, dear, they are simply lovely," the older woman managed to choke out.

"Here, Bonita, I got you two cards to play with," Harold said, shoving two cards over in front of her.

"Thank you, Harold," she returned stiffly but politely. "That was very thoughtful of you."

"See how nice he is," Courtney whispered supportively. "He bought you two cards to play with!"

"Nice my foot. He's a dirty old man."

"Mother!"

"He is! You just don't know the half of it."

"Shhh! He is going to hear you!"

"He couldn't hear himself break wind in a churn!" Bonnie said flatly. "He's deaf in one ear and can't hear out of the other one, let alone hear above the noise of this crowd." She looked bleakly at her two bingo cards and snorted disgustedly. "I never win anything in this stupid game."

Courtney picked up her bingo card and studied it seriously. "This looks like it's a lucky card. If I win anything, I'll give it to you," she promised solemnly. She figured she owed her mother that much for forcing her to come along that evening.

The caller announced a new game was beginning as

Bonita's eyes hurriedly searched the room for Clyde. When she spotted him, she could tell he had been looking for her too. Their faces both broke out in smiles and they waved at each other happily.

"Mother, watch your card and stop looking over there at Clyde! The caller said *B* six and you have *B* six!" Courtney pushed the red tag down over the number on Bonita's card curtly.

"I don't care if I have every *B* he calls all night. Look, there's some empty chairs over there next to Clyde and Graham. Let's go sit next to them."

"We will not! You stay right—" Courtney gasped as her mother rose swiftly and called to Harold. "Let's go sit in those seats over there! I can't hear the caller very well from where we're setting now!"

"What?" Harold held a hand up to cup his ear.

"I SAID, LET'S GO SIT IN THE CHAIRS OVER THERE. I CAN HEAR BETTER!"

Several rows of bingo players turned around to see who had spoken so loudly.

Bonita looked at Courtney smugly. "See what I mean? He can't hear it thunder, let alone hear me!" She turned back to Harold. "Okay?"

"Oh, well, if you want to." Harold picked up his card and trailed along behind Bonita's fast disappearing backside.

Bonita hadn't bothered to take her bingo cards with her when she left so it took several minutes for Courtney to gather up the cards and make her way over to the table where Harold and Bonita were now sitting.

Graham looked up as Courtney was forced to take the only seat left, which just happened to be beside him. Bonita had plopped down next to Clyde and was happily helping him watch his card now.

"Can you keep the racket down a little bit?" Graham

said sharply, straining to hear the caller. "What did he say?"

"*C* sixteen!" Courtney returned promptly.

Graham's eyes hurriedly scanned the card. "*C* sixteen . . . *C* sixteen . . . *C* sixteen . . ." he mused aloud, trying to find the number on his card. His eyes shot back to Courtney's irritably. "Very funny, Miss Spenser!"

"Thank you, Mr. Merrill. I thought so too." She smiled sweetly and pulled a red tag down over the number just called.

"What are you doing here tonight?" he asked under his breath.

"I came with my mother and *her* date, Harold Curtis. Do you mind?"

"Not at all. You'll notice that Dad has his own date with him tonight. The lovely Miss Mildred Mosely," he pointed out curtly.

"Yes, I noticed old dippy Mildred was with Clyde tonight. They make a lovely couple." Courtney pulled another red tag down on her card. "I'm only two away from bingo," she said smugly.

"How thrilling," Graham drawled blandly. "Did you get your beer?"

"I did, and I'd like to know what you think you're doing?" she replied coolly.

"Why, paying off my bet, Miss Spenser. Don't you remember?"

Courtney face took on a decidedly guilty look. "No . . . I don't remember much about last night except the sight of that beer this afternoon nearly made me ill!"

"What a shame. You mean you don't remember me carrying you to your bed and—" His words were interrupted before he could finish the sentence.

"Dr. Merrill!" Mildred Mosely scooted down next to him and took a deep breath. "I've been meaning to ask you about something all evening. My back has been killing me

138

. . . way down low, here in the middle." She turned in her chair so Graham could see where she was pointing. "Could you tell me what that is or maybe give me some medicine to make the pain go away?"

"I thought it was your arm that was hurting," Graham said politely, glancing at the spot Mildred was persistently jabbing with her fingernail.

"Oh, my arm's hurting too, but now my back's started paining something fierce. What do you think?"

"I'm not a medical doctor, Mildred. I'm a dentist. I think you should call your doctor in the morning and he'll tell you what he wants you to do."

"That won't do any good. I call him every day and he simply ignores me. Last week I told him the muscle in my eye was twitching and driving me up a wall. What number did the caller say?" She looked at Graham hopefully.

"*G* twenty-one."

"Oh, I don't have it. Anyway, as I was saying, he couldn't do anything for my eye and I suffered death until it decided to stop on its own. Well, the very next day . . ."

Graham slumped down in his chair and listened to Mildred drone on and on about her illnesses. Twenty minutes later Mildred was still complaining when Clyde finally managed to catch Graham's eyes. Clyde pointed to Mildred and his grin broadened as he mouthed a silent, but gleeful "I told you so" to his son. Graham frowned back at his father and averted his eyes hurriedly, refusing to acknowledge that Mildred Mosely was indeed a chronic complainer.

Courtney had watched the scene transpiring between Graham and Mildred, occasionally biting her lower lip to keep from laughing.

An hour later, it was Graham who was biting his lower lip. Harold Curtis had finally given up on Bonita and was now making his play for Courtney.

"Mr. Curtis. If I have to remove your hand one more time, I am going to get very upset," she warned between clenched teeth, pushing Harold's hand off her thigh for the third time.

"What?" He acted as if he didn't hear her.

"You heard what I said! Move your hand!"

"You're not going to get mad at me, are you? You're such a pretty little thing and after all, you're the one who actually wanted to go on this date tonight," he reminded with a sly wink. His hand patted her leg again. "Don't you like older men?"

"You should be ashamed of yourself! I'm young enough to be your granddaughter!" she scolded.

"I don't mind, if you don't." He grinned.

"Well, I mind! Now keep your eyes *and* your hands on your bingo card!" she warned, shooting an I-dare-you-to-say-anything glance at Graham, who was quietly taking in the whole conversation with a definite smirk on his face.

"Say, this is really fun, isn't it?" Graham grinned. "We'll have to all do this more often!"

While Courtney sat there and seethed, Harold burst out in a fit of wheezing and coughing. Courtney finally jumped up and pounded him on the back, praying that he wouldn't expire right there on his bingo card!

The other occupants of the table watched in concern as Courtney calmed down Harold and handed him a glass of water that Graham had put in her hand. "Are you all right now?"

"I'm fine now. This happens all the time." He coughed once more and took another drink of water. "I have emphysema. Have had for the last twenty years. Too many cigarettes," he said with a merry laugh.

Courtney sank down in her chair and drew a deep breath. She could see why Bonita found Harold less than exciting. He not only was a dirty old man, he could scare ten years off your life with each coughing spasm he had.

"Oh . . . oh, dearie me!" Mildred jumped up and started stomping her left foot wildly. She continued to bang her foot on the floor in a rapid fashion, muttering something under her breath about "pins and needles."

Graham had shot to his feet instantly and was watching her at a safe distance.

"Your foot gone to sleep again, Mildred?" Clyde called dryly. Courtney noticed that his eyes never left his bingo card as he talked.

"Yes, it's so irritating." Her foot stomped heavier, a look of grim determination on her face. "Nothing to be concerned about. I'll have it under control in a few minutes," she called optimistically.

Mildred knew her foot, because in a matter of minutes she was seated again, happily chatting away with Graham once more and vaguely watching her bingo card.

Courtney had noticed that Clyde and Bonita had spent most of the time whispering to each other. They had obediently played their cards, but it didn't take a magician to see that they were not interested in the bingo game. Finally, around nine o'clock, Clyde announced that he was going to the snack bar for some Cokes.

"I'll go with you, Dad," Graham offered, breaking in on another long verbalization from Mildred on her foot problems.

"You don't need to, Buddy. You just stay here and keep Mildred company." Clyde snickered under his breath. Yes sir, he owed his little son one, and now he was only too happy to be giving it to him!

"I really wouldn't mind, Dad."

"Nope! Wouldn't hear of it," Clyde brushed him off. "I'll bring you back some soft drinks. Come on, Bonnie, you can help me. Courtney can keep Harold company while we're gone."

Bonita sprang to her feet happily. "I'd be happy to, Clyde!"

141

Courtney leaned over and whispered to Graham. "Do you think it's safe to let them go off together like that?"

Graham shrugged his shoulders. "Where can they go? We're sitting right here watching them."

Where can they go? We're sitting right here watching them! That had certainly sounded reasonable enough, Courtney mused thoughtfully. But when thirty minutes had passed and Courtney had knocked Harold's hand off her thigh twice more, she had to admit that if anyone wanted any soft drinks he would have to go get them himself. Bonnie and Clyde had vamoosed!

"I think we'd better wrap this thing up," Graham suggested to Courtney a few minutes later, as Mildred started on a discussion of her gallstones. "The gypsies have given us the slip again. You'll probably have to give me a ride home. Dad surely took his car when they left."

"What will we do about Harold and Mildred?" Courtney asked, relieved that the night was finally coming to an end.

"We'll take them home, then you can take me home," Graham suggested uneasily. "Let's just get out of here. Mildred's illnesses are driving me insane."

"Oh, how nice," Courtney said lightly. "We'll be double dating!"

"You like that idea, huh?"

Courtney started to smile, but her eyes widened disbelievingly and the smile turned into an indignant gasp as Graham put his arm around her and pinched her soundly on her bottom.

"Just wanted to keep you on your toes, Miss Spenser," he explained with a devilish wink. "And I want you and old Harold to behave yourself in the backseat on the way home!"

CHAPTER EIGHT

The night air smelled cool and clean as they left the senior citizens' center and got into Courtney's small car. How small the car actually was had never entered her mind until she was forced to face the reality that she would have to be wedged tightly in the backseat with Harold Curtis. Somehow that thought sent her into a near panic.

"Harold, if you don't mind, why don't you and Mildred sit in the back and I'll keep Courtney up here with me," Graham suggested smoothly as he opened the car door for Mildred and Courtney. "I'll drive and she can point out the street markers. I don't see too well in the dark," he explained.

Courtney shot him a look of gratitude as Harold and Mildred climbed in the backseat and sat down.

"Did I tell you about the time I threw my back out while I was getting into a car and had to be in bed for a month, Dr. Merrill?" Mildred asked as she settled herself comfortably next to Harold.

Graham looked at Courtney and grimaced. "I don't believe so, Mildred. Tell me about it."

"I've heard it about ten times already," Harold muttered rudely. He had been looking forward to the ride home with Courtney and was very disappointed that she was riding in the front seat with that young Graham Merrill!

Harold and Mildred sparred angrily with each other all

the way home. By the time Graham and Courtney had deposited them at their houses, they drew a deep sigh of relief.

"Man alive! I can see why Dad isn't so crazy about spending his evenings with Mildred Mosely," Graham admitted as he gunned the car away from the curb. "She's a walking emergency ward!"

"You think she's bad! I can certainly sympathize with Mom on her feelings concerning Harold!" Courtney supplied readily. "You know, Graham, I've been thinking. Our parents are really lucky that they can still enjoy such good health at their age. If Mom has any aches and pains, I never hear her complain about them unless they get so bad she can't stand them."

"The same with Dad," Graham agreed. "His health isn't as good as it was even two years ago. I can see little changes in him every day, but he isn't one to dwell on the negative. He's always said that age is a state of mind and he's determined that he will never grow old."

"So far, neither one of them has grown old, have they?" Courtney glanced over at Graham, her heart beating faster as once more she mentally noted his rugged handsomeness in the dim lights shining from the dashboard. "And, after tonight, I'm not at all sure I want them to!"

Graham's deep chuckle filled the small car pleasantly. "They are both rather laid back, aren't they?"

"It's such a shame Mildred can't enjoy that same health and attitude," Courtney mused.

"She could. What Mildred needs is something to fill up all those lonely hours she's faced with every day. Her children and grandchildren all live in different states and she has lost the main ingredients in her life. Now she spends each new day dwelling on her aches and pains. What else is there for her to do?"

"What about volunteer work? There are so many worthwhile organizations that are crying for help."

"I thought about that earlier this evening. That's exactly what Mildred needs. To feel wanted and useful once again. I think I'll call the hospital tomorrow and speak to the head of the volunteer workers. With a little persuasion, I think I can get Lila to call Mildred and invite her to be a part of their organization."

Courtney smiled, a little surprised that he would take the time out of his busy day to try to make an old woman's life a little easier. "That's very thoughtful of you," she commented. "I'm so happy Mom has the shop to work in. I really don't know what she would do with all her time. Working has kept her in touch with the world, something a woman with her energy would have to be."

Graham chuckled pleasantly. "Yes, I know what you mean. After Mom died, Dad drifted for the next few years with no real interest in anything, not even his practice. After his last trip a few months ago, I talked him into taking on a few patients again. Since then he's bounced back and now he's the same old dad I had when I was growing up."

"Your father's a dentist too?"

"Sure. Technically he's retired but in my opinion he's still one of the best in the business," he said proudly.

Courtney sighed wistfully. "It sounds like they both went through the same period of adjustment after their spouses died. I'm glad they've managed to find a reason to go on living once more."

"Everyone needs a purpose in life, no matter what his age is," Graham said quietly.

"I still can't believe they gave us the slip again," Courtney fretted. "After all the trouble I went to to get Harold and Mother together . . ." Courtney paused.

"It doesn't surprise me a bit they slipped out together. In fact, I overheard them planning another motorcycle trip tomorrow morning."

"They what!"

"They're planning to ride down to Orlando and go to Disneyworld," Graham repeated calmly. "Dad thought I was listening to Mildred tell me about her tricky colon, but I was actually listening to him and Bonnie make their plans for tomorrow."

"Orlando! Good heavens! Do you have any idea how far that is from here? Surely they wouldn't try to ride a motorcycle that far."

Graham shot her a look of resignation. "You don't honestly think that a mere matter of miles is going to deter them, do you?"

"But it looks like it's going to start pouring any minute!" Courtney leaned forward and peered toward the churning sky. She noticed the flashes of bright lightning were continuing to increase rapidly. "The weatherman says it's going to rain for the next couple of days."

Graham shrugged his shoulders. "Dad has several rainsuits."

"Didn't you try to stop them when you heard what they were planning?" Courtney demanded incredulously.

"No, I did not! That would be a sure way to get Dad all bent out of shape and you could bet your boots he'd go then, come hell or high water!"

"Well, we've got to do something," Courtney said worriedly. "It's starting to sprinkle right now and by morning it will be a downpour. We can't let them ride hundreds of miles in a driving rainstorm on the back of a motorcycle!"

"What do you want me to do about it?" Graham grumbled.

"I don't know. Maybe we could steal his motorcycle wheels," she said impulsively.

"Steal his motorcycle wheels?" Graham swerved the car over to the side of the road and slammed on the brakes. "Brilliant! Absolutely brilliant, Miss Spenser! We'll steal his wheels and then they won't have any choice *but* to stay home."

146

"But they could take his car," Courtney pointed out hurriedly, amazed that he would take her impetuous suggestion seriously.

"No, they won't! That would take all the fun out of it if they had to ride in a car like people their age ordinarily do." Graham turned to face her in the small car, his eyes bright with excitement. "If we forbid them to go, naturally they will break their necks disobeying us. Now, all we have to do is sneak over there and steal both his motorcycle wheels and hide them. It would take awhile for him to buy new ones, and by that time, the day would be gone. It may not stop them permanently, but it will buy us a little extra time to come up with some other way to keep them from going!"

Courtney's face paled. "Oh, Graham, I was only kidding. I don't know how to steal motorcycle wheels!" Good heavens, beer in bottles last night, stealing motorcycle wheels tonight! This man was corrupting her systematically and she was standing quietly by with her mouth hanging open!

"You don't need to know anything. You can come along and hold the light for me," he brushed off hurriedly, the car squealing back out on the highway.

"But, Graham . . ." she protested feebly.

"No buts! This is an emergency," he said with grim finality.

They drove down the highway at an alarming speed as Courtney frantically gripped her door handle in case she was forced to exit unexpectedly, or if she was lucky, she would be granted an opportunity to jump out at the next stoplight!

The rain was starting to come down in sheets now, making visibility poor as they pulled up in a dark alley and screeched to a halt.

"Will you kindly stop driving my car this way," Courtney said as she tried to straighten her hair back into some

147

semblance of order. "I don't happen to be a dentist so I can't afford a new car every year!"

"This thing's doggy. You need to get rid of it and get something with a little more get up and go," he advised curtly.

"It has quite enough 'get up and go' to suit me," she said crossly. She looked around her, cringing at the sound of the rain pounding heavily on the roof of the car. "Where are we?"

"In an alley in back of my house. I'm playing it safe. Dad's bedroom faces the front of the house, so he won't be able to see us when he comes home." Graham reached over and unsnapped her seat belt. "Come on, let's go."

"In this downpour? You've got to be nuts! I can't get out with it raining like this!" Courtney protested.

"Oh, yes, you can, princess. You're not going to melt," he told her reassuringly as he dragged her across the seat and out the driver's side with him.

"Ouch! That hurt, you insensitive clod." Courtney fumed as she rubbed her backside that was still smarting from being jerked across the knob of the gearshift.

"Sorry, want me to kiss it?" Graham asked with a wicked grin.

"You have no idea how many times since we've met that I've mentally ask you to, Dr. Merrill." Courtney's smile was the very essence of sweetness as she looked up into his amused face.

The rain was pelting down on them in torrents. Their clothing quickly became plastered to their skin, and the water ran out of their hair in rivulets.

"Hey, Miss Spenser." Graham caught his breath as he held her soaked body out in front of him, his eyes eagerly exploring the enticing way her breasts were straining at the wet fabric of her blouse. The cold rain had indecently, but deliciously, exposed her to his wandering eye. His pulse beat faster as he slowly let his gaze follow the outline

148

of her small firm breasts, desire rising swiftly in him. "I knew there had to be some softness beneath all that hard exterior," he said matter-of-factly, "and I wasn't too far off."

Courtney felt her face turning warm at his intimate words and perusal of her body. Her stomach fluttered nervously and she knew she should slap his face for being so impudent, yet his eyes were holding her spellbound and she couldn't deny that the feel of his arms gently holding her at arm's length from him sent tiny shivers racing up her spine.

"You are being obscene, Dr. Merrill," she chastized in a weak voice.

"Now, what's obscene about a guy admiring a lady's—"

"*Dr. Merrill!* You are overstepping your bounds," Courtney warned, finally summoning up enough courage to pull out of his grasp. "It is certainly not very nice to make fun of my . . . assets . . . or lack of them," she scolded in embarrassment.

"Lack of them? They look pretty good to me—"

"You know what I mean," she interrupted curtly, trying to pull her wet blouse away from the objects of discussion. "I'm not very . . . you know . . . endowed," she admitted. She knew that most men preferred their women to resemble Dolly Parton. She had always looked more like Little Orphan Annie in that department!

"You look all right to me," he stated again, wiping the rain out of his face. "I happen to like women who are a little less . . . endowed." He grinned. "To be quite honest, I like your . . . er . . . just fine, even though they are the size of a grade-A large egg," he teased with a twinkle in his eye.

"Yes, a *fried* egg," she snorted disgustedly.

He laughed as he reached out and pinched her lightly under the chin. "No, they're not. They're beautiful, and I think they would fit in a man's hand just perfectly."

Courtney's breath caught as their eyes met in a serious moment. For the first time in her life, she was sorely tempted to play coy and invite him to be her guest.

"I think we better get on with our business," she finally murmured, tearing her gaze away from his. Gosh darn! he was cute.

Graham's hands fell away from her arms reluctantly. "Come on, the motorcycle's probably in the garage."

They ran through the bushes as the rain continued to pelt down on them. When they reached the front of the garage, Graham stopped, whistling under his breath softly. "Dad must not be home yet. His cycle's still sitting outside where he left it this afternoon."

Courtney's heart sank. She had been hoping it would be inside the nice, dry garage!

"This is better, though," Graham said hurriedly. "It will make it more believable. Stay here while I get some tools."

Courtney watched petulantly as he disappeared inside the garage, wondering why he hadn't been thoughtful enough to ask her to join him. At least she could have gotten out of the rain for a few minutes.

He returned shortly with his hands full of tools. "See those concrete blocks over there?" He pointed to a pile sitting next to the garage. "Go get me about four or five of them."

"Why do I have to do the heavy work?" Courtney complained, eyeing the blocks distastefully.

"Do you know how to strip the axle bolts off the wheels?" he asked.

"I'm sure I do." Courtney looked at the large motorcycle sitting before her. "What's an axle bolt?"

"Just go get the blocks," he said.

It took several trips for Courtney to drag the blocks back over to the motorcycle. In the process she managed to break two more fingernails, one clear down to the quick.

150

The bright flashes of lightning and the loud cracks of thunder prodded her onward. Never in her wildest imagination would she have thought she would be out in a monsoon, in the middle of the night, stealing motorcycle wheels with a dentist!

"Hey, come here!" Graham whispered loudly. "I can't see a thing I'm doing."

Courtney shuffled over to the cycle disgruntledly. "What do you want?"

"Hold the flashlight for me." He handed her a small cylinder. "Shine it up here on the wheel."

She obediently held the ray of light where he had demanded. "How long is this going to take?" she asked. She was beginning to get cold and she had sneezed a couple of times already.

"It won't take very long. I'll just slip the wheels off and prop the blocks underneath it. Turn the light more this way."

"What way! I have it where you said," Courtney whispered crossly.

"Shine it *here*." He grunted sharply, reaching up to grasp her hand to point it where he wanted it. The flashlight slipped out of her hand and rolled away into the darkness.

"Now look what you've done!" she hissed.

"Go get it," he snapped. "I can't leave or the whole cycle will fall!"

"Go get it!" she mocked nastily. "You seem to forget, I'm *not* your employee, Dr. Merrill!"

"Don't give me any static, just go get the darn flashlight . . . Oh hell! There's Dad's car pulling in the drive right now!"

"Will he see us?" Courtney got closer to the large motorcycle frame.

"No, he parks in the front drive. I don't think he'll bother to come around in the back. Just keep down low and don't turn on the light until he gets in the house," Graham said quietly.

"What if he comes out to look at his cycle?"

"He won't. Not in this downpour. Just go get the light and hurry!"

Courtney grimaced as she pulled herself through the mud to search for the flashlight. It took her ten minutes of wallowing in mud before she found it and crawled back over to Graham.

"If I ever live through this night, don't you ever call me to help you again," she chattered in a freezing voice. Her face and hair were covered in mud, along with every stitch of clothing she had on. She sneezed once more.

"Quiet down," Graham grumbled, sliding the back wheel off and handing it to her. "Hand me two of those blocks."

Courtney dragged the blocks over and helped him slip them under the cycle. "Are you about finished?"

"Just a couple more minutes," he whispered. "Hand me that smallest wrench."

Courtney looked around and picked up the tool he was pointing to. She walked over and started to hand it to him, the wrench nearly slipping out of her wet hand.

Graham instantly covered the front of his mud-soaked trousers with a protective hand. "Ah-ah! I'm catching on to your little tricks, Miss Spenser. If I have anything that interests you, I'd be more than happy to discuss it, but for heaven's sake, leave me my dignity!"

"I didn't *drop* the tool, Dr. Merrill. Stop crying wolf until he's at your door." She threw the tool down next to the cycle and scowled at him.

"If I left it up to you, I wouldn't be able to crawl to the door and fight the wolf away," Graham pointed out with a smirk.

"Is that right? Well, it so happens I have no interest whatsoever in what lies beneath that . . . that door. I admit

I have been clumsy lately, but I sure haven't intentionally singled your . . . I haven't singled you out to make a pass at and I want you to stop implying that I have! I don't even like you!"

"Good. Because I don't really care a whole lot for you either," he said flatly.

Courtney sat down on a concrete block and proceeded to ignore him. At the moment, that was the only way she could deal with his arrogance without resorting to physical violence.

A large, wet shaggy dog came wandering out of the bushes and sauntered over to where Courtney was sitting. Her hand came out to pet him, and she spoke softly to him for a moment. She glanced over at the masculine form lying beside the motorcycle, then grinned wickedly. She gently pushed the dog over in Graham's direction, pointing to where she wanted him to go. The dog looked at her, then moseyed over in the direction she was indicating. In a few minutes Graham was muttering under his breath as the dog affectionately lapped at his face.

"Come here and get this dog!" he ordered in a loud whisper.

"What dog?" she whispered back innocently.

The dog became even more affectionate, putting one muddy paw on Graham's chest and licking his face eagerly.

"Courtney! Get this damn dog!"

The dog jumped back at Graham's persistent voice, then decided that his kisses were not being appreciated. He stepped back and shook his heavily furred body, sending a stream of stinky water flying over in Graham's direction.

Graham rolled over and shielded his eyes from the onslaught, muttering a few selective, uncomplimentary phrases under his breath about the dog.

Courtney, unable to control her merriment one minute

153

longer, broke out in a fit of laughter. "What's the matter, Graham? Don't you like animals?"

"You better pipe down or you're going to be caught stealing Dad's motorcycle wheels," he warned, ignoring her laughter as he slipped the second wheel off and handed it to her.

"Me!" she gasped in disbelief.

"I believe *you* were the one who first mentioned it. I probably would never have thought of it." He shoved the last block beneath the cycle and stood up. "You have a real criminal mind, Miss Spenser," he complimented.

"I am here only because I happened to have had the horrible misfortune to be riding with you in the same car tonight," she pointed out angrily. She knew that he was deliberately trying to provoke her, but she was completely out of sorts to begin with and couldn't take his teasing at the moment.

"I only hope the police never find the wheels at your house," he continued nonchalantly, reaching down to pet the dog, who had decided to stick around after all.

"My house? What do you mean, my house!" She put her hands on her hips and glared at him piercingly.

"Well, think about it, sweetheart. We sure can't leave them here, now can we? And it would really be dirty for us to get rid of them completely." He shrugged his broad shoulders dispassionately. "That only leaves your house to store them at. Of course, the police would never find out unless someone informed them . . . which someone would never do," he pointed out reasonably.

"Which *someone* had better not!" She warned between clenched teeth.

"Now, honey, do you know of anyone who would be that low down, dirty, and conniving?" He leaned back against the cycle and crossed his arms smugly.

Courtney whirled and started marching angrily toward the car, dragging the motorcycle wheel along with her.

She was not going to stand out in the pouring rain and talk to that idiot one minute longer!

"Ya-hoo, sweetie, you forgot the other wheel. I would carry it, but my hands are full," he called in a loud whisper.

Courtney continued on her way, completely ignoring his heckling.

"Ya-hoo, sweeeeetie!" he called once more. "Are you mad at me, *again*?"

She stubbornly refused to answer him, making her way through the maze of bushes that kept slapping her wetly in the face. As she reached the road, she heard him come bounding along behind her, chuckling under his breath. She looked up, her eyes widening incredulously as he made a flying tackle and took them both down in a huge mud puddle that had formed in the road.

"Graham!" she yelled as he reached up and slapped his hand over her mouth hurriedly.

"Shh . . . Watch it! Dad will hear you!"

"Just look what you've done, your moron!" she sputtered, wiping thick gobs of mud out of her eyes and spitting the vile-tasting water out of her mouth.

"Hey, I've heard mud packs make a woman more beautiful. Here, let's work on you for a minute." He reached down and scooped up a handful of gunk and patted it neatly all over her face. "Why, we'll have you looking like a ten in no time at all," he assured her as he dedicatedly smeared it down her neck and arms.

Courtney sat Indian fashion, her arms crossed angrily as he applied her "mud pack." At the moment, she was too mad to even think, let alone speak. Never in her life had she sat in a mudhole!

"Say, I don't want to get your hopes up, but I think it's working," he said optimistically. "Uh-huh! I believe you're prettier than you were five minutes ago, although" —he looked her up and down critically—"your 'eggs' haven't changed any that I can tell. But it doesn't matter. I like you the way you are." He grinned as he looked at her.

"Oh, really?" Courtney reached down and scooped up a large handful of mud and smeared it on his face. "Well, I think your looks could use some sprucing up themselves!"

"Hey!" He rolled away from her, spitting out the mud with a stinging oath.

She crawled over on her hands and knees and shoved him down in the mud, and climbed up on his chest to pin him down. Before he could protest, she was stuffing the front of his shirt with mud, breaking out in giggles as he bellowed and tried to stop her lightning-fast hands.

"Miss Spenser, I thought you were a lady, and ladies don't wallow around in the mud like a bunch of hogs!" he scolded between bursts of laughter.

"You have a way of taking the lady right out of a woman," she told him, stuffing the mud down the back of his shirt eagerly. This was a heck of a lot of fun!

They tumbled in the mud playfully, each one slapping mud at the other in a wild frenzy. Her hands started to stuff a large mound of mud down the front of his trousers when she suddenly realized what she was doing.

His hands quickly captured hers, their gazes meeting intimately. "Hey, watch it, sweetheart," he teased softly. "I've told you if I have anything you're interested in, just let me know."

Her hands fell away instantly, her eyes dropping shyly. "Stop teasing me about that."

"Who's teasing?" he whispered suggestively. Their laughter died now as he gently pulled her down until she was lying on top of him. The rain was beginning to slacken as they gazed hungrily into each other's eyes. "I never tease about a thing like that."

Courtney grew almost lightheaded as his hand reached

156

out and tenderly pulled the few remaining pins out of her hair, letting the thick, lustrous, but muddy, mass tumble down over her shoulders.

"That's better," he murmured, as he gently ran his fingers through the strawberry-blond silkiness. "It's so beautiful. Why *do* you keep it pulled back in that horrible style?"

"I don't know . . . it's just easier to take care of that way," she returned in a small voice. He touched her with the gentleness one touches a newborn babe with and it made her senses stir, then spring achingly alive.

But moments later the intimate mood was shattered as he reached up and drew a large mask around the perimeter of her muddy eyes with his finger. Studying his handiwork critically, he said pensively, "You know, you wouldn't make a bad-lookin' bandit."

At Courtney's gasp of indignation, a mischievous smile spread across his handsome features once again. "To be quite honest, Miss Spenser, you're not half bad as an old maid either," he added tenderly, touching the tip of her nose jauntily, "and if it wasn't for the fact that I'm not particularly fond of the taste of mud, I would undoubtedly kiss you right now."

Her arms stole up around his neck sassily. "No sense of adventure, huh?"

"Oh, I don't know. Are you trying to tempt me into kissing you, you shameless hussy, you?" he teased affectionately.

That thought was more than tempting to Courtney as their eyes met and held suggestively. The rain had tapered off slowly to a fine drizzle, blanketing them in a dark, moist world of privacy. Stealing motorcycle wheels, drinking beer out of bottles, lying with a man in a mud hole at eleven o'clock at night in the aftermath of a blinding rainstorm . . . all those things seemed perfectly natural and desirable to her at the moment. Staid, reserved, always sensible Courtney Spenser had finally found the one man she was willing to do that for, and the thought was very disconcerting.

"Could I tempt you?" she asked softly, hardly daring to breathe as their gaze deepened and he drew her closer.

"Yes, I'm afraid you could," he murmured honestly, amazed at how perfectly she fit in his arms. What was it about this little scrap of a girl that sent his pulses singing and his senses into a state of carnage? he wondered uneasily as he continued to savor the feel of her softness pressed against him. Even though she was covered from head to foot in mud it still could not alter her special smell, the perfume of her hair, her delicate touch . . . all those things that served to bring out the male in him, yet there was something different about her—something he couldn't quite pin down, nor did he want to. He didn't like these new and different feelings. He was perfectly satisfied with the feelings Graham Merrill had lived with for the past thirty-seven years and he certainly didn't want a woman to come along and change things. Especially Bonnie Spenser's lovely, appealing daughter. How could he ever hope to break this attraction between Clyde and Bonnie if *he* got involved with Bonnie's child. Child? He scoffed softly to himself. Courtney was no child. On the contrary, he could feel her ripe, womanly curves pressing tightly into his muscular ones, and it was all he could do not to strip those muddy clothes off her and feast his eyes on the beauty that he had no doubt was hidden beneath.

With a reluctant groan, he gently broke their gaze and sat up with her still in his arms. "I think we better get you inside and out of these wet clothes before you catch pneumonia," he said regretfully.

"Inside your house?" she asked softly, finding it hard to come back down to earth after being in his arms again.

"Yeah, I can't take you home looking like that."

"But what about your father?"

"We have separate entrances to the house. Dad's quarters are up front, along with my office, and mine are in the back of the house," he explained as he pulled her up on her feet. "That way we both have our privacy. Come on, slowpoke, it's starting to rain again."

They quickly loaded the motorcycle wheels in the back of Courtney's car and before she could argue, Graham was pulling her back through the wet bushes, heading for the private entrance to his house. Not that she would have protested. At the moment, staid, reserved, always sensible Courtney Spenser would have accompanied Graham Merrill to a cock fight if he had suggested it!

CHAPTER NINE

By the time Graham let them in the back door, Courtney's teeth were chattering.

"The bathroom's down the hall on the right," he instructed, giving her a push in that direction. "You'll find towels and washcloths in the cabinet and there's a robe hanging on the back of the door."

Courtney didn't argue as she started down the hall. All she wanted was to get out of her wet, muddy clothes and into something dry and warm.

She walked into the bathroom and flipped on the light, stepping back momentarily when she saw the disarray the bathroom was in. It was decorated with the nicest of accessories, but someone, and one guess would do it, had been extremely careless when he last used it. Towels were thrown on the floor, the lids to the deodorant and aftershave lotion had been left off, and the mirror had enough toothpaste on it to brush regularly for a week!

"Don't mind the mess in there," Graham called. "My cleaning lady isn't due till tomorrow!"

A wrecking crew would be more appropriate, Courtney thought in dismay. "It looks fine," she yelled back, then grimly waded in and shut the door.

She stood under the shower for as long as she thought polite, letting the hot spray wash away the mud and grime, then she shampooed her hair and scrubbed with the big bar of soap that was in the tray. After toweling herself dry with the large, dark-blue towel she found in the linen closet, she reached up and removed the man's white terry-cloth robe hanging on the hook and slipped into it. Although it nearly swallowed her alive, it felt warm. Wrapping the towel around her head, she stepped back out and shyly walked into the living area.

Graham was just hanging up the phone as he turned and noticed she was back in the room. "Hi! Feel better?"

"Yes, much better, thank you."

"I was just checking with my answering service. I need to call a prescription in, then I'm going to hop in the shower." He picked up a pad and wrote something on it, then picked the phone receiver back up. "I thought while I was cleaning up you might order us something to eat. There's an all-night Chinese place down the road that delivers. How does that sound to you?"

"Fine. What do you want me to do with my muddy clothes?"

"The washer and dryer's next to the kitchen. Why don't you go put them in and they can be washing while we eat." He dialed the phone and within minutes was giving instructions to the druggist for the prescription.

Courtney went back to the bathroom and gathered up the muddy clothes that she had put neatly in the sink. Taking them into the utility room, she placed them in the washer, then decided to wait and wash Graham's along with hers. By the looks of the utility room, whoever did his laundry was due in six months ago.

Graham had left the name of the Chinese restaurant written on a pad next to the phone, along with the telephone number. His handwriting was as sloppy as his housekeeping, Courtney thought with annoyance as she tried to decipher the chicken scratches. She was finally able to make out the number and place their order. Having done that, she walked over to one of the sections of the three-piece sofa and sat down. Her eyes surveyed the room, noting that it was done in shades of soft blue. The furniture was expensive and tasteful and surprisingly not totally masculine. Courtney decided Graham must have had help in decorating. A strange feeling of jealousy shot through her as she mentally played a guessing game as to which one of the women he had mentioned would have been the one to decide on this particular, restful shade of blue.

"Could you read my handwriting?" Graham came walking down the hall, dressed in a clean pair of slacks and a red sport shirt. His hair was still damp from the shower and he smelled absolutely good enough to eat!

"Barely. You're penmanship is horrible," she pointed out lightly. She removed the towel from her head and began pulling a brush through the long thick mass of hair.

"Yeah, I know. I drive Schultzie straight up the wall with it," he agreed easily. "What did you order to eat?"

"Some cashew chicken, egg rolls, and sweet-and-sour pork. I hope you like that sort of thing."

"I love it." He walked over and sat down beside her, watching intently as she worked the tangles out of her hair and brushed it to a lustrous golden sheen. "Did you find everything you needed?"

"Yes. I put my dirty clothes in the washer and thought maybe you'd want to put yours in there too," she replied.

"Thanks. That's a good idea." He rose and went to get his clothes from the bathroom and start the load of wash.

When he returned, he walked over to the refrigerator and opened it. "Let's see, there's a dried-up piece of cheese, two bottles of beer, and some apple cider. Name your poison."

Courtney frowned. She certainly wasn't going to drink beer again. "Is that all you have?"

"That's it. Usually I don't have the piece of dried-up cheese," he teased, "but I think I went to the store a couple of months ago."

"How do you live like that?"

"I eat out a lot, or Dad cooks up some concoction and brings it over." He reached for the jug of apple cider and took the lid off to smell it. "This has been in here for a while but it smells good. Want a glass?"

"I suppose, if that's all you have." Courtney flinched as she thought of drinking apple cider with cashew chicken.

Graham reached into the cabinet and withdrew two glasses. After pouring them half full, he brought one over to Courtney and sat back down beside her. Taking a sip of his cider, he let out a low whistle and gave a fake shudder. "Wow! That stuff would put hair on your chest!"

Courtney continued brushing her hair. "Then I don't think I'll drink it. I've never had the slightest desire to have hair on my chest," she confessed.

"Oh, really?" He leaned back and closed his eyes wearily. "What have you had a desire to do, Miss Courtney Spenser?"

"Nothing really. I'm doing what I want to do," she returned easily.

"And that being?"

"Running my gift shop, having nice friends, leading my own life." Her hair snapped from the electricity in it as she drew the brush through one last time then laid it down on the coffee table in front of her.

"How old are you?"

"Thirty, why?"

"No special reason. I just wondered why a woman your age would still be living at home with her mother."

Courtney laughed softly. "I haven't always. I lived by myself until Dad died seven years ago. Mom took his death so hard that I began to worry about her. We came down here on a short vacation and she fell in love with the area. When she suggested that we both move here and start a gift shop, it seemed only natural for us to live in the same house."

"What did you do before you moved to Florida?"

"I was a beauty operator. I loved my work but it was such long hours that I decided the gift shop would be more to my liking. And it has been." She leaned back on the sofa and looked at him. "How old are you?"

"Thirty-seven and holding." He grinned.

"And why is a man your age still living with *your* father?" she asked playfully.

"For much the same reasons you're living with Bonnie. After Mom died, Dad knocked around by himself for the next few years. He only moved in here last winter," Graham revealed softly. "The old man's been terribly lonely since Mom died, but I think he's finally getting over it."

Courtney could tell by the tone of his voice that Graham loved his father very much. "You're very fond of him, aren't you?"

"Yeah, we've always gotten along pretty good. At least we did until lately." He took another sip of his cider. "Darn! Have you tasted this yet?"

"No, what's wrong with it?" Courtney picked up her glass and took a sip. It was very, very strong, but it had a yummy flavor.

"I don't know, it just doesn't taste right to me. I wish I could remember how long I've had the stuff."

Courtney took another drink of hers. "Tastes good to me!"

Thirty minutes later, she had drunk two glasses of cider, along with eating the Chinese food that had been delivered. Stuffing the last bite of eggroll in her mouth, she giggled and laid her head back down on the back of the sofa. "Gosh, that was good! Can I have another glass of cider, please?"

Graham looked up from his plate and frowned. She was sure hitting the cider hard tonight and he couldn't understand why. He had barely tasted his. He got up to go to the refrigerator, racking his brain to think how long that cider had been in his possession. Suddenly it dawned on him. Hell! He had had that cider since last Halloween. It had turned hard three months ago! The refrigerator door slammed guiltily as Graham rushed over and jerked the half-filled glass out of Courtney's hand. "Give me that!"

"What's the matter?" Courtney jumped back in surprise and giggled again. Her hand came over her mouth and she looked at him painfully. "Excuse me. I giggled again," she said, embarrassed. "I usually never giggle."

"Not unless you're drinking beer or *hard* cider," Graham said in a grim voice. "Come on, honey, it's time for coffee."

She broke out in another fit of giggles as he tried to help her to the kitchen. "I'm sorry. I don't know what's come over me, but everything seems so funny right now." She burst into another round of laughter.

"Oh, brother." Graham groaned. "You can't hold your liquor at all, can you?"

Courtney let out a gasp of indignation. "I do *not* drink, sir!" She looked at him coyly and giggled again. "I mean, *kind* sir!"

"Forget the coffee, Merrill, and head straight for a cold shower," Graham muttered to himself as he reached down and scooped her up in his arms.

"But I just had a shower," Courtney protested. "I don't want another one!"

Amid loud protests, Graham carried her into the bathroom and turned on the cold water faucet as high as it would go.

"I'm not getting in there," Courtney reminded him stubbornly, her arms wrapping tighter around his neck.

"Okay. This is going to hurt me as much as it does you, sweetheart, but here goes." Both Graham and Courtney let out a scream of agony as he stepped in the shower, still holding her in his arms tightly.

The icy-cold water beat down on them as Courtney

165

yelled in angry protest, but Graham refused to listen to her pleas. They stood under the running water for a full ten miserable minutes before he finally reached up and shut the faucet off.

"Still feel like giggling?" he asked warily, searching her face for any sign of merriment.

"No! Let me out of here!" she demanded crossly. "Are you trying to murder me?"

"No, just trying to sober you up. You know, for a woman who doesn't drink, it seems to me I'm spending half my time getting you back on your feet," he reminded her curtly as he stepped out of the shower and sat her down on the floor.

"What! What are you talking about? I was just sitting there minding my own business and drinking plain old apple cider."

"Yes, just 'plain old apple cider' that I've had in there since last October," Graham said, reaching in the linen closet for another towel.

"What! You were feeding me *hard cider!*"

"I didn't know it was hard," he dismissed curtly. "Here, dry yourself off and I'll go get you another robe."

She took the towel he offered and glared at him angrily. "Feeding me hard cider . . . beer in little glass bottles . . ." she grumbled heatedly to herself as he left the room. She jerked the wet robe off and vigorously rubbed herself dry. In all her thirty years she had *never* been drunk, and now since meeting Graham Merrill she had been soused *two* nights in a row!

The bathroom door opened a crack and a brown robe came sailing through the air, hitting her in the face. "Just stop your grousing. You should be happy I didn't let you continue your drunken spree," Graham taunted. "Hurry up and come out here. As soon as I get into some dry clothes we're going to have that coffee."

This time Courtney was forced to use the blow dryer on her hair. Her arm was too tired to brush it dry twice in one night. When she finally walked back out to where Graham was, it was soft and shiny once more.

"Why did you blow your hair dry this time?" he asked, handing her a cup of steaming black coffee.

"My arm couldn't stand the strain of brushing it dry twice in a row," she said curtly, still more than a little put out at him.

"I would have brushed it dry," he said softly.

Courtney's eyes flew up to meet his serious gaze. "That . . . I wouldn't let you do that."

"Why not?"

"Because—just because." She walked over to the sofa and sat down uneasily.

Graham picked up his cup and joined her. They both sat quietly sipping their coffee and ignoring each other. When the silence turned deafening, Graham sighed and set his cup down on the table in front of the sofa. Reaching in back of him, he flipped on a switch. The lights lowered and soft romantic music filtered through the air. He turned back to her and said softly, "Let's kiss and make up."

"What . . . ?" Courtney jumped at the sound of his words, thinking she had surely not heard them correctly.

"I said"—Graham pulled her over next to him and enfolded her in his arms—"I'm tired of fighting. Let's kiss and make up."

"You're an idiot," Courtney accused, her breath catching in her throat as he continued to draw her nearer to him. Instead of dressing this time, he had slipped on a robe, and Courtney could see his thick chest hair peaking out enticingly.

"That's not a very nice way to talk to someone who put you to bed last night and had to suffer through your very

167

. . . uh . . . colorful and elaborate thank yous," he scolded mockingly.

"What . . . what thank yous?" she asked warily, continuing to scoot away from his ever-tightening embrace.

"Are you going to try and tell me you don't remember thanking me for the bowling shoes, and commenting on how nice you think I would look in . . . certain clothes?" he pursued in a silky voice.

"I-I really don't remember very much about last night," she admitted as his hand came up to capture a strand of her hair and toy with it thoughtfully.

"You don't remember picking up that fantastic four-six split, or me betting you that case of beer in those 'cute little glass bottles' that you couldn't?"

"No. Was that the purpose of that case of beer you had delivered this afternoon?"

"I always pay off my bets." His eyes surveyed her flushed face, rosy and pink from her cold shower. "You sure you don't remember anything after we left the bowling alley?"

"I don't even remember *leaving* the bowling alley," she admitted miserably. She willingly let him draw her up against his broad chest now, knowing full well that it could be a mistake on her part.

"You don't remember the kiss, huh?"

"No . . . did I make a total fool out of myself?" She leaned her head on his shoulder and inhaled his intoxicating fragrance.

"I wouldn't say that," he mused thoughtfully. "I rather enjoyed it."

They both snuggled down contentedly into the plush upholstery of the sofa, forgetting for the moment that they supposedly didn't like each other at all. The soft strains of one of her favorite love songs filled the room intimately as they lay in each other's arms contentedly.

"You're all set up for these cozy encounters, aren't

you?" she murmured languidly as his fingers ran gently through the thickness of her hair.

"What? The music and lights? I had it installed for convenience' sake. I like to listen to music at night when I relax and it's much easier to flip one switch than run around the room flipping several," he reasoned smoothly.

"Of course. I'm sure Liza, Clarissa, Schultzie . . ."

"Schultzie!" Graham raised his head and looked at her in disbelief.

"Yes, Schultzie. Your office nurse, remember? The one who makes root canals pale to insignificance when she's around?"

Graham buried his face back in the fragrance of her hair. "Oh, *that* Schultzie. I'd forgotten you haven't met her yet."

"No, I haven't met her yet. But I have seen the blonde . . ."

"Ah. Are you perhaps becoming a little jealous of who I spend my time with—"

"Certainly not!" Courtney jerked away from him in anger but he firmly pulled her back into his embrace.

"Can't you take a joke? Come back here." He arranged them in the same position they had been in, only it seemed to Courtney that they were nearly lying down on the sofa now. "I know I'm not your type," he continued in a persuasive voice. "I believe you've made that clear on more than one occasion."

"That's right. And I'm not yours," she agreed as she suddenly found herself offering her mouth for his immediate possession.

He didn't refuse the invitation. His lips came down on hers lightly at first, then increasing in pressure as her arms cautiously worked their way up around his neck. They exchanged a series of long, lazy kisses, curling deeper in each other's arms. It occurred to Courtney to question herself on why she was lying there in his arms, thoroughly enjoying a necking session with a man who irritated her to no end, but the thought disappeared rapidly as his tongue merged softly with hers and sent cold chills racing down her spine. She stiffened slightly as she felt his hand reach for the tie on her robe and gently undo it.

"Where is your hand going?" she asked uneasily.

"I don't know. It didn't say," he returned innocently.

"It better not be going to gather 'eggs,' " she murmured in a quiet warning.

"Are you serious? It wouldn't do a thing like that," he assured her.

The hand in question quietly undid the tie and slipped inside the robe. He sighed softly as he hesitantly began to explore the soft, velvet texture of her skin. His fingers slid easily along her ribcage before reaching out to cover one small breast eagerly. "I was right," he said in a voice barely above a whisper. He gently stroked her soft breast seductively. "It fits in my hand perfectly."

"You said you weren't going to do that." Courtney's skin tingled where he touched her.

"I spoke for myself, not my hand," he excused lamely. He tugged the robe open wider and gazed at her beauty, his eyes darkening in passion.

Courtney's face flamed, yet something in his surveillance made her very proud to be a woman at that moment. "I wish you wouldn't do that," she told him weakly. Her thoughts were irrational, silently willing him to stop, yet longing for his touch.

"Then tell me to stop," he said simply. His gaze captured hers in a silent challenge. "I want you to tell me to stop," he demanded again softly.

That was very unfair to ask of her at this time and Courtney told him so as she buried her face in the front of his robe. Her cheeks could feel the wiry texture of the dark mat of hair that covered his chest so invitingly. Her fingers crept up to hesitantly explore the delightful feel of his skin beneath her fingers.

"If you're serious about me stopping, you're going to have to quit that," he warned, stealing another long, demanding kiss from her.

"I . . . this isn't something I do very often," she explained in a shy whisper, "and I honestly don't know what's making me do it right now."

Graham looked at her seriously. He didn't know if she meant she hadn't gone to bed with a man very often, or if she simply hadn't necked with a man this intimately. He decided not to pursue the statement since he had no intention of the situation developing any further than a few harmless kisses.

"I know this is not anything new to you . . ." she continued in a voice made breathless by the feel of her hands on his bare chest.

"No, it's nothing new," he agreed softly, "except contrary to your belief, I don't do this with every woman I happen to be attracted to," he confessed, sliding down to kiss the inviting brown crest that he held in his hand. He lovingly kissed each tip, then languidly kissed his way down to her navel before returning his attention to their conversation. "I've been teasing you pretty heavy about the number of women I date. But I'm rather discriminating about who I bring home with me."

Somehow that wasn't as comforting as Courtney had hoped it would be, but at the moment she was incapable of reasoning, as his lips continued to explore her ear and neckline alluringly.

"And I'm sure you do bring your share home," she added lightly, with just a slight touch of misery in her voice.

"At the moment I'm seeing two different women," he said defensively. "After all, dear, I'm an unattached male. What do you expect?"

171

"I don't expect anything," she said curtly. "I was merely commenting that you were much more experienced at this than I am."

He leaned up on his elbow and his gaze met hers in mute understanding. "Keep in mind I said I was *seeing* two different women, not necessarily bringing them home each night. You're going to have a hard time buying this, but I'm not a promiscuous sort of guy and I really have very little use for anyone who is." He paused and took a deep breath studying her solemn face before continuing. "And for the life of me, I can't understand why I'm explaining all this to you. I'm very happy with my life, Miss Spenser, and I have no plans whatsoever of changing it," he finished bluntly.

"You really are assuming a great deal, Dr. Merrill. I certainly have no thoughts of trying to change your life," she said. "You're not the only one who likes the way he lives."

He smiled, then leaned over and kissed her on the nose gently. "Just wanted to make sure you understood. Women have a strange way of making more out of a situation than what really exists."

"I don't," she assured as his mouth came down to take hers again in a lingering kiss. The stereo filled the quiet room with sounds of love as they lay locked in each other's embrace, totally shutting away the rainy, drowsy world. Just exactly when the kissing turned from simple necking to a more heated exchange, Courtney couldn't say. She hadn't expected it to change, although she knew she was playing with fire and was bound to get singed. At first, there were only the usual kisses. Slowly, they began to deepen, then turn smoldering, then hotly passionate.

By the time another ten minutes had passed, Graham groaned, then reluctantly rolled off of her. He buried his face in her hair, his hands refusing to relinquish their hold on her body. "I think it's time you went home," he panted hoarsely. This had gone on longer than he had ever intended it to. Courtney Spenser was not the type of girl you had one-night stands with. Never had he more painfully realized that than at this moment.

"I know . . . I'll get my clothes out of the dryer." Her head was in a hazy fog, her body crying out for fulfillment, but she knew that Graham Merrill was only interested in an impersonal act of love and nothing more. She started to sit up but was pushed back down impatiently as Graham's mouth took hers again in another hungry kiss.

It was several minutes before she could attempt to rise again. His kisses and touch had her in a world of smoky passion, one that she had no desire to leave.

It was Graham who sat up this time and pushed her away firmly. "Go get your clothes, Courtney . . . and hurry, damn it!"

Courtney blinked at his abrupt change of mood. Moments earlier he couldn't seem to get enough of her, but now he was urging her to leave as fast as she could.

"I-I don't want to go," she confessed in a miserably sad voice. She felt so totally confused she wanted to cry, to scream out her frustrations. She knew she *should* leave. She had never been one to engage in meaningless sex, nor would she ever. Like Graham, she avoided people who did and yet . . .

"Courtney." Graham's slumberous eyes met hers. "If you don't go right now, I won't be responsible for what happens. . . . I can't be . . ."

"I know. I'm going . . ." she whispered remorsefully, ". . . but you make me want something . . . you make me want . . ." Her voice trailed off weakly. She didn't know exactly what he made her want. She certainly didn't want a man permanently in her life. At least, not this man! Then what *did* she want? The security and peace of mind of the old Courtney or to spend just one blissful hour in infuriating Graham Merrill's arms? She bit her lip. Yes, as crazy as it was, that's exactly what she wanted. "Make me go, Graham." Her eyes pleaded silently with his for strength.

"I can't do that . . . I can't do that," he repeated huskily as he avoided her gaze. "But we both know you should." He could help her that much, but *only* that much.

She slowly pulled his head around until they were once more looking at each other, unable to avoid their feelings any longer. "Forgive me, but for the life of me, I can't find the words to say no."

Graham looked faintly surprised. "Uh . . . that cider has worn off, hasn't it?"

"Yes." She smiled sheepishly back at him. "I almost wish I had that to blame this madness on, but I'm afraid I'm perfectly sober at the moment."

His gaze was tender with silent understanding. "You're sure?"

She nodded. "I'm sure," she replied with a shaky laugh.

She didn't have to ask him again to pull her back into his arms. He did that most willingly. Their mouths met ravenously once more, dissolving all thoughts of either one of them leaving. They sank back in the soft folds of the sofa as he began to whisper all the sweet meaningless words lovers whisper to each other in the intimacy of making love.

Graham slowly began to work his way out of his robe, drawing her nearer to his masculine warmth as he kissed her deeply again and again. Her robe joined his on the floor in another few minutes as she closed her eyes in ecstasy and savored the feel of his body pressed intimately against hers.

It didn't make sense, she thought helplessly to herself as her desire grew to frightening proportions. Never had a man taken her to the heights of such sexual awareness, then kept her there like this man was now so breathlessly doing.

She had honestly thought that no man could ever make

174

her feel the thrill and excitement that the love stories she had read always spoke of, but Graham Merrill was proving her wrong. She was slowly but surely beginning to realize that he was different from any man she had ever met. Where was her common sense and her iron will when she so desperately needed them?

Their hunger and needs quickly overflowed their bounds as Graham unhurriedly joined with her in the act of love. He was a tender, considerate lover, taking them both to the realms of heaven before their passion erupted, sending them both spiraling into a world of oblivion. The rain fell softly on the roof as they drifted back to reality slowly. Graham still held her tightly in his embrace as he once more buried his hands in the thickness of her hair and kissed her long and tenderly.

"I won't say that I regret what just happened, but I want you to know that I didn't plan it," he murmured against the sweetness of her mouth as he ended the kiss.

"I know, and I'm sorry that I practically seduced you." Courtney's face felt warm as she thought of her earlier actions. "I don't usually . . ."

Graham stopped her words with another lingering kiss. "I'm well aware that you don't make a habit of this," he whispered softly.

"I think I better go home now," she whispered back. She needed time alone, to sort out all her feelings. Right now, she was puzzled and frightened at what had just taken place, yet she dreaded to leave the warmth of his embrace.

"All right. I'll get our clothes." Graham kissed her one final time before he reached for his robe. "It sounds like it's still raining. I'll have to look up that old umbrella I keep around here."

Courtney lay back on the sofa and stared at drops of rain running down the windowpane as Graham left the room to get their clothes. When he returned, he paused in the doorway and looked at the lovely strawberry blonde lying on the sofa, tears running quietly down her cheeks. Damn Merrill! Why couldn't you have put a stop to your actions before things got out of hand? he chastised silently. Had she been a virgin? He honestly didn't know because there had been no physical indication. One thing he'd bet his last dollar on. If she hadn't been, she was still very inexperienced. Not as much as she had been thirty minutes ago, but still very shy in her lovemaking.

With a silent groan, he stepped back out of the room to give her time to compose herself before he took her home. What kind of a mess had he gotten himself into this time?

CHAPTER TEN

"Can you believe that, Buddy! Stole my dad burn wheels!" Clyde Merrill was beside himself that morning as he stormed back in the kitchen. He had been outside with the police for the last half hour trying to find some clue as to who had stolen his motorcycle wheels.

Graham looked up from his morning paper and frowned at his father. "Why didn't you put it in the garage? If you had, then this might not have happened."

Clyde sank down morosely on the kitchen chair and stared out the window bleakly. "I forgot to." His eyes met his son's earnestly. "I was going to, Buddy, but the phone rang and I went in to answer it and then . . . I just forgot." He shrugged his shoulders philosophically.

With a deep sigh, Graham got up and got a cup of coffee for his father. Clyde looked so downhearted that morning it was all Graham could do to keep from telling him that his motorcycle wheels were safe in Courtney's garage and in this particular instance it wouldn't have made any difference if the cycle had been put in the garage or not. But of course he wouldn't. Clyde needed to take more responsibility for his possessions and if he didn't start at seventy years old, when would he? "Did the police find any clues?" Graham asked politely.

"No, none. The only thing out there now is Herb Mason's big old dog walking around. That thing's a sorry-looking mess," Clyde lamented as he spooned sugar disinterestedly in his coffee. "Looks to me like they could get the poor old thing in out of the rain. He's wet and smells like a sewer backed up on a hot fourth of July mornin'."

Graham's stomach rolled as he vividly recalled the smell and the way the dog had licked him in the face while he was trying to get the motorcycle wheel off. "Yeah, I know the dog you're talking about."

"Boy, this just burns me to the core. Stealing my motorcycle wheels! I still can't get over it!" Clyde stirred his coffee briskly. "And I had plans for today. Me and—" He broke off suddenly.

"Yes?" Graham looked at Clyde disapprovingly. "You and who had plans?"

"Me . . . and . . . someone." He picked up his coffee and quickly took a big gulp.

"I don't suppose you'd let me borrow your cycle for the day?" Clyde asked meekly a few seconds later.

"You guessed right. My cycle's clean, and staying in the garage today."

"Can't see why you can't share—"

Graham interrupted his father's grumblings. "By the way, Dad, thanks a lot for cutting out on me last night. Mildred and I had a simply stimulating evening!"

"That woman's runnin' about a quart low, isn't she?" Clyde smiled happily back at his son.

"She was *your* date!"

"She was not! It was *your* suggestion that we go to that stupid bingo party!"

"Where did you and Bonnie go?"

"Over to Georgios!"

"A disco club?" Graham asked incredulously.

"That's right!" Clyde jumped up and did a couple of disco steps in the kitchen, humming the fast pace music under his breath. "We got down and booooogied. You and that old-maid daughter of Bonnie's should go there some time. You two stuffed shirts would love it!"

178

At the mention of Courtney, Graham's face clouded and he grew quiet. He had spent a restless night after he had taken her home. They hadn't said very much to each other on the ride to her house. When they parted, he had kissed her lightly before she went in. They had made no promise to call each other or even to keep in touch. Graham didn't know why he had such a feeling of guilt this morning. After all, she had practically asked him to make love to her, hadn't she? He had given her the opportunity to back out but she had refused to take it. What else could he have done? Graham Merrill was a man, not a saint! Still, the nagging thought that there were women and then there were . . . ladies kept hounding him all night. And there was no doubt that Courtney Spenser was a lady.

"Don't you think?" Clyde stopped his dancing and glanced expectantly at his son.

"What?"

"Don't you think you should ask Courtney out? She's a nice-looking woman, and I figure if you can help me get her mind on something else . . ."

"You'll have more time to spend with her mother! I don't think so, Dad! In the first place, I'm not going to sacrifice my personal life for yours, and in the second place, I don't want you seeing Bonnie Spenser any more than Courtney does, and in the third place, Courtney Spenser is *not* my kind of woman! She doesn't like the same things I do, she doesn't go the same places I go, she's a love-and-marriage type woman and I'm not ready for that yet." Graham threw his hands up in the air helplessly. It seemed to him that he was trying to convince himself even more than he was his father!

"Hogwash! That's all a bunch of flimsy excuses. Besides, I'm not asking you to marry the girl, I'm just asking the both of you to leave me and Bonnie alone!"

"Yes, so you can run around wild as the wind and break both your necks! That's the only reason Courtney and I don't want you two together. We don't want to see you get hurt!"

"Bunch of party poopers! I've told you before, I'm not going to get hurt, and I am going to see Bonnie every opportunity I get," Clyde said defiantly. "You can't honestly say you'd prefer Mildred Mosely over Bonnie Spenser, now can you, Buddy?"

Graham's face paled. He couldn't actually say that. Mildred might be more reserved than Bonnie, but heavens, could he wish an acute hypochondriac off on his dad?

Clyde could tell by the look on his son's face he had hit a sore spot. "Well, Buddy? Old Mildred can bake the best damn apple pie you ever put in your mouth, and she can sure knit up a storm. Is that what you want for me?"

"I want you to hit a happy medium somewhere. Don't you know any woman your age who's . . . normal?"

Although the blue of Clyde's eyes was not nearly as bright as it had been fifty years ago, the look in them could grow just as tender, as they did now. "Bonnie Spenser is normal," he said softly.

"Come on, Dad." Graham shoved his coffee cup back irritably. "Excluding Bonnie!"

"Excluding Bonnie? Then there's no one I'm interested in and you just as well accept it, Buddy." Clyde pushed back from the table and stood up. "Now, if you'll excuse me, I'm going to go see about getting some wheels for my motorcycle. If everything goes all right, I hope to take a little spin on it tomorrow."

Little spin! Graham thought irritably as Clyde left the room. Orlando was hundreds of miles away, but to Clyde it was a little spin!

Graham's mind was never far away from Courtney as he went about his work. By the time he saw his last patient he knew that he had to see her again. If only to relieve his mind that what had occurred between them had been "just one of those things" and she had fully realized that and experienced no regrets that morning.

"You've been very quiet all day, dear." Bonita glanced over uneasily at her daughter as they tallied up the day's receipts.

"I'm tired today, Mother. I didn't sleep very well last night." Courtney punched the last button on the calculator and ripped the tape out of the machine. She had lain awake most of the night going over and over in her mind what had taken place earlier. It still surprised and puzzled her when she thought of how fast things had happened. It wasn't that she necessarily regretted what had happened. She hadn't allowed herself to examine her feelings concerning that yet. Although she had always dreamed of something similar happening with the man she would meet someday and fall hopelessly in love with, she never in her wildest dreams would have expected it to happen so spontaneously, so naturally . . . at least not with Graham Merrill.

"You must have gotten in very late. I didn't hear you come home."

"Yes, it was very late," Courtney murmured absently.

"I thought you might be mad at me . . . you know, for leaving you stranded with Harold. I hope he didn't give you too much trouble," Bonita apologized.

"That Harold Curtis is the typical 'dirty old man,' Mother. How could you!"

"I *told* you Harold was the pits! You just refused to believe me, so I thought what better way to prove to you what I was talking about. Anyway, I knew Graham would be there to protect you if Harold got too far out of line."

"I don't know why you would think that. I'm nothing to Graham Merrill. Why should he protect me?"

"Well, I didn't mean that he would fight rabid tigers for you, but he does seem like a nice young gentleman and I didn't think he would stand by and watch anyone try to take advantage of you." Bonita looked at Courtney hopefully.

"You do think he's a nice young gentleman, don't you?"

Courtney stared at her mother sternly. "No comment."

"He was nice to you last night, wasn't he?"

Courtney blushed. "Yes, he was nice to me, but we don't have anything in common except trying to keep you and Clyde . . . We don't have anything in common," Courtney said quietly, "so don't try to pair us off together."

"You're not mad about me and Clyde leaving last night?" Bonita looked sheepish.

"Yes, but what good will it do me?" Courtney sneezed.

"Oh, dear, are you getting sick? That's the fourth time you've sneezed today," Bonita clucked, reaching out to brush a lock of stray hair out of Courtney's eyes.

"I was out in the rain last night and I think I'm coming down with a cold," she explained.

"I noticed you're wearing your hair down this morning. It really looks pretty like that."

"Thanks, Mom, I—I didn't have time to put it up this morning." Courtney hated to admit, even to herself, that Graham liked it this way too.

Bonita gave a wistful sigh and walked over to peer out the front window of the shop. "It's still raining." She turned around and looked back at her daughter. "Did you know someone stole Clyde's motorcycle wheels last night?"

Courtney glanced up guiltily. "Really?"

"Yes. Now, who do you suppose would want to do a thing like that?" she mused. "We were going to . . . He was going to take a ride on it today," she amended quickly.

"Well, he probably couldn't have gone anywhere today anyway," Courtney pointed out. "The weather's too bad to be out on a motorcycle."

The bell over the door jingled as Rob Hanson entered, a bright smile on his handsome face. "Good afternoon, lovely ladies. How's it going today?"

"Slow. The rain's kept everyone away today," Bonita answered.

"Yeah, it's nasty out there." He walked over and propped himself on the counter next to Courtney. "How's the prettiest lady on the block today?"

"I think Mom's feeling fine." Courtney grinned impishly.

"Hey, what have you done to your hair?" Rob let out a low, appreciative whistle. "That's dynamite!"

Courtney shrugged indifferently. "I didn't have time to put it up so I left it down this morning."

Rob's gaze devoured the silky mass of blond hair. "It's beautiful, Court. You should never wear it up again!"

"If you don't mind, dear, I'm going to run along. I want to stop by the market and pick up some bread and milk on the way home. Will you be along shortly?" Bonita walked behind the counter and picked up her purse and umbrella.

"Not if I can persuade her to have dinner with me this evening," Rob said brightly.

Courtney covered the typewriter with its plastic cover and closed the register drawer. "Not tonight, Rob. I'm going home, taking a hot bath, and going to bed early. I've felt like I was coming down with a cold all day."

Rob's face fell. "Are you *ever* going to go out with me?"

Courtney laughed as she let her mother out the front door and pulled down the "Closed" sign. "Maybe one of these days."

"You always say that but when the time comes to go you always back out. You know you owe me one for breaking our date the other night."

"I know, Rob. And I will go to dinner with you one of these evenings, but not tonight." Courtney was trying to be as polite as possible, but she simply wasn't interested in Rob Hanson.

It was another twenty minutes before she was able to get rid of him and go home.

When she arrived, she ate dinner then went immediately to soak in a hot tub. Bonita had received a call earlier, then announced that she was going to the movies. Although that was a pretty tame evening, Courtney didn't need three guesses to know whom she was probably going with. But for that night she was willing to let it pass. She wasn't in the mood to spend another miserable night in the rain searching for them. She lay back in the tub, letting her mind drift lazily, wonderering what Graham was doing that evening. Would he be out with Clarissa, Schultzie— or both? Her eyes closed dreamily as she thought about the night before. It had been something special. If she lived to be a hundred she would never forget the tender yet exciting way he had made love to her. Granted, she didn't have much to compare it with, but she knew instinctively that he was a real pro when it came to making love to a woman. That thought disturbed her as she hurriedly sat up in the tub and reached for the soap. She had enough problems without dwelling on Graham Merrill's personal life.

Twenty minutes later she emerged from the bathroom wrapped in a warm, fleecy robe. The rain had made the air damp and chilly and she suddenly wished she was back in Indiana. There they had an old house with a large fireplace they could light on nights like this to take the chill out of the air.

The doorbell rang as she was walking out of the kitchen with a cup of hot tea in her hand. She frowned, wondering who it could be. Probably one of Bonita's friends, she decided as she unlocked the latch and opened the door.

For a moment Courtney's breath caught in her throat

when she saw Graham standing there in the wet night air. "Oh . . . Graham."

"Hi. I'm sorry I didn't call. I hope you weren't busy." His eyes uneasily surveyed her housecoat and slippers.

"No . . . no, of course not. I . . . just wasn't expecting anyone," she replied nervously. Her hand went up to touch her hair. She could have murdered him for dropping in like that.

"Do you mind if I come in?" he asked pleasantly. "It's a little wet out here."

"Oh . . . no, please, come in." She stood back as he walked past her into the house. She closed the door then turned to face him uneasily.

"You're sure I'm not disturbing you?" Graham walked over to the sofa and sat down, hoping to put her more at ease. He could tell that his unexpected appearance had unnerved her.

"No, not at all. I'm just surprised to see you, that's all." She walked over and perched on a chair next to the sofa. She couldn't help but notice how striking he looked. The tan corduroy sports coat with suede patches on the sleeves looked very attractive with his dark-brown slacks. Her eyes quietly admired the pair of dark-brown dress boots he was wearing, polished to a high sheen.

Graham reached up and loosened the dark tie he was wearing, his blue eyes meeting hers questioningly. "Do you mind?"

"No, please, make yourself comfortable." Her eyes fastened on his hands as they worked irritably at the knot in his tie, and she had to fight to keep her mind on the moment. It kept wanting to go back to the night before when she had lain in his arms and those hands had intimately acquainted themselves with every inch of her body. She self-consciously pulled her robe up tighter against her chin.

"Was your father very upset about his motorcycle this morning?" she asked conversationally.

Graham winced painfully at the thought of his father's anger. "You might say that. I thought he was going to blow a fuse!"

Courtney clutched her robe tighter. "I hope he never finds out who stole them," she replied.

"You and me both," he agreed readily. He glanced over at her. "You seem a bit nervous, Miss Spenser. Is there something wrong?" he asked casually.

"No, nothing! I'm just fine." The words tumbled out faster than she had wanted them to.

"Well." Graham chuckled. "I'm used to people being a little nervous when they're around me, but I assure you, I'm not here to extract any of your teeth tonight. This is strictly a . . . social call."

"Oh?" Courtney sat up straighter.

"Yeah." Graham picked a piece of imaginary lint off his trousers. "I've been thinking about you all day."

"Oh?" Courtney knew she sounded like a stuck record but her mind wasn't functioning too well at the moment.

"Yeah." He sounded like one now.

She cleared her throat nervously. "Uh . . . I hope they were nice thoughts."

His clear blue gaze met hers boldly now. "Very nice," he assured in a soft voice. He reached over and took her hand gently in his. "Would you think I was being impertinent if I kissed you hello?"

Courtney's gaze dropped shyly from his as her heart thudded painfully in her chest. "No."

Graham leaned over and holding her face with his hand kissed her lightly. His mouth tasted cool, clean, sweet, and very very inviting. The kiss lasted only a few seconds, but it had been long enough to send her blood racing warmly through her veins.

"I have to admit that I've been a little worried about you," he said as he gazed quietly into her bright eyes.

"Me?" She gave a shaky laugh. "Why would you be worried about me?"

"Oh, I don't know. Things just moved so fast last night . . ." He paused and let his hand drop away from her face. "About last night . . ." he began again hesitantly. "Any regrets this morning?"

"No, why?" She twisted her hands absently in the tie of her robe.

Graham stood up and walked over to the window restlessly. He stood with his hands in his pockets looking out at the rain falling heavily once more.

"Look, Courtney . . . I wanted you to know that if anything develops out of last night . . . you know . . . I didn't take any precautions—" He paused and glanced at her hopefully. "Did you?"

Courtney shook her head, embarrassed. "No." That was another thing, among the many, that she had been worried about all day.

"That's what I was afraid of," he responded bleakly. "I'm sorry I was so careless. It all happened so unexpectedly . . ."

"Yes, I know. I was as much to blame as you were."

"Yes, you were!" Graham swung around, irritation and guilt now flooding his handsome features. "Why didn't you leave when I told you to?" he demanded curtly.

Courtney's mouth dropped open. "Me! I told you I couldn't stop it! Why didn't you *make* me go!"

"Darn it, I couldn't have made you go! I was too far gone myself!"

"Then don't blame *me* for all of it!"

"I'm not blaming you, Courtney." His temper evaporated as suddenly as it appeared. "In any other circumstances I wouldn't have given it a second thought, but for some darn reason what happened last night has been nagging me all day."

"Why?" Courtney looked at him in disbelief. "I'm sure that wasn't the first time you ever . . ." Her voice faded weakly.

"No, it wasn't the first time I ever . . . but I've been wondering if it was your first time!" Graham's face was a mask of troubled concern.

Courtney stiffened her shoulders and sat up uneasily. "I believe you're getting a little personal, Dr. Merrill," she replied coolly.

"After what took place last night, don't you think I have a right to?"

"No, you certainly don't. Whatever happened between us last night has nothing to do with the past *or* the future. I'm very surprised that you would ask the question at all. You don't strike me as being overly protective of a woman's virtue."

"Now that's where you're wrong," he said sharply. "*Some* women don't have any virtue to protect. Those women, I don't worry overly much about. But I've always avoided any entanglement with the . . . other kind of women, which I have a strong suspicion you are!"

Courtney smiled serenely. "I thought men were able to tell one woman from another."

"Usually they can. I . . . was too busy to take inventory," he admitted gruffly.

"Too bad." Courtney rose and faced him aloofly. "Just exactly why did you come here tonight?"

Graham stepped back a few feet, surprised at her swift change of attitude. "I want you to give me a straight answer to my question!"

"Which is?"

"Were you . . . just exactly how experienced were you?" he demanded bluntly.

"I think it's time you left, Dr. Merrill!"

"Not until you answer my question!" He stalked back over to the window stubbornly.

"No!"

"No, you weren't experienced?"

"No, I won't answer your question. Whether I was or wasn't is none of your business! My *husband* will be the only one who will know my indiscretions, not some gigolo dentist!"

Graham gave a snort of disgust, then threw his hands up in the air digustedly. "What are you holding out for, Miss Spenser? A marriage proposal?"

"Of course! Do you feel guilty enough to issue one?"

He whirled around and confronted her angrily. "If it comes to that I wouldn't desert you."

"Ohhhh, now wait a minute!" Courtney's eyes flashed fire. "I wouldn't be associated with you under *any* circumstances, Graham Merrill! You get that straight!"

"Now *you* wait a minute!" The confidence that had shown so clearly on his face moments earlier disappeared. "I don't particularly like the idea of you referring to me as a 'gigolo,' and I'd like to know what you mean by 'you wouldn't be associated with me under any circumstances'!" He was definitely not used to a woman turning him down on anything he suggested. And since he had never even hinted at some sort of permanent commitment to another woman, Courtney's cavalier attitude irked him!

"Are you daft? It means exactly what you think it means. I don't want any part of you. Period. I don't like you," she added for extra emphasis.

"I wish you would have made that clearer last night, *Miss Spenser*!"

"I was waiting for *you* to speak up, *Dr. Merrill*!"

"Well!" Graham sucked in his chest and walked to the door in a haughty manner. "Let's just hope it never comes down to the fact that you may be *forced* into associating with me."

"You don't need to worry about that," she said easily, following along at his heels. "Even if it did come down to that, you'd never know."

Graham looked at her stonily. "I'll make a note to keep close check on you!"

"Suit yourself. So nice of you to drop by. You must come again when you can't stay so long." She opened the door and smiled at him sweetly.

"I'm not leaving here until I say what I came here to say tonight!" Graham slammed the door she had just opened. He crossed his arms stubbornly and glared at her.

"Then by all means, have your say then get out!" Courtney crossed her arms and faced him defiantly.

"Your damn hair looks prettier tonight than I've ever seen it look. You are a beautiful, sexy, and unusually appealing woman!" His words came out more like an accusation than an compliment.

Courtney blinked her eyes waiting for the rest of his tirade.

"So?"

"So, that's all I wanted to say!" He jerked the door open. "Good night, *Miss Spenser*!"

Courtney watched in disbelief as he marched angrily out the front door.

"Well! Good night yourself, Dr. Merrill!" She slammed the door on his hastily retreating back.

Leaning up against the door, she closed her eyes in relief that he had finally left. A small giggle escaped her as she thought of their stormy and strange conversation. She shook her head in amazement, then broke out in a burst of outright laughter. Now what in the world had all that nonsense been about?

CHAPTER ELEVEN

Clyde Merrill took a long, deep, appreciative sniff of the fragrant air that deliciously enveloped the kitchen he was standing in. "Now that has *got* to be the best-smelling apple pie anyone has ever baked!"

Bonita smiled happily as she scooped the peels of the apples off in the trash basket and wiped the counter clean. "I made an extra one just in case."

"Buddy would be thrilled to know you can bake a decent pie." He laughed sarcastically. Taking one last whiff, Clyde ambled over to where Bonita was standing and wrapped his arms around her waist affectionately. "You made an extra one just in case of what?" he teased, kissing her lightly on the neck.

"Just in case a certain man I know decides he would like to take one home for his dinner this evening."

"A certain man would rather take the baker home with him," he confessed sadly.

"I know." Bonita sighed sympathetically as she leaned back against his broad frame in contentment. "Do you suppose the children will ever accept the fact that we want to be together?"

"I doubt it. Buddy still watches me like a hawk every time I walk out the front door." Clyde turned her around and kissed her lingeringly. "What do you say we just hang it all up and get married anyway?"

"No, I couldn't do that to Courtney." Bonita's face grew worried. "She would never forgive me."

"Dag nab it! Why not?" Clyde moved away from her restlessly. "Courtney is a big girl who should be living a life of her own now instead of trying to run yours."

"It isn't that, Clyde. Courtney would never admit it, but I think she can't stand the thought of anyone replacing her father in my life," Bonita confessed thoughtfully.

"That's silly. I would never try to replace her father." Clyde's voice dropped abruptly. "Not that I wouldn't be honored to have a daughter as pretty and bright as Courtney. I've always wanted one, but I would never try to take Frank's place in her life. Not unless she wanted it," he added defensively.

"I think Courtney misses her father more than she would ever say. They had a very close relationship." Bonita picked up the teapot and poured Clyde another steaming cup full. "Someday the right man is going to come along and change her way of thinking on a lot of things," she predicted optimistically. "It won't take her long to realize that love finds you in strange ways. When that happens, she'll accept our love without any reservations."

"But what do we do in the meantime?" Clyde asked remorsefully. He picked up the sugar bowl and spooned two teaspoons into his tea. "Keep sneaking around like a couple of teenagers trying to outwit their parents?"

"I suppose so. But it hasn't been too bad, has it? We usually go where we want to," she pointed out.

"It still burns me up when I think about some maniac stealing my motorcycle wheels and knocking us out of our trip to Disneyworld!"

Bonita laughed. "Oh, well, it was raining that day anyway. We'll go another time."

"Yeah, maybe. If we can manage to sneak away from our guard dogs. What *are* we going to do about this, Bonnie?" Clyde turned pleading eyes on her.

Bonita seated herself across from Clyde and smiled secretly. "Well . . . I've been thinking. What if we sort of *helped* Courtney find someone she could fall in love with? Someone who would show her how wonderful life can be when you spend it with a man you love."

Clyde glanced up from his tea interestedly. "Oh? Do you have someone in mind?"

"Your son, Graham, might be rather nice," Bonita said pleasantly.

A spray of tea spewed out of Clyde's mouth before he could cover it with a napkin. "My Buddy!"

Bonita's face clouded up disapprovingly. "Is there something wrong with that idea?" she asked coolly.

A deep hoot of laughter filled the room. "My Buddy?" he asked again incredulously.

"Yes, *your* Buddy!"

Clyde sobered instantly when he saw the impatient scowl on Bonita's face. "Oh, now look, Bonnie. I didn't mean to imply that Buddy wouldn't find Courtney attractive but . . . my gosh, woman! I've tried to get him to settle down for years and he only laughs in my face!"

"So? Maybe he just hasn't found the right woman to make him want to settle down," Bonita pointed out sternly.

"Ha! He's looked at every eligible woman in this four-state area and he hasn't found one who's seriously caught his eye yet!"

Bonita picked up her teacup and sipped absently. "That doesn't mean that she isn't out there. I gather you didn't notice the way Courtney and Graham were looking at each other the other night at the bingo game?" she asked smugly.

"No, I didn't. It's hard to notice anything when Mildred is hanging all over me moaning about her corns killing her," he grumbled.

"Well, there was a definite interest on both their parts,"

Bonita said firmly. "And I know that Graham brought her home from the bingo game and she got in *very* late. Now obviously they don't play bingo until two o'clock in the morning, Clyde. What do you suppose they were doing?"

"I don't know and I sure hate to be the one to disappoint you, but I know for certain that Buddy doesn't . . . care a whole lot for Courtney." Clyde hung his head sheepishly. He hated to be so blunt, but he didn't want Bonnie getting her hopes up over something that was doomed to failure before it even began.

"Who said?"

"Buddy. On numerous occasions," Clyde said matter-of-factly. "He says they don't have anything in common."

"Monkey feathers! Courtney says the same thing but I think that's just a silly excuse to cover up the fact that they *are* attracted to each other," Bonita concluded. "Courtney has been anti-men so long that she naturally refuses to admit even to herself when one finally comes along that catches her eye."

"I don't know, Bonnie," Clyde said skeptically. "I think we're dealing with two hard-core cases of anti-involvement—"

"Oh, but it would be a real challenge to try, wouldn't it?" Bonita grasped Clyde's hand excitedly, her blue eyes sparkling mischievously. "They would make such a lovely couple if we could get them to notice each other!"

"Bonnie Spenser!" Clyde's eyes twinkled with amusement. "Do you realize you have just suggested we step in and try to run our kids' business! That's the very thing we've been trying to get *them* to stop doing to us!"

"Oh, I know, dear. But what could it hurt?" She leaned over and kissed him persuasively on the mouth. "After all, if we can get them to fall in love with each other, then our problems will be over. They couldn't object to our marriage if they were going to be married themselves!"

"Boy, I don't know." Clyde's face clouded with apprehension. "Buddy gets really mad when I butt in his personal affairs . . ."

"Poo! He'll never even know what hit him," Bonita assured as she stood up and went over to the stove to check on the progress of her apple pie. "Now, we're going to have to be sly about this little caper—"

"I'd say we are," he interrupted as he slumped down defeatedly in his chair. "Do you realize what will happen if they ever catch us on this one!"

"They won't catch us," Bonita said happily. "You watch. If this works out like I hope it will, they'll be thanking us!"

"And if it don't, we'll be sitting home knittin' and whittlin' for the rest of our lives," Clyde predicted glumly.

When Courtney let herself in the house that evening she was tired, hungry, and out of sorts. The smell of fresh baking assaulted her as she set her purse down on the hall table and wandered into the kitchen. Bonita had begged off work earlier in order to stay home and clean house.

"Hi, Mom." Courtney kissed her mother and sat down at the table where Bonita was peeling carrots.

"Hello, dear. Did you have a nice day?"

"Fair. What smells so good?" Courtney glanced around the kitchen, trying to locate the tantalizing aroma filling the air.

"I baked pies this afternoon. How does that sound?"

"Good. I'm hungry." Courtney rose and went over to the refrigerator and opened it. She stood studying the contents for something to tide her over until dinner.

"Don't spoil your dinner, dear. I have chicken and dressing tonight," Bonita warned absently.

The door to the refrigerator closed slowly. Courtney ambled back to the table and sat down once more. "So, what have you done today?" she asked, reaching for a carrot.

"Oh, a little cleaning, a little baking, nothing too interesting. What about you?"

"Nothing. The store was busy this morning, but by afternoon it had slowed down. We're going to have to reorder more of the shell windchimes," she mused, crunching on the vegetable thoughtfully. "I sold the last three just before I closed."

Bonita laid the paring knife down and got up to rinse the carrots off with cold water. "That's nice. Did anyone I know happen to come by today?"

Courtney thought for a moment then replied absently. "No, no one in particular. Were you expecting someone?"

"Oh . . . no, I just thought that perhaps that nice Graham Merrill might stop by," she said casually.

Courtney stiffened at the mention of Graham's name. She hadn't seen him in more than a week and she certainly had no plans to do so anywhere in the near future. "Why would *he* stop in?" she replied crossly.

"Oh, I don't know." Bonita finished washing the vegetables, then sliced them up carefully and put them into a saucepan. "I just thought he might want to come and get Clyde's motorcycle wheels that you and Graham hid under those blankets in our garage," she announced calmly.

Courtney nearly choked on the bite of carrot she had just taken. Bonita walked over and carefully whacked her on the back a couple of times. "Are you all right, dear?"

"How did you know about those . . ." She was still finding it difficult to breathe let alone speak.

"The motorcycle wheels? Oh, I've known about them since the night you and Graham put them in there. I was looking out the window when I saw a light in the garage. I put on my robe and went out to investigate, but when I heard you and Graham talking I knew it was nothing to worry about. I do think that was a pretty rotten thing to do to Clyde, but I suppose you had your reasons."

"Mother! How could you sneak around and spy on me!" Courtney gasped indignantly as she frantically searched her mind on what she and Graham had been discussing while they were in the garage that evening. She prayed they hadn't been talking about anything that had happened earlier!

"You were only talking about the motorcycle wheels, dear, and where to hide them," Bonita assured her. "After all, wouldn't you have been curious if you had seen a light in the garage at two in the morning?" she asked innocently.

"Does Clyde know we have his wheels?"

"No, I didn't tell him. I knew he wouldn't take it as well as I did."

Courtney slumped back in her chair in relief. "Thank goodness! I think you're probably right. Graham said he was pretty upset."

"Yes, he was," Bonita agreed smoothly. "And if I ever catch you doing anything that ridiculous again, I will personally tan your bottom, no matter how old you are, do you understand?" Bonita glared at her daughter sharply.

"It wasn't . . . exactly my idea . . ." she said weakly.

"Whosoever's idea it was, I don't want it repeated. Is that clear?"

"Yes, Mom."

"If Clyde and I want to 'break our necks' on that cycle, they're our necks to break. Right?"

"Right."

"Good. Now that that's all settled, I want to ask you a personal question." Bonita pulled up an extra chair and sat down beside her daughter. "What do you honestly think of Graham Merrill?"

Courtney looked at her mother suspiciously. "Not much. Why?"

"Honestly? You really don't think he's handsome, devil-may-care, interesting . . ."

". . . stuck on himself, a real gigolo, an arrogant romeo? Yes, I think he's all those things, why?"

Bonita sighed and crossed her hands tolerantly. "You're too picky. You'll never find a husband at this rate."

"Are you suggesting that I might be . . . romantically interested . . . why, that's preposterous! Where *do* you come up with all these wild ideas!" Courtney's face flamed when she remembered just how "romantically" involved she had become with Graham Merrill.

Bonita sighed again and looked at her daughter tolerantly. "Let's just say I'm a romantic at heart. I want to see you find someone and settle down. I want to see my grandchildren while I'm still able to see them."

"Just stop worrying about it, okay?" Courtney asked uneasily, knowing that what her mother wanted was neither unusual nor unreasonable. It was, at the moment, merely impossible. "You don't want me interfering in your life, so please show me the same courtesy. There is no man that I'm interested in and I really don't see any prospects in the near future, Mom. Now, you're going to have to accept that and stop trying to line someone up for me!"

"I would not try to do anything that wasn't in your best interests, dear. I hope you know that," Bonita said defensively.

"I know you wouldn't, Mom. All I'm asking is that you stay out of it. And for heaven's sakes, don't even imagine anything romantically developing between Graham Merrill and myself. The last thing in the world that man wants is a permanent relationship. If, and mind you I did say *if,* I ever find a man I thought I could love, he would be the exact opposite of Dr. Merrill. He is not my type!"

"Well." Bonita rose and walked back over to the stove. "I think you're entirely wrong about him."

"Be that as it may, it's my opinion and I'm entitled to it. Now promise you won't mention Graham Merrill's name in my presence again."

"All right. I promise," Bonita said obediently. "I won't mention his name."

"Good." Courtney reached for the evening paper and scanned the front page quietly. Conversations like the one she just had always put her out of sorts. Not that she needed anything to do that today. She had been in a bad mood all week, puzzled and very confused about her turbulent feelings concerning Graham. Courtney refused to admit, even to herself, that she could become very attracted to that arrogant dentist. She forced her mind to concentrate on the bold print of the headlines. More rumors of wars in foreign countries. She flipped on toward the women's section, determined she had enough bad news to live with without indulging in more. It irritated her that a man like Graham could warrant even a second thought. He hadn't bothered to call or try to see her in any way since the night he had dropped by last week. Of course, they hadn't exactly parted friends. . . .

"Oh, dear, I'm afraid my arthritis is trying to flare up on me again." Bonita wiggled her fingers and looked at them accusingly.

The paper lowered a fraction as Courtney peeked up over the sheet to look at her mother. "What?"

"I said, my arthritis is trying to flare up on me," Bonita repeated firmly. She lifted her hand in front of Courtney's face and wiggled her fingers again painfully. "See."

"I didn't even know you had arthritis," Courtney said. "Has it just cropped up?"

"No, I've had it off and on for a long time. I just haven't said anything about it."

"Well, call Dr. Raymond in the morning and see what

he suggests." The paper reclaimed Courtney's attention as Bonita drummed her fingers irritably on the kitchen table.

A few minutes later, the paper landed on the table sharply. "Mother! If your arthritis is bothering you, I would suggest you stop banging your fingers on the table like that!"

"Oh, I'm sorry, dear. I was just trying to figure out what I'm going to do about my friend in the morning," Bonita answered worriedly.

"What about your friend?"

"A lady who works in my friend's office has had a personal crisis and can't be at work tomorrow. I promised that since things were a little slow at the shop that I would come in and help tomorrow." Bonita looked at her hands and sighed wistfully. "But the job requires some typing, and now I'm afraid I'll have to disappoint my friend and not be able to go."

"That *is* too bad," Courtney agreed. "Maybe you can call your friend tonight and she can find someone else to take your place."

"No, she can't. She's already tried everyone she knew. I was a last resort," Bonita said resignedly.

"Boy, that makes you feel good, doesn't it?" Courtney laughed.

"Oh, I'm sure she didn't mean it that way, dear, but I really feel bad about having to disappoint her like this."

"If you call her tonight, I'm sure she'll be able to come up with something," Courtney dismissed lightly.

"What about you?" Bonita blurted suddenly.

Courtney looked surprised at her mother's swift outburst. "What about me?"

"I was just thinking, why don't *you* go work for my friend tomorrow and I'll take care of the shop? That sounds like a good idea, huh?" Bonita peered back at her daughter hopefully.

"Mother! Really, that's ridiculous. I don't want to work

for someone I don't even know," Courtney protested with a groan.

"Oh, it's easy work, dear. You'd probably enjoy the change of pace! All you have to do is answer the phone and do some light typing. Simple. You'll simply love it." The elderly woman's face beamed angelically.

"I bet!" Courtney eyed her mother suspiciously. "What kind of business is this?"

Bonita's face grew decidedly devious. "I think they fix things."

"That's it? They fix things?"

"Yes. That's all I really know about it. They just fix things," Bonita confirmed happily. "Will you do it?"

"Oh, Mom." Courtney groaned again. "I really don't want to."

"But you will? Oh, good!" Bonita jumped up from her chair and clapped her hands in glee. "Now I won't have to disappoint my friend!"

With a resigned sigh, Courtney reached for the paper once more, defeat written on her face. Tomorrow she would go work in her mother's "friend's" office. An office where they "fix things." Whoopeee! Some days it just didn't pay to get out of bed.

It was very early the next morning when Courtney pulled her small car up in front of the address her mother had given her and braked to a halt. She glanced down at the slip of paper, then back up at the bold letters on the front of the house. Her eyes narrowed suspiciously. There was something about this house that looked vaguely familiar to her. Slipping out of her seat belt, she left the car and walked up the brick walkway, still trying to determine if she had been there before. She was sure she hadn't been to any business that had its offices in a home. The only business she knew that fit that description would be

201

. . . Her footsteps halted. Gad! Surely her mother wouldn't be conniving . . .

The front door of the house flew open and the tall, imposing figure of Clyde Merrill stepped quickly through the doorway. Courtney's heart leaped to her throat as the full impact of how much Graham resembled his father assailed her. That was exactly what Graham would look like in another thirty years, she thought weakly, trying to still her thudding pulse. It was no wonder her mother found Clyde appealing. He was a striking, virile man, even in his waning years.

Clyde hurried down the walk, a smile of welcome on his face. "Hi. Glad you got here a little early. I have a patient coming in for a lower impression this morning." Clyde grinned nervously. "She . . . she's having her lower denture relined and in order to have it back to her by this afternoon, we have to start early in the morning." His voice trailed off as he saw the look of panic cross Courtney's rather sickly features. "Oh, you don't have to help me do that," he assured hurriedly. "All you have to do is answer the phone and make appointments."

"Mother said I was supposed to be helping a friend," Courtney said in a small voice, still refusing to believe she was standing here in front of Graham and his father's dental office.

"Well, I am her friend," he said matter-of-factly. "Since you and Graham have decided we can't be anything else, at least afford us that luxury," he said, smiling.

Clyde had taken her arm and was hurrying her up the walk before she had an opportunity to oppose. "I sure do appreciate you coming in to help today. Buddy and I have a full schedule—"

"Does he know I'm coming?" Courtney skidded to an obstinate halt and turned around to face Clyde stubbornly.

"Not exactly," Clyde admitted, shuffling his feet

around nervously. "But he won't mind. He doesn't care who's here as long as the phone gets answered."

"Oh, really." Courtney looked at him disdainfully. "Well, I'm sorry, Dr. Merrill—"

"Clyde. You're welcome to call me Clyde if I can call you Courtney."

Courtney met his serious gaze hesitantly. "Yes . . . I don't care if you call me Courtney . . . but as I was saying, I'm afraid there has been a mistake. I'm not going to be able to work for you today. Mother never said a word about working . . . here . . . and I don't think I want to do it."

Clyde had once more taken her arm and led her up the walkway. Before she knew it, they were stepping inside the front door, into the plush offices of Merrill and Merrill, D.D.S.

"As I was saying," Courtney continued frantically as Clyde took her purse, poured her a cup of coffee, and sat her down at the desk, "I don't think I'll be able to stay. I have to go. Right now." She looked helplessly at the typewriter and ringing telephone before her.

"Oh." Clyde's face fell in disappointment. "Could you just stay for maybe an hour or so? I'll call one of the temporary employment agencies and see if they can send someone over in the next hour or so, but until then I sure would appreciate your answering the phone for me." He looked at her pleadingly.

"Well, maybe for just an hour. . . ." She looked up as he grunted a grateful thanks and ran like a scared jackrabbit in the direction of his office.

Courtney stared at the ringing phone, hoping it would give up. When it didn't, she jerked up the receiver and answered it. For the next thirty minutes she tried to make appointments and intelligently give the caller a reason for her not being able to answer any questions that were asked, as the office filled with patients. She had accummulated five calls for Graham already but as yet hadn't seen any trace of him.

A few minutes before nine, she heard the door next to the office open, and Graham stepped in. The clean, sexy smell of his aftershave preceded him as he stepped into the office and stopped abruptly. His blue gaze fell on her, holding her eyes hostage for a brief moment before he finally spoke. "What are you doing here?"

Courtney's knees had grown weak at the sight of him. His hair still was just a little damp from his shower, and the pale blue of his doctor's jacket made him seemed more tanned and handsome than she had remembered.

"That's what I've been trying to figure out," she replied weakly.

"Where's Florence?"

Courtney shrugged. "If Florence is the one that I'm suppose to be replacing, then she had a personal crisis today."

Graham looked puzzled. "Florence doesn't have any family in this area."

"I'm afraid you'll have to ask your father," Courtney replied coolly, forcing her eyes off his broad chest. "I'll only be here until he finds a replacement for me."

Graham walked over and poured himself a cup of coffee, still clearly puzzled over the turn of events. "I still don't know why you would be here," he said.

"I'm afraid I have been duped, Dr. Merrill. Mother said I was to be filling in for a friend of hers. She neglected to say who the friend was. Stupid me forgot to ask." The phone shrilled loudly again as she angrily jerked it up and answered in her most pleasant voice. "Good morning, Drs. Merrill and Merrill's office."

Graham smiled and toasted her sweetly with his cup of coffee as she hastily scribbled down a name. "One moment please. I'll see if the doctor is available."

Courtney pressed a button then turned to Graham. "Are you available for personal calls?"

Graham grinned, then took another casual sip of his coffee. "How personal?"

Courtney noticed how enticingly his blue eyes crinkled at the corners when he smiled. Her hands turned clammy and she unconsciously wiped them on her skirt nervously. "She didn't say, but she's called three times already and made it abundantly clear that it was a personal call." Courtney smiled back at his amused expression. "Perhaps it's Schultzie calling to say she had too big of a night last night and won't be able to make it to work this morning."

"You could be right," he replied smoothly. "I'm sure when ol' Schultzie has a big night, it puts her under for a week." He stood up and picked up his coffee cup. "I'll take the 'personal' call in my office where I'll have more privacy." He winked at her suggestively. "In the meantime, why not ask Schultzie what she did last night? She's just now walking in the front door."

Courtney glanced up as the front door opened and Schultzie exploded into the room. Looking as if she was nearing at least sixty years old, she was around six foot two and looked for the world like an ex-marine sergeant. She hustled in the office and threw her purse in one of the drawers in the desk Courtney was standing at.

"Morning, boss," she called out brightly to Graham.

"Good morning, Schultzie." Graham walked toward his office whistling merrily, leaving Courtney there without any introductions whatsoever.

Schultzie zipped on a blue jacket, then turned to face a stunned and silent Courtney. Schultzie was not quite what she had expected. Graham's words rang home in her ear: "Besides Schultzie, a root canal pales into insignificance." Courtney could now see the truth of his statement!

"Who are you?" Schultzie barked out briskly.

Courtney jumped at her sharp words and swallowed hard. "I'm . . . replacing Florence."

"What's the matter with her?"

"Personal problems . . . I think."

"Well, you better park it, sweetie, and get to work. We have a long day ahead of us," she advised as she started off down the hall with a cup of coffee in her hand. "We have an impacted molar this morning, two abscesses, eight fillings, a deep scaling . . ." She was still listing the morning work schedule as she disappeared in a door on the left and slammed it soundly. Courtney sank back down at the desk and looked at the light on the phone. Graham's personal call was sure taking a long time! He was still on the line. An unreasonable feeling of jealousy shot though Courtney as she drummed her fingers irritably on the desk. She answered one of the other lines as it rang, still keeping her eyes on line one.

Clyde stepped out of his office, walking along beside his patient, who was talking very little. "Your denture should be ready by around four this afternoon, Mrs. Poe. Come back then and we'll have you ready to go."

Mrs. Poe covered her mouth with her hand and mumbled embarrassedly, "I hope I don't have a wreck on the way home!"

Clyde laughed and patted her on the back. "See you at four."

When Mrs. Poe had left the inner office, Clyde turned back around to Courtney. "You can send Mrs. Hart into room two now."

"Yes, sir—Dr. Merrill?"

Clyde turned and looked at her. "Yes?"

"Uh, have you called the employment agency yet?" she asked hopefully.

Clyde snapped his fingers. "Boy! I've been so busy I forgot all about it. I'll do that the first chance I get. You doing okay?"

"Not very well, but I suppose I'm not destroying too much of your business. Be sure and call the first chance you get though," she reminded politely.

"Oh, I will," he said obediently as he disappeared back in his office.

Courtney ushered Mrs. Hart into room two. "The doctor will be with you in a minute," she assured the woman in a professional manner. She smiled as she closed the door and took a deep breath. She was actually beginning to sound like she knew what she was doing!

When she returned to her desk she saw the light on number one was still lit. Her temper fairly sizzled as she thought of Graham wasting the whole day on a personal conversation when he had an office full of patients waiting for him! Glancing around her sheepishly, she spitefully pushed the button down and picked up the phone, then dropped it in its cradle, severing the conversation on line one. Smiling, she withdrew a nailfile from her purse and calmly went to work on one of her nails. The door to Graham's office opened and he strolled out nonchalantly. He walked up to the desk and sat down on the end dispassionately. "Sorry to disturb your work, Miss Spenser." He watched her file her nails for a few seconds. "I can see you're hard at it, but I was wondering: Did you happen to cut my conversation off a few minutes ago on line one?"

Courtney continued filing, ignoring his disturbing presence perched on her desk. "I might have. I'm new, you know."

"I know. I'm sure it was an accident, but in the future watch what you're doing, okay?"

Courtney shrugged. "Okay." She agreed. "I know it's not my place to point this out, Dr. Merrill, but you *do* have several patients waiting to see you. I don't think they appreciate having to sit out there and waste their valuable time while you make time over the telephone," she pointed out.

207

Graham crossed his arms and stared down at the top of her head aloofly. "I was 'making time,' as you so elegantly put it, with a pharmaceutical salesman, Miss Spenser. That is part of my job, you know."

"She had a marvelously sexy voice," Courtney complimented disinterestedly as she continued to work on her nail. "I bet she sells a lot of . . . stuff."

"I was talking to a *he,* and his voice didn't do a thing for me," Graham said calmly.

"I answered the phone, remember? That was no male voice."

Graham's arms dropped down to his side, a look of amusement spreading over his features now. "My, my. Are we jealous, Miss Spenser? You shouldn't be. I only talked to Melodie for a few minutes—"

"Don't get funny!" Courtney threw her nail file on the desk and stood up. "Go call the employment agency and have someone come over here and replace me," she demanded curtly.

Graham looked stubborn. "Why should I do that? That's not my job, man!" he scoffed in an exaggerated drawl.

"Your father's too busy to call. You go call!"

"I can't. I'm too busy myself," he said. "Good grief, woman, can't you see I have a whole office full of people sitting out there wasting their valuable time waiting on me?" He tossed her an arrogant salute and walked back in his office whistling unconcernedly.

Courtney gritted her teeth to keep from screaming. He was the most clod-headed man she had ever met! She sat back down at the desk, her temper simmering. It was apparent she was going to be stuck here all day. Well, Drs. Merrill and Merrill! If they wanted to play dirty pool, so could she. She smiled wickedly as she picked up her pencil and waited for the next phone call. If father and son thought they were busy now, wait until tomorrow! For the next few hours, she religiously booked everyone who called for the following day five minutes apart. By afternoon she had decided that there were not enough calls coming in to complete her plan so she methodically went through the appointment book and politely called all the people booked for the next two weeks and asked if it would be possible for them to come in tomorrow since the doctors would be on vacation at the time of their original appointment. By the end of the day the two doctors were booked to see a total of forty patients apiece on Thursday.

By five o'clock that evening, she gleefully closed the appointment book secure in the knowledge that by Thursday night, Clyde and Graham Merrill would know the true meaning of being too busy!

CHAPTER TWELVE

"Gee, Dr. Merrill, you look like you've been busy today." Courtney stood in the doorway of Graham's office on Thursday evening, smiling. Graham was sprawled out in his chair, his blue coat a rumpled mess. Rearing back in his chair, he stared blankly up at the ceiling.

"You are a real comedian, Miss Spenser. Do you realize that I just saw my last patient ten minutes ago and it's now"—he sat up and peered bleary eyed at his watch—"nine o'clock?"

"No kidding?" Courtney walked on in the office and sat down. "Did I schedule too many patients yesterday?" she asked innocently.

"I could break your neck! Do you realize that not one patient got mad over the wait! In fact, the majority of them were thrilled to death to get an earlier appointment." He smiled sickly. "Several have promised to recommend me to their friends and family because of the marvelous way I can run so many patients through my office a day."

"I guess my neck deserves to be broken because I have been feeling a little guilty over what I did to your innocent patients, but now you know exactly how I felt yesterday when everyone was so busy they didn't have time to call and get me a replacement," she said, clucking her tongue sympathetically.

"You better not let Dad see you," Graham warned, laying his head on the desk in exhaustion.

"Is he still here?" Courtney asked uneasily. She had come by just to gloat, not for any confrontation.

"I don't know," Graham said in a muffled voice. "I think he passed out around seven and Schultzie took him in to lie down."

Courtney's face grew concerned. "Not really?"

Graham sat up and rubbed the back of his neck tiredly. "No, not really. He held up better than I did."

A small smile escaped Courtney as she rose and went over to stand behind Graham's chair. She reached out and began to firmly massage the tight corded muscles in his neck. He went weak with pleasure as he groaned and relaxed under her gentle ministration.

"You keep that up and it just may save your life," he murmured in pleasure.

"Is your father very mad at me?" she asked, working her fingers deeply along his shoulder muscles.

"I couldn't say. We didn't have time to talk about it." He moaned and slid deeper into his chair. "What are you doing here anyway? Come to gloat over your victory?"

"Uh-huh. Pretty rotten trick, wouldn't you say?"

"Uh-huh. I'd say." Suddenly Courtney found herself pulled into his lap unexpectedly. "I think I'll have to demand retribution."

"Oh?" Her hand reached up to run through the thick mass of his hair affectionately. "And suppose I won't give it?"

He shrugged as a tiny grin came over his tired features. "Then I suppose I'll have to take it forcefully."

"Then I suppose there's no reason to fight it," she relented softly. Their eyes met for a moment in silent communication.

"It wouldn't do you any good," he whispered huskily. "I've wanted to kiss you ever since I saw you sitting there in the office yesterday morning." His mouth brushed teas-

211

ingly across hers, causing her insides to flutter wildly. "Weren't you just a little bit glad to see me?"

"Um . . . a little," she admitted coyly.

His mouth captured hers in a hungry kiss now, sending them both reeling from the impact. They kissed long and deep as he drew her up closer to his broad chest. She could feel the imprint of his maleness stirring as she sat on his lap. That, coupled with the familiar clean male smell of him, sent her blood racing hotly through her veins. Reluctant to end the kiss, they broke off exchanging short, teasing kisses with each other.

"By the way, how did you like Schultzie?" he asked with a wry grin.

"She was stunning." Courtney grinned back. "She was everything and more than I had expected!"

"No kidding, why are you here?" he asked between brief intervals of smoldering affection. "I didn't think I would see you again this soon."

"I do feel bad about what I did. After Mom and I went round and round over how she tricked me, I wanted to see if your father made it through the day all right."

"Are you sorry for being such a witch?" he teased sternly.

"No, not where it concerns you," she said positively. "My only concern is for your father."

"Like I said, he made it a lot better than I did." Graham winced painfully. "Really, Miss Spenser. Forty patients in one day?"

"A real bummer, huh?" She pulled his mouth down for another long, pleasant kiss. It was at least another five minutes before they resumed their conversation in a normal tone of voice.

"I gather you weren't here on your own accord yesterday." Graham chuckled, nuzzling her mass of fragrant blond hair. "And what are you doing with your hair back up in that unattractive wad at the back of your head?"

"I like my hair this way," she said irritably, "and I'm not trying to please you anyway."

"Why not?" He kissed her on the tip of her nose. "I'm an easy guy to please."

"She tricked me." Courtney ignored his teasing and went back to their original discussion.

"Who?"

"Mom. She tricked me into coming to your office yesterday," Courtney explained. "I had no idea it was your office I was supposed to work in or you wouldn't have caught me within a hundred miles of here."

"Is that right?" Graham grinned affectionately. "What do you want to bet that both gypsies were in on this?"

"My last dollar. Only I can't figure out why. Why would they cook up something like this? They apparently weren't planning on sneaking away again. Your dad was booked solid with patients all day."

"Who knows? Maybe they're trying to matchmake." Graham chuckled again. "Now wouldn't that be a crock! We're trying to break them up and they're trying to get something started between us!"

"Ridiculous," Courtney agreed, joining in his laughter.

Graham's face sobered instantly. "What's so ridiculous about it?" He was beginning to tire of her irritating immunity to what he considered his immeasurable charms.

She leaned in closer and kissed him playfully on his nose now. "You're simply not my type, Dr. Merrill."

"Nor are you mine," he reminded, returning the kiss. "You're only a pleasant distraction from a hectic day."

"My sentiments exactly. I'm well aware I have no affect on you whatsoever." She buried her face in his neck and smiled provocatively. Even she knew better than that!

Graham stirred uncomfortably against her. "Miss Spenser, I'll confess I'm not immune to your considerable . . . charms." He moved suggestively against her, giving her proof that she did indeed affect him powerfully. "But before this gets out of hand again, I think you better let me take you to dinner."

"I've already eaten," she whispered teasingly, reveling in the affect she seemed to be having on him.

"Then you can watch me eat," he murmured grimly, his hand casually loosening the button on her blouse and reaching inside to gently caress one soft mound.

Their mouths met again hotly for a few minutes as Courtney fought to bring her whirling emotions under control. "You're right. I think we better stop this," she reminded when they finally broke apart a few moments later. This was quickly getting out of hand.

"We will. In just a few minutes." His hand sent waves of desire coursing through her now.

"I think we better stop *now,*" she murmured weakly against his mouth once more.

"Oh, you're turning chicken now, huh?" he taunted, kissing down the length of her lightly perfumed neck. "Are you wearing Chloe again?"

"Yes, I'm surprised you remembered the name."

His hold tightened on her almost painfully. "Anything that smells that good, I remember. I hope you have a big bottle of it."

"No, I really don't." She laughed softly.

"You will have by tomorrow," he said, kissing her again aggressively. "I'm going to buy you the biggest bottle they make."

The kissing got out of hand again rapidly. It took all of Graham's willpower to finally bring a halt to it. He had made himself a promise that past week that he had every intention of keeping. He was not going to go to bed with Courtney Spenser again. Granted, it had been unexpected the first time, but he knew enough now to guard against another such incident. He was becoming increasingly unnerved by the fact that here was a woman whom he was afraid he actually *could* fall in love with. Before, he never had to worry. He had never met a woman who had made him look twice other than for the obvious reasons. Courtney was different and he was a smart enough man to realize it. He was going to have to keep her at a distance, which shouldn't be all that hard to do, he reasoned. She was really no more eager to be with him than he was to be with her. This physical attraction they had for each other was only temporary and would pass. As soon as they managed to break up the relationship between Bonnie and Clyde, they would have no reason to keep seeing each other. He paused in his wanderings, a shaft of fear shooting through him. The thought suddenly occurred to him that he no longer was as concerned about his father and Courtney's mother as he once was. After meeting Bonita Spenser, it was rather hard to dislike her personally. She was a lovely lady in every respect. Maybe it wouldn't be such a bad idea if Clyde settled down. . . . Graham sat up abruptly, nearly knocking Courtney to the floor with his swift actions. That way of thinking was dangerous! His goal was what it had always been: to break up the elder couple's courtship and get his life back on a normal path. Just because Bonnie Spenser had a daughter who was beginning to turn his insides to jelly every time he encountered her had to be overlooked as a purely physical reaction between a male and female.

Courtney grasped the desk for support and steadied herself quickly. "Goodness! When you decide to stop, you decide to stop, don't you?" she noted crossly.

"I'm hungry," he excused lamely. "Come on, you can keep me company while I grab a sandwich."

Courtney helped turn out the lights in the office and close up. They walked through the doors to Graham's living quarters.

"If you don't care, I think I'll take a quick shower before I eat," Graham told her as he unbuttoned his blue

215

coat and pulled it off over his head. At the sight of his broad chest, Courtney's knees went weak.

"I don't mind, I'll just read a magazine while I wait."

"I won't be but a few minutes," he promised, heading toward the bathroom.

It was exceedingly hard for her to keep her mind on the article she was trying to read. Her eyes kept wandering over to the sofa where she and Graham had made love that rainy night. Biting her lip painfully, she forced her mind back to the magazine. She could almost taste his demanding kisses and feel the touch of his hands against her feverish skin. . . . She was staring sightlessly at the same page when Graham returned to the room fifteen minutes later.

"Hope you didn't mind the wait." Graham sat down on the sofa to tie his shoelaces.

"No, I've hardly noticed you were gone," she assured hurriedly, refusing to meet his gaze. Why did he have to sit there of all places!

"Well." He finished his task and stood up. "I'm ready if you are."

Courtney laid the magazine down on the table and rose. "All ready!"

Their gazes met and locked as they stood in the quiet room, each one trying to ignore the other's disturbing presence.

"I'm really hungry. I didn't have time for lunch today." Graham's gaze held hers captive.

If only he wasn't so handsome and didn't smell so darn good, Courtney thought resentfully, she wouldn't be having these crazy feelings about him. "I'm sure you must be . . . if you didn't eat lunch." She swallowed nervously. Why couldn't they just walk out of the room and go? Why were her feet glued to the floor like this?

Graham took a hesitant step toward her. She was beginning to be a real thorn in his side! Why in the devil

216

couldn't he get his mind on anything but how soft and warm she felt when he held her in his arms, or the smell of her perfume . . . ?

"If you're ready, I am," Courtney reminded him again weakly. The look of longing in his eyes both frightened and thrilled her beyond all reason. She knew that if they didn't leave now, they wouldn't be going.

"Oh, yeah . . . I'm ready." Graham's steps retreated hastily.

"Will you hand me my purse?"

"Sure, where is it?"

Both sets of eyes now focused on the place where she had lain her purse earlier. Courtney froze as Graham looked at the sofa then quickly glanced away. It was plainly written on his face that he was fighting with the same memories that had been washing over her all evening. Courtney watched uneasily as Graham fought to control his emotions, and lost. He turned slowly, his eyes pleading with hers for help.

"Courtney . . ." He held out his hand in a mute plea for her to come to him.

She shook her head helplessly. "I thought you were hungry . . ." she murmured inanely, and moved forward to accept his hand.

He pulled her masterfully into his arms and lifted her off the floor, kissing her ravenously. She returned his kiss with full measure, drowning in the touch and feel of him. It didn't make sense, but she knew she wanted him more than anything she had ever wanted in her life. Reaching out, Graham impatiently pulled the pins from her hair, letting the silken mass fall round her shoulders as he groaned and deepened the kiss. The world suddenly disappeared and there was no one but the two of them.

"Tell me the truth, sweetheart," he pleaded in a ragged voice. "Were you experienced or not? I have to know."

Courtney buried her face in the warmness of his neck.

217

"Does it really matter to you, Graham?" That question seemed to occupy all his thoughts when they were together, and Courtney couldn't figure out if it was just his sense of responsibility or if it really made a difference to him. The last thing in the world she wanted from him was chauvinism!

"No . . . not in the way you mean. It doesn't matter to me if you had been or not. I just don't want to feel that I've been the one . . ."

"If that were true, then we *both* would be responsible. If you remember, I had no objections," she reminded him softly, as he set her on her feet again.

"It's not the same." He groaned. "Tell me the truth, Courtney!"

"Figure it out for yourself, Graham. After all, I am thirty years old," she taunted.

"I know, I've taken that all in consideration. So you must have had some experience!" He let out a long sigh of relief and pulled her close for another demanding kiss. They kissed eagerly for a few minutes before they parted breathlessly once more.

"Then on the other hand, I am an 'old maid,' " she felt obligated to point out.

"Oh, hell!" Graham spit out disgustedly. "Then you were inexperienced?" His blue eyes looked distressed.

"I didn't say that either."

"Is this some game with you, Miss Spenser?"

"No, but it seems to be with you!" She had no idea why she was tormenting him so on this absurd subject, but in her opinion, he was asking for it!

"Why won't you just come out and give me a simple yes or no? That's all I'm asking!" He threw up his hands in exasperation. "The answer doesn't mean a thing, but I want a straight answer out of you before we go to bed again!"

"Oh." Courtney smiled up at him coolly. "Is that the point of this ridiculous conversation?"

"No!" Graham pointed out quickly. "We're . . . not going to do that again. That was just a slip of the tongue."

"I don't appeal to you?"

Graham's shoulders sagged defeatedly. "Now you know that isn't true. Of course you appeal to me."

"Then why? Even if I was inexperienced then, I'm certainly not *now,*" she persisted.

"Are you wanting me to make love to you again?" he asked incredulously.

"No! No . . . of course not." Courtney flushed beet red. "I was just curious why you would be so dead set against it, that's all."

"You just don't seem like the kind of girl you can kiss and run with . . . and I'm strictly the kiss-and-run type," he confessed hurriedly.

"I know that," she said softly. "I knew what happened between us wasn't anything you took seriously, and you don't have to be concerned anything lasting will come out of it. I . . . that danger has safely passed."

"It has?" He looked immensely relieved. "Thank goodness. Because I have been worried." His face softened. "I didn't mean for it to happen . . ."

"I know that too."

"And it won't happen again, I promise you."

"I know it won't. We're both smart enough to keep that from happening," she agreed.

His arms reached out and pulled her back to him. "I'm glad we can talk about this like two responsible people, Miss Spenser. A lot of women wouldn't look at it the way you do."

"Thank you. You seem very adult about this also," she complimented as his mouth came back down to tease lightly with hers.

"We'll allow ourselves a few innocent kisses, then we'll

219

go get me something to eat," he reasoned against the sweetness of her mouth. "No harm in that, is there? After all, we are two reasonable adults."

"None that I can think of," she consented readily.

They moved toward the sofa, locked tightly in each other's embrace, their kisses growing longer and more demanding by the second.

"Doesn't it seem rather warm in here to you?" he murmured, his fingers systematically unbuttoning each small button on her blouse.

"A little," she agreed, her breathing turning ragged.

"I thought we might be cooler if I took off my shirt and you took off your blouse," he suggested, tugging the material off her shoulder. He kissed the newly bared flesh longingly.

"Yes, I think that would be cooler," she acquiesced gracefully. Her hands eagerly helped him remove his shirt. She could feel a rippling shudder go through him as her softness met the wiry texture of his chest.

It was mutually decided five minutes later that the room was still too warm and they dispersed with all clothing, their kisses raging heatedly, and neither one caring in the least.

Graham moaned and rolled over with her, drawing her up on his chest and pressing her tightly against his overpowering need of her. "I'm afraid it's going to happen again, Miss Spenser, and there's no way I can stop it," he warned hoarsely, covering her mouth with each heated word.

"You want me to try?" she whispered shakily.

"Are you more in control of yourself than I am?" he asked hopefully.

"No."

He moaned quietly and captured her mouth again passionately. "You understand now, you're not my type of woman. You're too soft, too vulnerable . . . I don't know

220

how in the hell this keeps happening . . ." He groaned miserably, melting in the wake of her soft exploring touches. His words were stopped by her mouth claiming his eagerly once more.

"And you're not mine either," she reiterated clearly, as his mouth continued to brand hers fervently. Her body seemed to melt into a running puddle as he joined his body with hers, sending them both skyrocketing into oblivion.

If Courtney had thought he was a tender, passionate lover before, he took her to worlds she had never been this time. It was like a beautiful dream the way he held her, caressed her, and whispered intimately into her ear. Just when she thought she would explode from sheer joy, he would slow his pace, then begin again to leisurely show her the unbelievable delights of being in his arms. When they both could no longer hold back the tide of passion that flooded their very souls, he took them over the mountain of ecstasy together.

It was a few minutes before either one could speak, neither one wanting to break the strong thread of desire that still flowed through them. It was as if they couldn't get close enough to each other or quench the fires that were barely banked now. The exacting kisses of moments earlier had turned soft and leisurely as they lay in each other's arms exchanging whispers of gratification.

"I have a confession to make, Miss Spenser." Graham sighed in contentment.

"And what might that be?" she asked in a drowsy voice.

"I don't know why it keeps happening, but this time I don't regret it one iota."

Courtney rolled over and wrapped her arms around his neck, meeting the blue of his eyes solemnly. "And you really did the last time?"

Graham gazed at her tenderly for a moment before he spoke. "I tried to tell myself I did." He reached out and brushed a lock of hair away from her face, which was flushed warm and pink from their passion. "You're different somehow, Courtney, and to be honest, I think you scare the hell out of me," he admitted in a quiet, husky voice.

"I don't mean to."

"But you do. That's the problem."

"As long as we're confessing, I'll admit that in many ways you scare me too, Graham. I have never been affected by a man in the way that . . . well, I guess it's no secret that I'm attracted to you. But," she hastened to add as she noted the look of distress come over his handsome features, "I know that it's only a temporary attraction, one that will pass as soon as we aren't thrown in each other's company so often. I want you to know that I don't expect or want anything out of you. This crazy physical thing we have for each other . . . Well, I don't know how to explain it other than to say you don't have to worry about it. I know that it's just something that's happen . . ." Her voice trailed off weakly.

Graham rolled over on his back and covered his eyes tiredly with his arm. "Sure! Don't worry about it. Do you realize we are right back where we started?"

"What are you talking about?" Courtney sat up and reached for her blouse irritably. Why did he always have to spoil things by getting practical? She knew exactly what his next words would be.

"I didn't take any precautions again. Did you?" he asked bluntly.

"I don't go around looking for this sort of occurrence, Dr. Merrill. No, of course I didn't."

"Do you know the chances you're taking by being so darn careless?" he asked incredulously.

"I'm sorry, I'll start carrying a pharmacy with me every time I think our paths might cross," she told him heatedly. "Now get off me, I want to use your bathroom if you don't mind!" Suddenly he was placing all the blame squarely on

222

her head. She shoved him irritably off of her and snatched up her skirt.

"You don't have to get sore about it. I'm telling you this for your own good," he pointed out in a gruff tone as she headed toward the bathroom in a mad huff.

"Spare me the 'facts of life' sermon!" She slammed the bathroom door loudly.

Ten minutes later she reappeared and waited patiently for him to re-dress to go out for the long-delayed sandwich. If he hadn't made her promise to stay, she would have left while he was in the bathroom. Using the excuse that he had something important to say to her, he had enticed her to stay around long enough to listen.

She had to sit through two ham and cheese sandwiches, an order of French fries, and a piece of chocolate pie before she finally found out what he had to say.

He had driven them back to his house, then walked her to her car, his arm draped lazily around her neck.

"I believe you had something important you wanted to say to me," she reminded curtly, hating herself for responding to even his slightest touch.

"I believe I did." He pulled her around to face him, trapping her between the car and his large frame. The moonlight shone brightly on their faces as he surveyed her loveliness with a long sigh. "You make this awful hard to say, Miss Spenser."

"Just say whatever you think you need to say. I want to go home." Her gaze dropped stubbornly from his.

"Okay. It's this. I think from now on, we should avoid each other as much as possible."

Courtney's eyes flew up to meet his painfully.

"Now don't look at me like that," he warned in a husky whisper. "This thing between us is getting out of control and we're going to have to put a stop to it. If you remember, our main goal is to break up the relationship between Bonnie and Clyde. We are not going to be able to do that

223

if we keep letting our personal feelings get in the way . . ."

"Plus the fact, you're scared to death of me," Courtney interrupted angrily. "Well, you needn't be. I have no desire for any permanent relationship with you."

"Yes, darn it! I'm scared to death of you." He reached down and kissed her roughly. "Now let's just wrap this up in a friendly way and go our separate paths. Any effort to keep Dad and Bonnie away from each other, we'll do alone. No more joint efforts. Agreed?"

"Agreed!"

"Fine!" His voice softened. "Naturally, you will let me know if anything should develop. . . ."

"Naturally. I will not," she said curtly.

His face clouded worriedly as his arms dropped down to his side. "You're a stubborn witch!"

She opened the car door and got in the driver's side. "Good night and *good-bye*, Dr. Merrill. Hope you have a pleasant life."

"Good night, and *good-bye* to you, Miss Spenser. I certainly intend to!"

He stood under the warm nighttime sky, long after the red of her car's taillights disappeared into the darkness, thinking about her. What he had suggested was the only way this sticky situation could be handled. He was about to fall deeply in love with Courtney Spenser, and he planned to fight that tooth and nail.

He closed his eyes and smelled deeply of the faint traces of her perfume that still lingered in the air and on his clothes. He would fight it, but he had the sinking sensation in the pit of his stomach that he had lost the battle long before it even began.

CHAPTER THIRTEEN

If there was one thing that burned Courtney to a crisp, it was when someone threatened something that went against her wishes, then kept his word! In the unsettling case of Courtney Spenser and Dr. Graham Merrill, that is precisely what was taking place.

She had known from the moment she had angrily stormed into her car and driven home that night a little over three weeks ago that she didn't really agree with Graham's point of view concerning their precarious relationship, but she had been too darn stubborn to admit it. Somewhere along the line, Graham had suddenly become much more important to her than she had realized. There was no way she could point out the moment and say, "This was the particular minute when I fell in love with him," but she knew without a doubt now that that minute had occurred. For all she knew, that moment could have come as early as the first day he had stormed into her gift shop and demanded that she keep her mother away from his father. Then again, it could have come the first time they made love so sweetly and so unexpectedly on that wet, rainy night they had stolen Clyde's motorcycle wheels, or it was entirely possible she had fallen in love with Graham Merrill the first time his unusual blue eyes had met hers in a serious moment and he told her he didn't think it was wise for them to continue to see each other even on the indifferent basis they had been. All she knew for certain was that she *had* fallen in love with him. The thought didn't hold any happiness or any thrilling elation for her. On the contrary. It infuriated her!

Graham had been very true to his word. She hadn't heard from him in over three long weeks. He had sent one of those enchanting balloon-a-grams to her shop last week with the simple message: "Is everything still all right?" It hadn't taken a genius to know what he was referring to. He apparently was running scared over his impetuous actions the last time they had been together and was frightened that it could have lasting repercussions.

She sincerely hoped that he had gotten the message when she had angrily burst every balloon and sent them back to his office still hanging limply on the strings. She might secretly want a lot of things from Graham Merrill, but *that* kind of attention she didn't welcome at all.

Life had been so much simpler before he came on the scene, she mumbled crossly to herself as she plugged in the vacuum and started her part of Saturday morning house-cleaning. She had even taken what she considered drastic steps by accepting two dates with Rob Hanson and one with a salesman who came into the shop regularly. On all occasions, she had come away feeling that both her time and the man's had been wasted. There was only one man in the world who seemed to turn her in to a quivering heap, and that one was not interested in a permanent relationship at the moment, and certainly not with her!

"Did you say something, dear?" Bonita walked into the room, a colorful beach bag slung over shoulder.

"No, I was just talking to myself." Courtney straightened up and looked at her mother suspiciously. "Where are your going?"

"To the water slide. I have my part of the housework done," she defended quickly as she saw the swift look of disapproval surface on her daughter's face.

"The water slide! You are hopeless." Courtney sank

226

down on the sofa and readjusted the bandanna she had tied around her hair earlier. There was no need to ask who Bonita was going with. She knew without a doubt that Clyde Merrill would be involved. It was strange, but Courtney had done nothing to prevent the gypsies from seeing each other lately. It seemed she had lost all heart for breaking up the elderly couple.

"You're still in a bad mood, aren't you, dear?" Bonita walked over and gave Courtney an affectionate hug. "Is there something you would like to talk to me about?" She looked at her daughter expectantly. Courtney had not been herself recently. She had been moody and irritable for the last three weeks.

"Of course not, Mom. What makes you think there's anything wrong?" Courtney scoffed uneasily.

"I know there is," Bonita persisted quietly. "Don't you want to tell me about it?"

Courtney sighed defeatedly and laid her head on her mother's shoulder for a brief moment. "No, not right now, Mom. Maybe someday."

"I'm always here," Bonita said in a comforting voice. "You know that, don't you?"

"You always have been and I want you to know I love you, Mom. I hope you know that."

"Well, of course I know that," the older woman said with a gentle laugh. She lifted Courtney's troubled face up to meet hers. "Every cloud has a silver lining. Always keep that in mind."

"It's always darkest before the dawn. At the end of every rainbow there's a huge pot of gold, et cetera, et cetera. I know, I know, Mom." Courtney laughed, wiping quickly at the tears that threatened to overflow.

The phone rang, interrupting Bonita's next words. She walked over and picked up the receiver, giving Courtney time to regain her shattered composure.

The call was obviously for her mother so Courtney

decided to fix herself a glass of tea before she ran the sweeper. When she walked back in the living room, holding her glass, she noted that Bonita had discarded the beach bag and was now wearing jeans and a bright-red baseball cap.

"Let me guess. Your plans have been changed and you're not going to the water slide after all. You're going to play ball instead." Courtney sat down on the sofa and propped her feet on the coffee table, grinning in disbelief at her mother. This woman had more energy than a nuclear power plant!

"Now how did you know that!" Bonita asked in surprise.

"I'm a mystic, didn't you even guess?" Courtney whispered mysteriously.

"Oh, you! Stop your teasing!" Bonita readjusted her cap pertly.

"Need any help practicing your spittin' and scratchin'?" Courtney continued to tease as she took a drink of her tea. "All good ballplayers have to learn that before anything else."

"I'll leave that to the men," Bonita said brightly, unaffected by her daughter's playful banter. "I get to play first base today!"

"Wow! Some people have all the luck."

Bonita turned around and looked at her daughter sternly. "I'd rather play first than have to go out in right field. It's always so hot out there and there's not a whole lot of action."

Courtney shook her head sympathetically. "That's the breaks. I guess you take what you can get and be grateful."

"Why don't you come with me today?" Bonita's face lit up expectantly. "I'm sure we could use an extra player and the outing would do you good!"

"No, thanks! I have to run the sweeper." Courtney stood up swiftly and reached for the vacuum. The last thing she wanted to do was go wallow around on some dusty ball diamond.

"No, now really. I mean it, dear." Bonita swooped over and took the sweeper out of her hands firmly. "I'll run the sweeper while you go get ready. You've moped around this house for the last three weeks. You need to get out and have some fun for a change. Now run along and change your clothes like a good little girl." She switched the vacuum on and began to run it across the plush green carpeting quickly.

"Mother!" Courtney had to practically yell over the whine of the sweeper as she trailed her mother around the room helplessly. "I don't want to play ball . . . for heaven's sake. Who's going to be there?"

"Just the usual gang! Go get dressed and stop arguing! The fresh air and exercise will do you a world of good!"

Courtney jammed her hands on her hips irritably. There were a million things she would rather do than spend one of her only free days playing baseball!

"How long do I have to play?"

"We usually cream the opposing team real quick. It won't take long," Bonita assured, making Courtney do a hopping dance as she ran the sweeper under her feet zealously.

Fifteen minutes later mother and daughter were walking out the front door. One was still grumbling about her fate, while the other was smiling broadly.

"For heaven's sake, put your cap on right," Courtney said curtly as they got in her car and she backed out of the drive. Bonita was wearing her hat backward now, whistling merrily under her breath.

"I like it better this way. It's more comfortable," Bonita protested as Courtney put the car in gear and left a streak mark of rubber fifty yards long in front of their house.

When the small car pulled up to the empty lot that was used regularly as a baseball diamond, Courtney noted that most of the two ball teams seemed to be present. Clyde Merrill gave a friendly wave and loped over to open the car door for Bonita.

"Hi there! We've been waiting for you," he called in a friendly fashion. He took the ball glove and bat that Bonita handed him and helped her out of the car.

Courtney held her breath as she got out. She hadn't seen Clyde since she had worked at his office that one day, and she hoped he wasn't still angry with her over the inconvenience she had caused him and Graham and their patients!

If he was, he showed no signs of it. He smiled at Courtney and bid her hello pleasantly. Taking Bonita's arm, he walked with her up to the ballfield slowly. When they reached a large oak tree, he swiftly pulled her behind the spreading branches and stole a hurried kiss.

"Clyde," she protested when she could catch her breath. "Courtney will see us!

"Let her. I want to kiss my woman." He pulled her back for another lingering kiss, secure in the knowledge that they were well hidden behind the green foliage. It was a few minutes before they both remembered where they were and called a reluctant halt to their show of affection.

"I have something for you," Clyde said as he withdrew a small jeweler's box from his pocket.

"Oh?" Bonita's eyes shone brightly as she surveyed the black velvet box he had shyly put in her hand. "What is it?"

"If I tell you, it wouldn't be a surprise," he reasoned with a soft chuckle. "Open it and see."

Her fingers trembled slightly as she opened the box and her eyes gazed at the lovely cameo pendant lying in the box. "Oh, Clyde." She sighed softly. "It's beautiful."

"Do you like it?" he asked expectantly. "I don't know what you call it, but I thought it was awfully pretty . . . just like you," he added tenderly. "I knew it would look even lovelier on you."

"It's a pendant, Clyde, and yes, I do love it." She reached down and lifted the golden chain out of its box carefully. "Will you put it on me?"

"Here? On the ballfield?" He sounded very embarrassed.

"Sure, why not?" she said happily. Her heart was nearly bursting with pride at the thought of the lovely gift he had given her.

Clyde's hands seemed large and clumsy as they undid the delicate catch and slipped the chain around Bonita's neck. "I seem to be all thumbs," he confessed in a gruff voice. He fastened the clasp and let out a sigh of relief. "There, I got it on."

Bonita turned back around and placed her arms around his neck fondly. "Thank you. I'll treasure this gift for as long as I live," she whispered sincerely.

Clyde chuckled again and drew her closer. "Well, you won't get to cherish it as long as I *wish* you could, but I'll settle for what time we have left as long as we can spend it together." His blue eyes met hers solemnly. "And no one is going to stop me from sharing that time with you."

"Of course not, dear, no one will," Bonita assured him lovingly, as she lay her head on his broad shoulder and smiled in contentment. And she would personally make sure that no one did, even if she had to turn a certain thirty-year-old over her knee and show her who was still boss in the Spenser household.

Courtney had wandered up to the ball diamond disinterestedly. She kept trying to see around the tree Clyde and her mother had disappeared behind but was meeting with little success. The hot sun was beating down on the empty lot, making it less appealing by the minute. She had noticed that senior citizens comprised about eighty percent of the two teams. Some were playing catch with each

231

other while another group seemed to be having a practice game.

Courtney sank down on one of the dusty bleachers and watched morosely as a man who looked to be around seventy took a nose dive as he slid into homeplate.

She shot to her feet, ready to go over and apply first aid until they could call an ambulance and get him to the hospital. The man jumped up, kicking his heels in the air gleefully as he shouted out that he was safe. He had a strip of dirt running down the center of his face, but his eyes were twinkling brightly.

Her knees went weak with relief when she realized the elderly man was perfectly fine and having the time of his life. Several of his teammates ran out and were patting him on the back as she sank back down wearily on the bleachers.

She looked up as she saw another car pull into the empty lot and a tall good-looking man emerge with a stunning redhead following in his wake.

Her heart nearly stopped as she watched Graham walk toward the ballfield. He looked devilishly handsome in a pair of blue jeans and a red T-shirt. He had a red cap, one like those Bonita and Courtney were wearing, stuck rakishly on the back of his blond head. Courtney swallowed hard. She had forgotten just how sexy and appealing he was, but her heart painfully reminded her she hadn't forgotten at all. Even though the temperature was hovering close to ninety, she froze as he glanced up and his blue gaze met hers. If she had been given the slightest inkling that *he* would be there today, she certainly wouldn't have gone.

He looked as surprised as she felt, but he recovered quickly and nodded curtly in her direction as he took his bat over to the rack and placed it there.

Courtney slid off the bleachers and walked quickly over

to where Bonita was now standing as the redhead seated herself on the bleachers.

"Hello, dear. Guess where you get to play?" By the look on Bonita's face, Courtney knew she wasn't going to like the answer. Her mother was trying to be too positive about it.

"Probably the highly coveted position of right field?" she guessed accurately.

"How did you guess!"

"It figures. Why can't I play one of the bases?" Courtney pleaded.

"There's no positions open except center field," Bonita said patiently.

"Then I'll take center field."

"You can't. Graham always plays center. We didn't know if he was going to come today or not, but since he's here, he gets his regular position," Bonita apologized.

Courtney glared at her mother. "I believe you forgot to mention that Graham might be here today, Mother."

"I did? Huh." Bonita's face grew innocently pensive. "I must have overlooked that little item. Does it matter?"

"It does if he gets to play center and I'm stuck out in right field!"

"Yeah, well, Graham always plays center," Graham taunted as he walked up to stand beside Courtney. He shoved his hat farther back on his head and grinned engagingly. "Right field is always too hot and not enough action. It's the perfect position for you, Miss Spenser."

Courtney gave him a cool look of distaste and then ignored him. "I don't like this, Mother."

"Don't be cranky, dear, and don't worry. I might let you play first after a while." Bonita shooed Courtney out in the direction of right field hurriedly.

It had been a long time since Courtney had played baseball so she was pretty rusty. After the fourth ball flew over her head and she had to chase it, she was hot and

233

sweaty and losing her patience rapidly. It didn't help matters at all that Graham kept shooting her dirty looks as the other side continued to score on her errors.

Once when he ran back to try to catch a ball that was in her territory, they collided violently, with both of them falling to the ground as the left fielder ran for the missed ball.

"Why don't you watch where you're going, you clumsy oaf!" she sputtered as she tried to spit dirt and grass out of her mouth. Graham's large frame had landed on hers, nearly burying her nose in the ground.

"You're the lousiest excuse for a right fielder I have ever seen!" he shot back curtly. "When they hit the damn ball, will you at least try to make a *small* effort to catch it, Miss Spenser? Don't just stand there with your mouth gaping as it sails over your head!"

"I'm trying as hard as I can! If you don't like the way I play my position, let me play center and you play right field." She got up and dusted off the seat of her jeans angrily. "You're a big hog and trying to play both positions anyway!" she reminded hotly. "Just stay where you belong and leave me alone."

She couldn't believe her eyes when he childishly thumbed his nose at her and stalked angrily back to his position. That blockhead!

He was back running after one of her balls ten minutes later. He streaked by her, grinning wickedly as the ball roared over her head like a jet. She whirled and ran after him, completely forgetting the ball. She was furious to think he was deliberately making her look inept. Since she was smaller, she easily overtook him in record time. Hurling herself at him angrily, they both went down, tumbling end over end before they finally came to a stop. The ball rolled to the fence, and the other team scored two runs as Courtney and Graham's teammates scampered to retrieve the ball before another run came home.

"What in the hell do you think you're doing!" he roared, rolling over on his back and throwing his ball glove up in the air in complete exasperation.

"That was my ball," she panted, trying to regain her breath. For such a large man, he could run like a gazelle!

"Your ball! Then why didn't you catch it?" he bellowed incredulously.

"I was going to! *You* didn't give me enough time," she railed. She reached over and whacked him painfully in the chest with her glove.

"Ouch! Darn it! Now you cut that out!"

She staggered to her knees and crawled over to where he lay gasping for breath. Pressing her head down on his forehead, she stared sternly into his astonished blue eyes. "You keep *out* of my territory, Merrill. Is that clear?"

"But you can't play ball worth a—"

"I said *out!* Keep O-U-T!"

"Okay," he agreed abruptly, staring eyeball to eyeball with her. "Whatever makes you happy."

"*That* would make me immensely happy." She stood up and jammed her cap back on. "All we have to do is get one more out, then we're up at bat. Get up and get back to your position!"

Graham stood up, then leaned down to pick up his hat and glove. He wiped his sweaty forehead with his arm and stuck his hat back on his head, scowling at her disgustedly. "Next ball that comes through your territory and it isn't caught, you're going to the bench! And I sure hope to Bessie you can hit a ball better than you can catch one. Thanks to you, the score's now fifteen to nothing!"

"You just worry about your ball-playing abilities. Not mine." She turned her nose up in the air and stalked back to right field regally while he once again thumbed his nose at her retreating back.

It was another twenty minutes of hard playing before Courtney's team got the last out. She walked over to get a drink of water out of the Thermos, trying to wipe the sweat and dirt out of her eyes. Pieces of her hair had tumbled down from beneath her cap and she knew that she must look like a disreputable sight. A streak of jealousy shot through her as she noted Graham standing over at the bleachers talking to the redhead. Leaning tiredly against the backstop, she watched as the woman reached out and wiped a smudge of dirt off Graham's nose. The sight of some other woman touching him hurt so badly she thought she was going to cry. Turning away from the painful scene, she walked over to look at the bats.

"Do you even know how to hold one?" Graham's deep voice asked as he walked up behind her a few minutes later.

"I'll manage," she replied coolly.

He shrugged his shoulders and walked out in the direction of third base once more. "I'm coaching third. If you happen to make it that far, I'll see you." He smiled pleasantly. "I won't hold my breath though."

"Oh, please do. For the next two hours, if you can." Her smile was pure sarcasm.

Her first time at bat, Courtney struck out. She could physically feel the look of disgust coming from the direction of third base. When it was her turn to bat again, Clyde stepped up and offered her some gentle coaching. He showed her where to put her hands and how to stand. Surprisingly, Courtney didn't resent his help but rather sincerely appreciated it. It brought back pleasant childhood memories of when her dad would spend hours with her out in the backyard playing ball.

"Now you can do it," Clyde told her encouragingly as he stepped back from the plate.

"Maybe you better put a pinch hitter in for me," she said uneasily. There were two runners on base and she knew their team desperately needed a base hit right now.

"Nonsense. You're just as capable of pulling us through as anyone else on this team," Clyde said firmly.

"Maybe Mom can hit better than me." She looked at Clyde pleadingly.

"Bonnie's a clean-up batter. You just get us a base hit then we'll let her bring them home. Come on, now, do it for me, girl."

Courtney glanced over at Clyde once more, her heart softening as she saw the look of complete trust written clearly in his eyes. Giving him a radiant smile, she stepped up to the plate and grasped the bat solidly. In the distance she could hear Graham whistle and start to chatter, urging her on.

The first two balls were strikes, but the light of hope never faded from Clyde Merrill's eyes. He knew that Bonnie's daughter was no faint-hearted weakling. She would come through for the team.

Minutes later a broad smile broke across his weathered features as he heard the crack of the bat and saw the ball go whizzing out toward center field. Yessir! He knew his girl would come through!

Graham nearly swallowed the wad of bubble gum he had been chewing on as he watched the ball hit the fence and roll toward left field. He finally snapped out of his stupor and ran toward second, waving his arms wildly at Courtney's streaking figure.

"Hold up! Hold up on second," he shouted, watching as the fielders ran to retrieve the ball.

Courtney rounded second, glancing up only once to see where the ball was.

"I said hold up." Graham blinked his eyes as she shot by him, totally ignoring his coaching. He sped after her and raced her to third. Stepping on the bag at the same time, third baseman, coach, and runner all went down in a heap.

The ball reached base just as Courtney regained her

237

balance and crawled over to the bag and grasped it. "You idiot! Why didn't you hold up on second?" Graham bellowed. "You almost cost us a run!"

Shooting her a murderous look, he helped up the elderly man who was playing third base and brushed him off politely.

"You okay, fellow?" he asked concernedly, never once bothering to see if Courtney had broken her neck.

"I'm fine, sonny. Let's play ball," the old man assured with a toothless grin.

Graham turned back to Courtney and repeated his earlier charge. "Do you realize you almost cost us this inning?"

"But I didn't, did I?" she said smugly. She called time out and calmly tied her shoelace. "I believe I scored two runs, isn't that so, Dr. Know-It-All-Merrill."

"You were lucky, Miss Piggy-Headed Spenser!"

"You worry too much," she scoffed, motioning to the umpire that she was ready to play again.

Graham shot her an angry warning. "Don't you step foot off that bag until I say you can go!"

It was Courtney who thumbed her nose at Graham this time.

As the game proceeded, she kept darting off the bag every few seconds, keeping Graham's nerves stretched to the breaking point. Their team had finally managed to make a comeback and at the moment only two runs separated the teams. If Bonnie could hit a grand slam, which Graham knew she was more than capable of doing, Courtney could come home and the score would be tied.

"Get back on base!" he gritted between clenched teeth, as she once again made a motion as if she were going to steal home.

"No, I think I'll try to make it," she taunted in a whisper.

Graham swore nastily. "You do and I'll break your neck! Stop clowning around!"

"I can do it! I run real fast," she tormented, knowing full well that she wouldn't dare endanger the team's chances by doing anything that foolish, but it was so much fun to see his face turn red and angry!

"Hey, Doc," she hissed a few minutes later. He diverted his attention momentarily away from the batter's box, his face a mask of agony. The count was three balls, two strikes, two outs, last inning. It was now or never.

"What do you want?" he asked gruffly.

"I think I'm going to try and make it to homeplate right now. Now, while the pitcher's spittin' on the ball again!" She jumped off the base teasingly.

Graham panicked, his foot coming out to trip her as the third baseman whistled for the pitcher to throw the ball to him. The ball zoomed into the third baseman's glove as Courtney fell on her face, missing the base entirely with her groping hand.

"*Out!*" the umpire shouted jubilantly.

A roar of disappointment went up from Courtney's team as she sat up and looked around her dazedly. "*Graham Merrill!*" she shouted angrily. "Look what you've done! You've made us lose the game!" It never occurred to her that she had been just as responsible.

"*Me?*" he roared. "If you hadn't been horsing around, we *would* have won it!"

She jumped to her feet, grabbing the sandbag they had used for third base and swinging it angrily at his large, imposing frame that seemed to be hovering over her menacingly. She hit him square in the stomach, the unexpected impact knocking him flat on his rear. He was on his feet in seconds, swiping embarrassedly at the bottom of his dusty jeans.

"Now, I think that was totally uncalled for, Miss—" He didn't finished his sentence because she swung the base

239

again and whacked him back off his feet soundly. He hit the ground with a jarring thud this time.

The two teams were walking off the field, totally ignoring the warring couple where third base used to be.

When Graham came to his feet this time, Courtney had decided by the look on his face that she probably *had* gone too far in knocking him down the second time. The blue of his eyes was definitely not friendly as she turned on her heel and started running. Fast.

"Don't you think you better make your daughter stop beating my son with that third-base bag?" Clyde asked Bonita as they strolled across the ballfield, hot and tired.

"No, dear. I don't think she'll hurt him. Isn't it nice that they've finally noticed each other?" Bonita smiled up at Clyde happily.

"Yeah." Clyde stopped and watched his son come swiftly to his feet and take off in hot pursuit of Courtney. "It sure is. I was beginning to think they never would," he confessed. Draping his arm around Bonita, they walked off the ballfield content in the knowledge that love was beginning to bloom between the young couple right under their very noses.

Where does one run to hide on an empty ball diamond when one is in fear for one's very life? That question loomed large in Courtney's mind as she glanced back over her shoulders in hopes that Graham had given up the chase. Unfortunately, he hadn't, and he looked none too happy as he gained ground on her. Darting behind the same tree Clyde had pulled Bonita behind earlier, Courtney crouched low and peered around the branches anxiously. There was no sign of Graham now. She backed up slowly, holding her breath. Thank goodness, she had lost him! Her body stiffened as she backed into a hard wall of resistance. Turning around, she grinned sheepishly as she looked into cold blue eyes glaring at her insolently. "Hi there," she said weakly.

"Hi there," he mimicked in a decidedly unfriendly voice. "Miss Spenser"—Graham began to advance ominously in her direction—"never in my entire life has a woman beat me up with third base. How do you think that makes me feel?"

"I wouldn't have had to do that," she explained in a shaky voice, still backing away from him, "if you hadn't tripped me. You have to admit yourself, Dr. Merrill, it wasn't nice of you to do that either!"

"I thought you were going to try to steal home. That's what you said, wasn't it?"

"I was only teasing you." She forced a laugh. "Can't you take a joke?"

"No."

"I was afraid you couldn't." Courtney whirled and started to run again, but one large hand reached out and jerked her to an abrupt halt. Resisting with all her might, they tumbled back down to the ground as she tried valiantly to break his iron hold on her.

Graham's strength quickly overpowered hers as he pinned her to the ground and lay down on top of her. She looked up into his eyes expecting to find great anger there. Her breath caught as she realized what she was seeing was not anger, but another emotion she had seen twice before in those beautiful azure depths. A look of hunger had replaced the anger now. Hunger for her.

"Damn it, Courtney, keep still so I can kiss you," he murmured softly as he reached up and gently took off her cap, letting her hair flow loosely around her shoulders.

"Well, why didn't you say so?" She sighed contentedly, wiping at the dirt on his nose as she had seen another woman do earlier. Only this time she had the supreme pleasure of touching him.

His fingers threaded their way through the thick mass of her blond hair as he drew her mouth up to meet his. Their kiss was explosive and passionate, hot and wanting, yet tender and reacquainting. They kissed long and deep, breaking apart only for brief seconds to regain their breath. Instead of three weeks, it seemed like they had been apart more like three years.

"Why haven't you called me lately?" she cried out softly as he buried his face in her neck and breathed in her achingly familiar scent.

"I wanted to. Darn, how I wanted to . . ." he confessed, taking her mouth again almost roughly. They kissed again fervently, trying to draw even closer to each other's bodies. The magic and fire between them burned brightly, begging to be quenched.

"Are you all right?" he asked, kissing her nose, her eyes, then capturing her mouth again ravenously.

Courtney groaned irritably. "If you're asking what I think you are, stop it!"

"Honey, you're not being fair with me. I have a right to know if anything resulted from our being together." Her kiss cut off his angry words abruptly. Minutes later she whispered repentantly in his ear. "We were lucky again. Nothing happened," she confessed.

"Why are you so darn stubborn about telling me?" He groaned huskily against her ear. "You won't tell me if you've been with a man before . . . you probably wouldn't have told me if you found out you were expecting a baby. What's with you anyway?"

"When you think of me, Graham, I want it in a much different way. I don't want to be a constant source of worry to you. What we have shared together is just that. Something wonderful we've shared *together*. I have always been as much the culprit as you have in this relationship, so stop worrying about it."

"I don't worry about it," he murmured as his hand slipped beneath her T-shirt and gently cupped her breast, stroking it lovingly. "But I would like to know."

"Know what?"

"Were you—"

"Forget it, Graham. It's none of your business." She ran her tongue around the outline of his lips. "Umm . . . you taste good, just like grape bubble gum!"

"If you're not going to give me any answers, then you have my permission to taste away," he invited in a low, suggestive voice.

"I'd really like to, but have you forgotten there's a redhead sitting in the bleachers waiting for you?"

"Clarissa!" Graham groaned, burying his face on her shoulder.

The mere mention of her name sent jealousy raging through her body. "Graham?"

"Huh?" he murmured, kissing her neck affectionately. "I never did buy you that big bottle of Chloe, did I?" he asked in a muffled tone.

"No, but that's not important," she dismissed hurriedly. "Graham, you told me one time you were seeing two different women. Are you serious about either one of them? I mean *really,* honest-to-gosh serious?" For the first time since she had met Graham Merrill, that question had a very overriding importance to Courtney.

Graham was silent for a moment. "No. Neither one of them is of any particular importance to me, Courtney. Actually, I've seen several different women in the past three weeks." He sat up and ran his fingers through his hair absently. "I don't know, maybe I've been trying to prove something to myself, although I don't know what it is I'm trying to prove." He laughed ironically. "All I know is I've missed seeing you like hell."

Her face broke out in a radiant smile. "If that's a compliment, I'll take it."

"Look." He reached over and took her hand in his. "What would you think of the idea of us seeing each other some . . . you know . . . none of the heavy stuff. Let's just date for the next few weeks and really get to know each other."

Courtney's heart fairly sang with joy. "I'd like that, Graham." She squeezed his hand tightly.

"Well, we'll have to keep it from your mom and my dad. I still think it would be best if that relationship was broken up, and if they found out we were dating they would be mad as the devil because we don't approve of them seeing each other. And I think we should go ahead and date other people."

"Oh, that will be easy. Clyde and Mom won't ever have to know," Courtney assured readily. "And you're right. We should continue dating other people. After all, this is just sort of a . . . testing period. . . ."

"Right! And who knows? We may discover we don't actually like each other, that it's all simply a . . . physical thing," Graham said lightly, hoping against hope that was all it was.

"That's very possible," Courtney agreed. "But I think we should agree . . . no physical relationship in the coming weeks. That way we'll be sure."

"Yeah . . . yeah, I had it figured the same way. Let's just get to know each other and then we'll see what happens." His blue eyes assessed her hungrily.

"That sounds very reasonable to me. We can kiss, though, don't you think?"

"Oh, sure, I don't see where that would hurt anything," he said sensibly.

Courtney closed her eyes, brushing her lips against his in reassurance that this wasn't a dream. "I think I should bring up the fact that we both don't feel like either one of us is the other's 'type,' " she teased playfully.

"I'm willing to reevaluate that assessment, if you are," he teased back.

"I'm willing. Then it's agreed. We'll see each other without letting our parents know about it. At least for the

244

time being," Courtney reiterated. "And naturally we'll continue to see others too."

"Yeah, let's start with dinner Sunday night. You're not busy, are you?" he looked at her hopefully.

"Oh, no! Not at all. Dinner sounds lovely. What time?"

"Five o'clock too early?" He hated to sound eager but it had been three long miserable weeks since he had last seen her!

"I could be ready by four thirty," Courtney accepted impatiently.

"Okay."

They came back into each other's embrace, their mouths meeting eagerly.

It was Courtney who came to her senses first, several minutes later. She reluctantly broke away from his hungry kisses as she felt his passion pressing demandingly into her side. She knew there could be no repeat performance of the ecstasy they had shared twice before until some kind of a commitment could be spoken of. And Graham would have to be the one to ask for that commitment. Her heart was heavy when she realized how very slim that chance would be.

"We really have to be going," she whispered regretfully. "It's shameful for you to be with me and have Clarissa waiting . . ."

"She's the one who came by my house as I was leaving this morning. I didn't have a date with her today," he defended quickly.

Pressing soft kisses against his neck, Courtney smiled happily. "I know this will go straight to your egotistical head, but I'm glad," she admitted softly.

"And I'm glad you're glad. Now kiss me one more time, then I do have to go."

Courtney complied with his request willingly and in a few minutes he had disappeared back around the tree.

She lay looking up at the sky, hugging his remembrance

close to her heart. She had no idea where things would go from there, and at the moment she wouldn't let her mind dwell on the future. She was hopelessly in love with Graham Merrill, she knew that without the slightest doubt. Now all she had to do was sit back and wait until he fell in love with her.

Elementary, my dear Watson! Or was it?

CHAPTER FOURTEEN

"Things are moving entirely too slowly." Clyde sat the teacup back down on the table and looked at Bonita seriously. "At the rate they're going, Buddy and Courtney are going to be as old as we are before they decide to start getting serious about each other!"

"I don't understand what's taking so long," Bonita agreed absently. "I know my daughter inside and out and I could swear she has deep feelings for Graham, yet I know she's been dating other men lately. That's the puzzling aspect of this. She has never cared much about dating, but the last two weeks she's been gone every night with first one, then the other."

"Has Buddy been over much?"

"Not at all! That's what worries me. Oh, Clyde, what if she falls in love with another man before we can get her and Graham together! She's been getting flowers and candy and someone sent her a mushy singing telegram yesterday morning."

"Aren't any of the gifts signed?"

"No, not a one of them. I was hoping they would be from Graham, but since they don't seem to be seeing each other at all, that would be unlikely."

"They're probably not from Buddy. I don't think he gets mushy," Clyde observed morosely.

Bonita glanced over at Clyde and winked suggestively.

"Don't bet on it. I'll wager he can be as sweet and affectionate as his father."

A faint blush covered Clyde's face as he hastily spooned more sugar in his tea, trying to ignore Bonita's teasing. "So, what are we going to do about this situation? I'm getting tired of waiting, Bonnie. I want to get married soon, while I still have the strength to enjoy it." He winked at her now.

"I know, dear. I do too. And if we can't get those two children of ours together, we'll never get them to accept a marriage between us." Bonita stood up and reached for the tea kettle. "You know it isn't just that I want Courtney to accept our marriage, I really want her to fall in love with Graham for her own personal happiness. He's such a dear boy, and I think he would make her a wonderful husband."

"If she manages to get that boy to the altar, she'll be doing something no other woman's even come close to," Clyde said glumly. "He's been footloose and fancy free all his life, and I don't think he's too crazy about the idea of a woman changing his ways."

"The right woman will make him want to change them in five minutes. In fact, she'll have him begging for a trip to the altar," Bonita predicted happily. "But in the meantime, I think it's time we did something to try to speed up their decision that they were meant for each other."

"Oh? Do you have an idea?" Clyde perked up.

"Yes, I do." She crossed her hands and stared at Clyde intently. "Now what do you think their reaction would be if they thought you and I were going to elope?"

"I don't know about Courtney, but I think Buddy would lay an egg!"

"Good. That's what I was hoping. Now if Graham lays an egg, we want to make sure that Courtney is there to pick it up and put it in her little basket!" Bonita's eyes sparked devilishly as she motioned for Clyde to lean closer. "Now here's the plan. . . ."

The front door opened that evening and Courtney breezed into the house breathlessly. "Mom! Are you home?"

The silence of the house answered her question. She shrugged, then took an apple out of the bowl of fruit sitting on the coffee table and took a large bite out of it. Humming a happy tune under her breath, she walked into her bedroom and opened her closet door. She stood surveying her wardrobe, wrinkling her nose in distaste. Someday she was going to throw out everything and buy new clothes. Sexy, feminine new clothes.

Crossing the room, she flopped down on the bed and stared up contentedly at the ceiling. For the first time in her life she wanted new clothes. Lately she had been feeling very feminine and very lovely. She smiled lazily. A certain dentist had a lot to do with those new, happy feelings. Oh, Rob Hanson had been surprisingly fun to be with, and Brad Reasoner, the salesman she had been seeing, had courted her with flair, although neither could hold a candle to Graham. A secret smile overtook her features as she thought about the way Graham had begun to court her in earnest. He had sent her enough flowers to start a greenhouse and enough candy to start her own factory in the last couple of weeks, and that ridiculously mushy, sentimental singing telegram he had sent yesterday had her walking on air all day long. Rob and Brad were tolerable, but it was Graham who sent her pulses racing and her knees turning to pure jelly every time they went out. Courtney couldn't help but marvel at how much fun they had together. They still sparred back and forth over their parents and how they both felt they would be better off seeing someone else, but when it came to their own personal feelings, they would both go weak with

249

wanting as they struggled to keep their relationship on a strictly platonic level. So far, they had been successful but only due to the tight rein Graham held on their necking sessions. He had teasingly told her he had taken more cold showers in the last few weeks than any one man should have to in a lifetime, but he remained firm in his word that this was a time of discovering, of learning between them. For Courtney it was enough. For now. She had every hope that someday he would realize that what existed between them was rare and beautiful and could have no other destiny but a lifetime commitment to each other. A smile of complacency crept over her pretty features. Graham didn't want to admit it, but he was just as jealous of her seeing other men as she was of him seeing other women, even though it had been his suggestion. It nearly killed both of them to run into each other when they were out on a date with someone else, yet they each stubbornly refused to verbally acknowledge to each other how deep their feelings had grown. Courtney rolled over on her stomach and hugged her pillow tightly. But he would. Given time, Graham Merrill would be hers and hers alone.

After a brief rest, Courtney took a shower and readied herself for her date with Rob that night. They had agreed to go to the skating rink so Courtney could keep an eye on her mother and Clyde. It seemed impossible to keep the two gypsies apart so she had opted to be there should Bonita fall down and hurt herself. At least she would be there to pick up the pieces!

The rink was crowded and noisy when Courtney and Rob arrived a little after seven.

"Are we seriously going to skate?" Rob asked, disappointment seeping through his voice. He looked at Courtney pleadingly. "I can think of a lot more things I'd rather be doing with you than skating!"

Courtney smiled and took his hand. "Ah, come on.

Where's your sense of adventure? How long has it been since you've been on a pair of skates?"

"Not since I was a kid," he admitted, letting her drag him to the counter where they rented skates, "and to be perfectly honest, I prefer to keep it that way."

They exchanged playful banter as they got their skates and took them over to one of the benches running along the wall and put them on.

Bonita came off the floor like a speeding bullet and rolled up to where they were sitting. "Hi, you two!"

"Hi, Mom." Courtney stood up and tested her rusty skating abilities. "Whoa!"

She groped wildly in the air as Bonita came to her rescue.

"You be careful, dear. You haven't skated since you were a child," her mother warned worriedly.

"Don't worry about her," Rob scoffed. "Skating's like riding a bicycle. Once you learn it, you never forget." He came to his feet and was lying flat on his back in the middle of the floor a few seconds later.

Both Bonita and Courtney broke out in laughter as he struggled to get back on his feet.

"You do make it look simple," Courtney complimented teasingly.

In another half an hour, both Courtney and Rob were whizzing around the skating rink, falling only occasionally. Around ten, she glanced up to see Graham and his date for the evening standing at the rail watching the skaters. She nearly lost her balance as she smiled and waved at him, but unfortunately she hit the wall on the back turn trying to see who he was with. The girl didn't look familiar, but that didn't ease the agony of seeing him with another woman. She wasn't sure what hurt worse—the pain in her heart at seeing Graham with another woman or the bump on her head from running into the wall.

Courtney made a couple of more spins around the rink

when she noticed Graham's date disappear into the bathroom. Seizing the opportunity to speak to him alone, she skated up to the rail and stopped. "Hi, good-lookin'. Want to fool around?" she teased brightly.

He looked around curiously. "Yeah, you see anyone I might have a chance with?"

"Me!"

"You?" He frowned and grinned at her affectionately. "No, thanks. Girls with lumps on their foreheads don't turn me on."

"I'll remember that the next time we're together, fellow!" She leaned against the railing, trying to play it cool as her feet nearly slipped out from beneath her once more. He reached out to steady her, his arms going round her waist firmly. He pulled her up against the rail, but he refused to let her go.

"Don't you believe a word I say, lady. Any chance I get to fool around with you I'm going to take, lump or no lump." His eyes met hers, sending a very intimate and loving message.

She pulled back from him reluctantly, fighting the overwhelming urge to kiss him. They had been together only the night before but to her it seemed much longer.

Graham smiled, reading her thoughts because they were his also. "Me too, sweetheart, but it will have to wait," he whispered softly.

Courtney's hand trembled as he picked it up and kissed the palm suggestively, his gaze never leaving hers.

"What are you doing out here?" she asked in a shaky voice, pulling her hand away from his mouth swiftly. He already had her to the point of attacking him.

"Looking for Dad and your mom." He straightened up and tried to regain control of his warring emotions.

"Oh? Why? Did you tell him not to go out with Mom tonight?"

"No, but I was a little uneasy on what their plans were for the evening."

"Skating? What's to worry about? They go skating at least twice a week."

Graham looked at Courtney solemnly. "I don't want to alarm you, but I think they may be planning to elope tonight."

He had to reach out and steady her again as her feet nearly flew out from under her once more. "Elope!" she gasped.

"I could be wrong, but there are too many clues that add up this week. Yesterday I found a slip of paper totaling up both of their social securities, there's a sign out in the garage reading 'Just Married, Tampa or Bust,' and tonight I found a note lying next to the telephone with the name of a justice of the peace written on it and the hour eleven fifty, today's date, and the name of a motel about five miles out on the highway. That, coupled with the fact I saw Dad put a suitcase in his car just before he left tonight, sounds a little suspicious, don't you think?"

"You mean they are planning to be married tonight?" Courtney and Graham's eyes fastened intently on the elderly couple who were skating a fast-paced disco dance, backward, and appeared to be loving every minute of being the center of attention.

Clyde glanced over at the railing and leaned down and whispered to Bonita smugly. "Unless I miss my guess, the suckers are taking the bait right now, hook, line, and sinker!"

"Shh, dear, they might suspect. Just keep skating." Bonita looked over at the rail and waved at the young couple innocently. "I only hope what we're doing is right. I trust your son to be honorable and not take unfair advantage of my daughter in the situation we're going to be putting them in," she added sternly.

"Any woman who can beat up a man with third base

doesn't have to worry that she's going to be taken advantage of," Clyde said, chuckling. "From now on, those two are on their own!"

Courtney smiled weakly and waved back at her mother. Out of the corner of her mouth she whispered frantically to Graham. "Well, we have to do something! We have to stop them!"

"That's what I thought," he answered grimly. He looked around the rink. "Are you by yourself?"

"No, I'm with Rob."

Graham's face fell. "Rob Hanson? You were with him the night before last," he accused tightly.

"Yes, that's right. And I'm with him again tonight." She smiled.

"Where is he?" Graham questioned curtly, as if he didn't believe her.

"Lying out there in the middle of the floor."

Graham's eyes followed in the direction her finger was pointing to the man sprawled out painfully in the center of the rink after taking another bone-shattering fall.

"I hope he broke his—"

"Nasty, nasty," Courtney scolded. "Do I make bad remarks about your date?"

"Hell, Courtney. Why do you have to see that creep twice in one week?" he demanded hotly.

"He isn't the only man I've been seeing. I see *you* more than twice a week," she pointed out.

"Get rid of him so we can find out what Dad and Bonnie are up to," he demanded gruffly. "I'll take Lila home and be over at your house in thirty minutes."

"Please?" Her laughing eyes met his distressed ones.

"Please . . . sweetheart." His eyes gazed back in longing at her.

"I'll meet you in thirty minutes," she relented, giving his hand a reassuring squeeze. "If Mom and Clyde are eloping, we don't have much time."

"Give me a kiss before we go," he said huskily.

"No, I can't do that, Graham," she protested, her heart doing triple somersaults at his delicious suggestion.

"Why not?" He pulled her up closer to the rail, his arm going around her waist demandingly.

"Because we are both with other dates and that wouldn't be very respectful to them."

"I don't care who you're with."

"Well, you should." She pulled away from him firmly. "After all, Dr. Merrill, it was your suggestion that we date other people."

Graham gave a sigh of defeat. "Okay, but when I get to your house in thirty minutes, you won't have that flimsy excuse to fall back on." The tone in his voice warned her she would be spared no mercy when he had her alone.

Placing a kiss on the tips of her fingers, she pressed them against his lips intimately. "I have no desire to use an excuse when it concerns you."

He caught her fingers with both hands and kissed them hungrily. "Make that twenty minutes."

"Twenty minutes," she confirmed in a loving voice.

It was actually close to forty-five minutes before both dates were shed and Graham knocked impatiently on Courtney's front door. When she opened it, he pulled her into his arms and kissed her as if he hadn't seen her in months. Ushering him into the room, Courtney returned his kisses fervently. It was several minutes before they parted long enough to draw a deep breath. They stood in the middle of the room hugging each other. Graham was fighting to overcome the strong desire to lock the door and carry her into bedroom. Both knew that would be foolish, but it was hopeless to deny that was what they really wanted.

"Graham," she murmured against the warmth of his neck. The smell of his aftershave was doing wild and crazy

255

things to her senses. "If Mom and Clyde are eloping at eleven fifty, we don't have time for this."

"Do you know that right now that doesn't seem important to me at all," he confessed in a husky voice. "All I want to do is hold you in my arms and feel your softness against me." His mouth returned to capture hers in a demanding kiss, sending all thoughts of protest fleeing from her mind. In a few minutes it was apparent someone was going to have to be strong enough to stop this madness because it was swiftly getting out of hand. In the end, they both pulled away shaken.

"We have to stop this." Graham panted, moving away from her. "We made ourselves a promise and we're going to keep it if it kills me."

"Us," she corrected. "Kills us!"

Graham ran his fingers through his hair. "Now, back to Dad and Bonnie. I have the name of the motel they're going to. They probably will go there and change their clothes before they get married. We'll go there first and try to talk some sense into them." His hands were trembling as he shoved them deep in his trouser pockets and walked over to the window. Courtney could tell it was taking him an unusually long time to regain control of his emotions.

"It's nearly eleven now. We better get started," Courtney said softly, wishing with all her heart she could ease his agony. All he had to do was ask.

He stood staring out into the darkness for several more minutes before he turned around and walked slowly back over to her. Leaning down, he kissed her tenderly once more before he picked up her sweater and handed it to her.

"I think I'm losing the battle." He laughed mirthlessly.

Courtney reached out and touched his face yearningly. "Would that be so bad?"

He shook his head and helped her put her sweater on. Arm in arm they walked out to his car and got in.

Traffic was light at this late hour so they were able to

reach the motel in less than ten minutes. Graham went to the office and found out that Clyde and Bonita had registered earlier in the day. On the pretext of wanting to leave some champagne for the newlyweds, Graham obtained a key to their room and minutes later they were turning on the lights in the empty room.

"There's Dad's suitcase," Graham said in a disapproving tone.

"Yes, and look, they must have planned on celebrating pretty heavily." Courtney groaned, taking note of the three bottles of champagne sitting in buckets of ice on a table next to the bed.

Graham walked over and looked at the label. Emitting a low whistle, he was duly impressed with the vintage. "Good year."

"I don't know anything about champagne." She shrugged disinterestedly.

"Well, we might as well make ourselves comfortable," Graham said, casually. "It's too late to stop the ceremony, but we can try to prevent the . . . consummation." He glanced at her uneasily.

Courtney sank down on the bed. "I hadn't even thought about that."

Graham yawned and lay down on the bed next to her. "Don't look so shocked. In Dad's own words, 'there may be snow on the rooftop, but there's still fire in the old furnace' or something to that effect."

Courtney laughed. "Are they ever going to be surprised to find us here." She lay down next to him. "What do you think they'll say?"

"I'm in the presence of a lady, I can't say what Dad's exact words will be," he teased.

They lay quietly for a moment, each one lost in his own private thoughts.

"You know, you could very easily take advantage of me in a situation like this," Courtney pointed out, not very

257

discreetly. "I mean, here we are, alone, just the two of us, in a motel room . . ." Her voice trailed off suggestively.

"Isn't that odd?" Graham said dryly. "I was just thinking the same thing."

"Oh?" Courtney sat up and leaned on her elbow. "What did you decide?"

"That I wasn't going to."

"Oh." She lay back down and stared up at the ceiling, feeling somewhat rejected. "Why do I have the strange feeling that other women would have more luck with you in that department than I do?"

"Other women are . . . other women. You're you."

"That sounds very deep and philosophical." She pouted. "Does that translate down to 'You don't appeal to me, Miss Spenser'?"

Graham wasn't about to let her goading affect his better judgment. "I don't think you're honestly worried about that. You know all too well how you appeal to me."

It was clear he wasn't going to fall for her bait. He was going to need a little more enticement. Since, unlike Eve, she didn't have an apple to offer him, she'd have to find another way. But what? She had never tried to encourage a man in her life, and at the moment the mere thought turned her cold. She glanced nonchalantly at his good-looking body lying next to hers and swallowed hard. Her eyes fastened on the bottles of champagne. If she drank any of that, she wouldn't have any problems seducing him! The clock on the bedside table said eleven twenty. If Clyde and Bonita didn't get married until almost midnight, then it would take a few minutes to sign papers, drive back to the motel . . .

"I'm thirsty," Courtney finally said.

"There are glasses in the bathroom," Graham muttered in a drowsy voice.

Courtney slid off the bed and walked into the small green-tiled bathroom. She scooped up the glasses that were sitting on the tray and rolled them up in a towel, then put the bundle in the wastepaper can. If there were no glasses she couldn't drink water, but she could sip champagne straight from the bottle! And voilà! Instant stewed brains and then she would have the nerve to make a very unladylike pass at him.

"There's none in here," she called innocently.

"There were five minutes ago. Where did they go?"

Courtney cringed. He must have checked the bathroom when they first got in. "Oh, here they are," she said as she dug the glasses back out of the wastecan and sat them back on the tray, mumbling under her breath about her rotten luck.

"Did you say something?" he asked.

"No, nothing," she called brightly.

She shuffled disheartenedly back to the bed and lay down again.

"Find them?" he ask pleasantly.

"Yes, thank you. The water was delicious."

"I'll bet," he murmured in a relaxed tone. "I always say there's nothing like a glass of warm tap water to get your evening off to a roaring start."

"What time do you think they'll be here?" Courtney asked, an hour later. They had watched an old movie on TV, but it was now over.

Graham looked at his watch. "Darned if I know. They should have been here by now."

"I'm thirsty again," she complained.

"What's with you tonight? That's the third glass of water you drank since we got here. Did you eat something salty for dinner this evening?"

"I don't know why I'm so thirsty. The water just isn't quenching my thirst." She sat up and looked at the bottles of wine chilling in the ice buckets.

"Maybe I should drink something else?" she commented meekly.

"There isn't anything else *to* drink except the wine and there's no way you're going to get a glass of that," Graham said sternly.

"Why not?" she asked indignantly.

"Because, my dear, you and I both know you can't hold your liquor! I have purposely kept my hands off you while we've been in this . . . tempting position."

"I'd noticed," she said glumly. He hadn't kissed her once since they entered the room, and he had stayed as far on his side of the bed as possible without rolling off the edge.

"And besides that, it's Dad and Bonnie's wine—not ours."

"They have three bottles, for heaven's sake. It wouldn't hurt if we had a couple of little sips out of one of them, Graham." She reached over and touched his arm lightly. "Please. One tiny sip isn't going to make me drunk."

He pulled away from her touch like she had stuck a hot iron on his skin. "No, Courtney."

She got on her knees and crawled over to his side of the bed.

"Get away," he warned ominously. "I said no."

"I will take off all my clothes and throw myself at you shamefully if you don't let me have a tiny little sip of that wine," she threatened grimly.

"You wouldn't . . ." He moaned as she leaned over and softly brushed her lips against his. "Don't start anything, Courtney. I'm trying to handle this the best way I know how." The pressure of her lips increased on his.

He rolled away from her and jumped off the bed hurriedly. "All right. One little sip and that's it!" He reached for one of the bottles and proceeded to open it. A loud pop filled the room as the cork flew off, and he filled two of the glasses from the bathroom with the bubbling liquid. Handing her the glass with the least amount of wine in it,

260

he warned firmly, "Enjoy it because that's all you're getting."

"Yes, sir!" She saluted him and took her glass. It was empty after the first swallow. The wine tasted absolutely vile, but, she reminded herself, she wasn't doing this for the flavor of it! She frowned unfavorably at the bottom of her empty glass. "Graham, that's not fair. Your glass had more in it than mine did," she accused.

"Tough. I can hold my liquor better than you can," he replied callously.

Before he realized what was taking place, she shot off the bed and poured her glass full of the sparkling wine.

"Courtney!" Graham sprang to his feet and tried to take the glass away from her. She gulped the contents down swiftly while she tried to hold him back.

"Are you nuts!" he exploded. "That will go straight to your head."

She took the last swallow and handed her glass back to him meekly. "I was really thirsty, Graham."

Giving her a distinctly cold glare, he angrily poured another glass of wine for himself and sat back down on the bed. "You're crazy," he grumbled.

The room was tilting slightly now as Courtney strolled back over to the bed and wrapped her arms around his neck repentantly. "Are you mad at me?"

"Go away. No, I'm not mad." Graham tried to remove her arms but his efforts were halfhearted and he failed miserably. With a long sigh, he pulled her down on his lap and let her snuggle against his broad frame. "You're looking for trouble, aren't you, lady?"

Courtney kissed his neck contentedly. "I want to be with you, if that's what you mean."

"You're trying to make this as hard on me as you can, aren't you?" He finished the last of his wine and set the glass back down on the table.

Courtney reached over and filled both glasses again. "Isn't this yummy?"

"Real yummy," he agreed, beginning to feel the relaxing effects of the wine himself.

"I don't usually like this stuff, but it sure tastes good tonight." Courtney took another long swallow. "What time is it now?"

Graham glanced at his watch. "Nearly one."

She giggled. "Do you think we've been . . . hic . . . oh, 'scuse me, what was I going to say?" She took another drink of wine before she continued. "Oh, yes, I 'member now. Do you think Mom and Clyde duped us again?"

Graham was pouring his third large glass of champagne now. He looked up and his handsome features darkened. "I hadn't thought about it. Why would they want to do that?"

"Who knows?" Courtney shrugged. "They're weird lately." She rolled over on the bed and giggled again. "Really weird!"

"What's so funny?" Graham looked at her disapprovingly. "See, I told you you would get drunk."

Courtney sat up and drew a deep, exasperated breath. "I am *not* drunk! The first little giggle, I happen to giggle . . . hic . . . you always accuse me of being intoxicated. You are an old fogey, Dr. Stick-In-The-Mud Merrill! Why can't you learn to laugh and have fun like me?"

"I don't see anything particularly funny," he said in a hurt, petulant tone.

"Nothing funny!" She gasped incredulously. She took another long drink out of her glass. "Co' mere. I'll tell you something so funny you'll die laughin'."

He slumped over on her lap and looked at her expectantly. "Tell me something hilarious, Miss Spenser. I can hardly wait to hear what you consider uproarious at this moment."

"Okay. Are you ready?"

He nodded in eager anticipation.

"Do you know how you can tell if an elephant's been in your 'frigerator?"

He thought for a moment. "No, how do you know if an elephant's been in your 'frigerator?"

"By the footprints in the Jello!" Courtney doubled over with laughter as Graham looked at her blankly.

"You said you were going to tell me something funny," he said irritably.

"That was funny!"

"It was not. I know a funnier one than that," he said sullenly. He sat up and drained his glass dry again.

Courtney was still laughing at her own corny joke, but she managed to bring herself under control and say peevishly, "Oh, yeah? That's the funniest elephant joke I've ever heard. You tell yours and we'll just see which one's the funniest." She pitched her glass down on the floor, picked up the half-empty bottle, and took a long, deep swig. In a few minutes, she was going to seduce him, but she was going to let him tell his dumb joke first or he would have his feelings hurt.

Graham popped the cork off the other bottle of champagne and drank out of it. Coming back over to the bed, he set the bottle down and looked at her smugly. "Do you know why an elephant's ankles are so wrinkled?"

"No, why?" She raised the bottle to her lips and drank thirstily.

"Because he ties his tennis shoes too tight."

A spray of champagne shot out of her mouth, drenching Graham, as Courtney doubled over with delight once more.

"That's nothing." Graham chortled, beginning to get in the swing of things now. "Do you know how you can tell if an elephant is in bed with you?"

"No, how?" Tears were streaming down her face. At

any other time, Courtney would be mortified and bored to death with such cornball jokes, but at the moment she thought they were the funniest things she had ever heard in her life.

"You can smell the peanuts on his breath!" They both dissolved in rollicking laughter as he fell on the bed and they gasped for breath.

"You know why an elephant paints his toenails red?"

"So he can hide in a strawberry patch!"

"Oh, darn! You've heard it!" They rolled around on the bed holding their sides in mirth. By now they were both roaring drunk and enjoying every minute of it.

"Do you know how many elephants it takes to screw in a light bulb? . . . No, now wait a minute." Courtney's laughter receded as she thought for a minute. "I don't think that's an elephant joke."

"I don't think it is either." Graham grinned happily. He reached out and grabbed her once more, tickling her unmercifully.

"Wait!" She gasped, trying to stop his plundering hands. "I just thought of another one."

His motions ceased as she fought to regain her voice. "What's gray and sings calypso songs?" she asked seriously.

"Dunno. What?"

"Harry Elephanté!"

"Oh, brother." His groan was pained.

Her eyes sparkled brightly and her face was flushed a pretty pink by the wine. "You didn't like it? How about this. What's green, sings, and wiggles?"

"I wouldn't have the slightest idea."

Another giggle escaped her. "Elvis Parsley!"

"Okay, smartie. What's green and used to dance in old movies with Ginger Rogers?" Graham fired back.

She reached up and pulled his mouth down to hers, and they kissed for a moment before she answered expectantly,

"I give up. What's green and used to dance in old movies with Ginger Rogers?"

Graham stole another kiss, then grinned smugly. "Are you ready for this?"

"Shoot."

"Fred Asparagras."

That one was too much for both of them. They broke out in laughter again and rolled over the side of the bed in a tumbled heap. Courtney landed on Graham with a thud, bringing on even more gales of mirth. It was several minutes before they could speak. When they regained their senses, Courtney wrapped her arms around his neck and whispered in his ear shyly, "I have a confession to make, Dr. Merrill."

"Go ahead and confess, Miss Spenser," he offered generously.

"I drank all that champagne so that I could have the nerve to seduce you."

"You're shameful." He gasped, shocked. "But go ahead and seduce me anyway."

"I can't." She yawned in disgusted. "I'm too sleepy now." She snuggled down deeper into his arms.

Reaching up over his head, Graham dragged the blanket off the bed and covered them both snugly. "Maybe later," he promised as he wrapped his arms around her tighter. "I have a confession to make myself. I'm not in any condition to be seduced at the moment," he admitted drowsily.

"Are we going to sleep on this floor?" she asked dazedly.

"I think so." He pulled her mouth down for another long kiss. "Night."

"Night."

They were just about to doze off when she murmured, "There's no doubt in my mind, we've been duped for sure!"

265

* * *

Dawn was barely breaking when Courtney awoke. Graham was still sleeping soundly. She felt like she had been run over by a truck as she sat up and looked around. She could barely remember what had taken place last night, but she knew instinctively she wouldn't like it, whatever it was. The empty wine bottles were mute testimony to why her head felt like someone had split it open with an ax.

She pulled herself up and straightened her clothes. At the moment she didn't have the nerve or the desire to face Graham. He must think she was an absolute idiot to have drunk that much champagne against his wishes. She blushed furiously trying to remember if she had carried out her plan to seduce him. For the life of her, she couldn't remember. And why were they both sleeping on the floor with all their clothes on? Grabbing her purse, she let herself out the door and closed it quietly. She called a cab from the phone booth around the corner from the motel and a few minutes later was speeding home, wondering what in the world had happened the night before, yet dreading the answer!

CHAPTER FIFTEEN

Long before the cab stopped, Bonita was at the curb opening the door for Courtney. For the first time her daughter could ever remember, Bonita Spenser looked every day her sixty-eight years.

"Come on, dear, let me help you in the house."

"I don't need any help, Mom," Courtney returned crossly. "I think you've done quite enough!"

Bonita looked properly chastised as she trailed along behind her daughter meekly. It had been the most miserable night of her life, wondering if in her zeal to seek her daughter's happiness, she had instead foolishly put her in harm's way.

When Courtney entered the house, she paused, her eyes growing stormy as she saw Clyde Merrill sitting on the sofa. By the looks of the empty cups and dark circles under their eyes, both her mother and Clyde had waited up all evening for Courtney to return home. Slamming the front door angrily, she walked on in the room heading for her bedroom.

"Stop right there." Clyde's authoritative voice boomed out strongly in the early-morning stillness.

The no-nonsense tone in his voice gave reason for Courtney's footsteps to falter hesitantly. Not since her father had died had she been spoken to in such a decisive manner.

Clyde rose to his feet, looking to her very much like a

tall, forbidding giant at the moment. "Now you turn around, young lady, and go right back over there and open the door for your mother."

The young woman's eyes stared at him defiantly, debating whether to obey or continue on to her room. His next curt word made the decision for her.

"Now!" The blue eyes that stared back at her were stern but loving.

With the fight suddenly drained out of her, Courtney meekly backed up and opened the door for her mother. Bonita stepped in, casting a worried glance in Clyde's direction.

"Now, before anyone says anything they might regret later, let's all sit down and talk about this calmly. Bonnie, I know you're tired, but would you care to make us a fresh pot of coffee? I think we're going to need it."

"No, of course not, dear." Bonita glanced at Courtney. "Are you hungry? I could fix you something to eat."

Courtney's head still throbbed painfully from all the champagne the night before. She slumped down on the sofa and closed her eyes. "No, Mom. Just coffee, please."

Bonita scurried out of the room as Clyde walked over to the chair facing the sofa and sat down. The only sound that broke the silence in the room was the steady tick of the grandfather clock that sat in the hallway.

Even with her eyes closed Courtney could feel the penetrating gaze of the man who sat opposite her.

"Stop looking at me that way," she grumbled in a cranky tone.

"I'm sorry. I was only wondering if you were all right. Your mother and I have been very worried about you, Courtney."

"Really? How strange. I'd bet my last nickel you knew where I've been and who I've been with."

"Yes," he admitted tiredly, "we knew where you and

Buddy were. But we honestly didn't expect things to turn out this way."

"That's reassuring." Courtney opened her eyes and faced him at last. "It's rather disconcerting to think your own mother and her—"

"The man she's going to marry," he supplied calmly.

"The man's she's going to marry." Courtney paused and looked at him helplessly. "Honest?"

"Honest. We're all through playing games, Courtney. I love your mother and I have reason to believe she loves me." He paused for a moment as a flash of pain crossed the young woman's features. Rising slowly from his chair, he came over to the sofa and knelt down in front of where she sat. "I don't want to hurt you. God knows, that's the last thing in the world I want to happen. I know how hard it is to see another man step in and take the place your father always held in this household, but I won't be trying to take Frank's place, Courtney. All I'm asking is for a chance to make a place of my own with you and your mother. I have no idea how many years I have left," he confessed, "but I'm lucky enough to enjoy good health right now, I have a more than substantial bank account, and I love your mother more than I can express with mere words. I promise, if you'll entrust her to my care for whatever time we both have left, she'll want for nothing."

The hand that reached out in mute appeal for hers had lost all its youth, but none of its strength, and courage. The small hand that took it hesitantly at first, then grasped it eagerly, still had all its youth, but many long years of learning lay ahead. The blue-veined, wrinkled hand grew wet with tears as Courtney buried her face in it and sobbed her repentant acceptance of his most gracious offer. If the last few weeks had taught her anything, it was the fact that apparently there was a love for all seasons, and she was tired of trying to deny it. If Bonita and Clyde could find

269

a deep, abiding love in the December of their lives, then who was she to stand in the way of such happiness?

Clyde withdrew a large snowy-white handkerchief from his pocket and extended it to her. His eyes were misted with tears as she gratefully accepted it.

"I don't know why I'm giving you this. I need it more myself," he said gruffly, dabbing at his eyes guiltily.

Courtney laughed and took the clean tip of the handkerchief and offered it back to him. "Here, we'll share."

"Thank you. That's all I'll ever ask, Courtney." His eyes told her he was talking about more than the sharing of a handkerchief.

Courtney reached over and gently traced the weathered features of his face. "I'll be more than happy to share my life with you. To be honest, I've missed having a dad to talk to. You must understand, Clyde, I've never really objected to you personally. My only concern was that you and Mom were too wild—"

"For our own good? Don't let that worry you. We haven't lived to our ripe old ages without exercising some caution," he dismissed lightly. "The old rocking chair will catch us soon enough."

"I doubt that." She laughed. "I doubt that very seriously!"

"Well, it sounds like things are going all right in here!" Bonita walked in the room with a tray of coffee and sweet rolls, glancing expectantly at her daughter and Clyde.

"Things are fine, Bonnie, just fine." He glanced at Courtney and winked conspiratorially before he stood up and helped Bonita set the silver coffee tray on the table. "I do think we owe Courtney an explanation about last night though, and I've been waiting for you to get back so we can give her one."

"Oh, monkey feathers." Bonita sank down on the sofa uneasily. "I was rather hoping you had already explained all of that to her, dear."

"No way!" Clyde said sheepishly. "After all, you were the brains on this particular caper!"

"Yeah, Mom," Courtney said matter-of-factly, reaching for her coffee, "if you're gonna be a gangster, you're gonna have to learn to take the consequences."

Bonita smiled serenely. "Speaking of gangsters, Clyde, dear, did I ever happen to mention what I found out in my garage the other day?"

"Oh, now, Mom," Courtney interrupted hastily, nearly choking on her coffee. "Clyde doesn't want to hear about the junk in our garage." Graham Merrill was going to have to be the one to tell his father about those stolen motorcycle wheels! She wasn't about to take all the blame!

Her mother's face was solemn now as she handed Clyde his cup of coffee. "Courtney, about last night . . . ."

Courtney's insides fluttered. "Yes?"

"Well, I'm afraid I did a terrible thing. You see, we deliberately made you and Graham think we were eloping."

"We arranged everything so that you and Buddy could have some time alone together," Clyde broke in. "Not that we expected you to spend the *whole* night together."

"I can assure you, it was all perfectly innocent." Courtney winced. "Your son is a perfect gentleman . . . when he wants to be," she added miserably. She crossed her fingers, hoping that she wasn't telling a story. Actually, she had no idea what had taken place last night!

Bonita reached over and touched her daughter's hand affectionately. "If I'm going to be honest with you, I have to tell you that at first, we were trying to get you and Graham together simply to get you off our backs, but somewhere along the line I began to realize what a nice man Graham was and what a perfect couple the two of you would make."

"Mother. Shame on you." Courtney smiled lovingly. "Graham and I are as different as day and night, definitely

271

not each other's type." She grinned wickedly. "Now I'll be honest with you. We have been trying our darnedest to break you and Clyde up!"

The three broke out in relieved laughter. "You think that comes as a surprise to us?" Clyde chuckled.

"Probably not. We haven't been very discreet about it, have we?" Courtney conceded. "All this time, you two have been trying to get us together, and we've been trying to keep you apart!"

"Has it worked?" Bonita's serious voice broke hopefully in on their merriment.

A look of pain replaced Courtney's laughter now. "No, at least I don't think so. Oh, you've done your job well where I'm concerned," she confessed sadly. "I'm very much in love with . . . Buddy." She looked at Clyde knowingly. "But he's been a little slower to make that decision than I have."

Bonita's face mirrored regret. "I'm so sorry."

Courtney stood up and stretched tiredly. "So am I, Mom, but things happen that way sometimes. Life isn't always a barrel of laughs. I'll just keep on truckin' until a certain stubborn man sees things my way." She winked playfully at Clyde. "Buddy can be a real pain in the you-know-where at times."

"I know exactly where." Clyde winked back.

"Mom, I think we should keep the shop closed today. I don't know about you, but I'm going to take the day off. As soon as I take a shower I'm going down to the beach and sun all day." Courtney hoped the sun would help rid her of the splitting headache she had. She leaned down and kissed her mom, then shyly placed a hurried kiss on Clyde's forehead. "See you all later."

"Did you see that?" Clyde exclaimed happily as Courtney left the room. "I think she's beginning to like me!"

"Why, of course she likes you, dear. All the Spenser women are suckers for good-looking dentists," Bonita assured him happily. "I just hope your son realizes that before it's too late."

"Oh, don't worry about Buddy." Clyde stood up and strolled casually over to where she was bending over to clean up the remains of their coffee session. He pinched her affectionately on the fanny. "He may be stubborn, but the boy's no fool!"

Bonita straightened up abruptly, her face flushing a pretty red. "Why, Clyde Merrill, you old fool!"

"Why, Bonnie Spenser! You loved it and you know it!" He captured her in his arms and hugged her tightly. For all who cared to take notice, Clyde Merrill was one happy man.

The sun was beaming down warmly on the deserted stretch of beach as Courtney shook out her blanket and placed it on the sand. Slipping off her terrycloth beach towel, she looked around cautiously to make sure that no one else had discovered her private domain. The black, two-piece string bikini she had chosen to wear was extremely skimpy and she had no desire to encounter anyone. She lay down on the blanket and closed her eyes contentedly. The hot sun beat down on her aching body as she lay dozing peacefully, willing her mind away from the handsome young dentist who had stolen her heart. She wondered fleetingly if they had made love again last night and berated herself for being such an idiot with the champagne and missing out on the pleasure of remembrance if that had occurred! Quickly she forced her mind away from last night and back to the present. She and her mother spent many hours there on that remote part of the beach on weekends; they would bring a picnic lunch and get away from the crowds for the day.

For over an hour she lay daydreaming, soaking up the warm rays of the sun. The pain in her head had lessened somewhat as she drifted off to a peaceful slumber.

273

The feel of sand being trickled slowly down her stomach caused her to open her eyes slowly.

"Hi. You know why an elephant has red eyes?" a deep, masculine voice asked.

Courtney turned weak at the sound of his voice. She smiled, then asked softly, "Why?"

"So they can hide in cherry trees."

"That's ridiculous, they don't have red eyes and they certainly couldn't climb a cherry tree," she scoffed. She had always hated those corny elephant jokes.

"You ever see one hiding in a cherry tree?" he asked indignantly.

"Well, no . . ."

"Then it works, doesn't it?" Graham leaned over and kissed her a warm and sexy hello.

When they parted, her heart was beating so loudly she was sure he could hear it. "How did you know I was here?"

"Your mom told me. When I woke up and found you gone this morning, I went home and cleaned up, then came by your house." He kissed her again lingeringly. "Why didn't you wake me up this morning before you left?"

"I think I was too embarrassed," she admitted, her breath catching slightly as she realized he was wearing tight shorts and a casual open-neck shirt which he hurriedly pulled over his head. He sank down next to her on the blanket and pulled her into his arms. The feel of his bare skin next to hers sent shivers of delight racing up her spine.

"Did I make a total fool out of myself last night?" she murmured in a small voice.

"Yes, I'm afraid you did," he murmured honestly, his mouth toying with hers in a tantalizing fashion.

"You don't have to be so honest."

"Why not? I strive to be an honest gent," he defended.

"Was Clyde still over at Mom's when you went by?"

"Yeah." He propped himself up on his elbow and traced her nose playfully. "I hear you're going to be my new sister."

Courtney's faced paled. "Oh, gad! I hadn't even thought about that!"

Graham's grin was contagious. "A real bummer, huh? Well, no problem." He sighed, reaching behind her neck and undoing the strap on her bikini. "I think I have a solution that will cancel that relationship out."

"What do you think you're doing?" she asked curtly.

"I've come to seduce you, my dear, sweet Miss Spenser." The top fell away and his blue eyes darkened with passion. "By the way, I like this bathing suit, what there is of it." His gaze scanned her bare, feminine curves lazily. "Someday when we're not getting ready to do more important things, I want you to model it for me, then we're going to burn the damn thing because I don't want anyone else seeing you in it." He leaned down and kissed the tip of each breast seductively. Flames of desire ignited swiftly between them as he rolled her over and untied the bottoms of her bikini.

"Are you crazy? What has gotten into you?" she protested weakly as he slipped the black material off her and discarded his shorts at the same time.

Leaning back, he looked at her hungrily in the broad daylight, his face growing tender. "I told you, I've come to purposely, very deliberately, premeditatedly make love to you. This time it won't be by accident, nor on the spur of the moment," he warned softly. "This time it's been planned right down to the last detail."

Courtney's smile was smug as her fingers wrapped lovingly in the thickness of his dark-blond hair. "You mean for once you won't have to sweat out a month of waiting to see if your rash actions would get you in hot water?"

"Nope, not this time." His blue gaze met hers lovingly.

"Not that I don't intend to get you pregnant quite a few times in the coming years, but for right now I want to have the next few months just getting to know and understand my wife. Do you mind?"

Courtney looked at him in puzzlement. "Are you trying to tell me something, Dr. Merrill?"

"Yeah, I'm trying, but it's a little difficult." He slid on top of her and hugged her nude body up close to his. The feel of his hair-roughened chest against the bareness of her soft skin was delightful to the both of them. Another round of long, fiery kisses were exchanged before he was able to speak again. "I've promised myself that before I make love to you again, there is going to be a very real and binding commitment between us. I know that you've felt over the last few weeks that I didn't love you, or desire you . . . not the way you thought I should. You'll never know what agony you've put me through, Miss Spenser, and I hope you're prepared to make up for all the time we've lost," he said huskily, kissing her again impatiently.

"That was not necessarily my fault," she pointed out, running her hand down the length of his muscular body.

"I know, but it was something I felt we should do, Courtney. We're dealing with a lifetime commitment here and I didn't want any mixups in our feelings. If I had taken you to bed every time I wanted to, I would have never done any serious thinking. I'll be the first to admit, you're the only woman I've ever felt that protective of, but I wanted to be sure that what we had was a very real and lasting thing, not just a physical affair."

"And what have you decided?" she asked, love shining brightly in her eyes now.

"I've decided it's very real, very lasting, and very wonderful." Graham's tender gaze told her the words he spoke were from the heart. "I knew I was hopelessly in love when I could spend the night with an old maid, drinking champagne straight out of the bottle and listening to the corniest elephant jokes I have ever heard in my entire life, then waking up the next morning and wanting to hear more as long as she was the one telling them."

"Me tell elephant jokes!"

"Yes, and I don't mind telling you, they stunk!"

"Oh, gosh, what else did I do, Graham? Did we . . . ?"

"No, we didn't. I told you, I have a question to ask before we do that again."

Courtney ran her hand suggestively through the thick mat of hair on his broad chest, letting her finger trail playfully lower each time. "Then get on with it, Dr. Merrill. I can't wait to give you my yes answer."

He moaned softly as their mouths met hungrily and her hands roved exploringly over his naked skin. She could feel his ever-growing need pressing intimately into her side and she thought she would burst with happiness.

Graham's breathing was ragged as he broke apart from her and cupped her face protectively in his hands. "I want you to . . . I think we could be . . . don't you think it's time we got . . ."

"Graham. Are you having a hard time asking your question?" Courtney asked.

Graham grinned boyishly. "A little. The words I'm trying to say have never been in my vocabulary. In fact, I may have to have you help me."

Courtney reached up and cupped his mouth with her fingers. "Now look. Repeat after me: *Will you marry me, Courtney?*"

"*Will you* . . . M-A-R-R-Y"—he made a strangled sound—"*me, Miss Spenser?*"

Courtney's smile was radiant. "Now, see? That wasn't hard, was it? You didn't say it right, but it wasn't that hard."

"No, not at all," he said in a relieved voice.

"Now, say it right," she demanded softly.

"Will you marry me, Miss Courtney Spenser?" he said easily.

"I surely will, Dr. Graham Merrill."

"Good. As soon as we make love, we'll discuss all the gruesome details." He grabbed her to him and rolled happily on the warm sand with her, then moved away to fulfill his promise of protecting her as he found what he needed in the pocket of his shorts. He came back to her and took her in his arms again. Their playfulness evaporated quickly as they came together in the glorious act of love. This time was different from the times before. There was something to say for the word commitment, Courtney thought fleetingly as Graham once more became one with her and they soared together in joyful ecstasy. And it was all good! The exhilaration of being in love and someone returning that love was an event well worth waiting for.

Graham's hands explored the gentle curves of the woman he loved, murmuring words of intimacy, as they poured out their love for each other with words and fevered caresses.

"I love you, my beautiful, adorable Miss Spenser," he whispered as their bodies sought and at last found sweet release together.

When the tides of rapture had subsided, they lay locked in each other's arms, letting the rest of the world drift lazily by. The sound of the ocean lapped gently against the sandy beach as they exchanged long, languorous kisses.

Another hour passed before Graham looked at his watch and groaned. "Do you know what time it is?"

"No." Courtney pulled him back in her arms, not caring in the least. "Does it matter?"

"The gypsies will think we've gotten lost. I was supposed to come down here, get you, and be back in a hour."

"What's the rush?" she protested.

"Would you believe it if I told you we were getting married tonight?"

"What?" Courtney sat up and brushed the sand off her arms.

"We're eloping with Bonnie and Clyde. Isn't that exciting?" He grinned and flipped her bathing suit at her.

"You're not serious." She looked at him suspiciously.

"I'm always serious. It won't take you long to find that out." He leaned over and pushed her down on the blanket and kissed her soundly once more. "If you want a big wedding, we'll have one later. But, right now, I want to be sure that you're all mine. I want to marry you today, now, in the next fifteen minutes if possible."

"Are you trying to tell me I'm doomed to a lifetime of seeing my dentist regularly?" she teased, kissing him back zealously.

"Very regularly," he confirmed, returning her kisses.

"Graham. Are you saying you don't mind if Mom and your dad get married?"

"No, I don't mind." He lay back and gazed contentedly up into the blue sky, dotted with fleecy white clouds. "I don't think I've minded for a long time, to be honest. Those two gypsies are really in love with each other, and who am I to argue with love?" He rolled back over and touched her face reverently. "I want the whole world to know the joy of love, just as I do at this moment."

"You know for a man who's fought so hard to avoid the altar, you don't seem the least bit upset about losing the fight," she said in a puzzled voice.

"Hey, I'm going to let you in on a little secret. I have known all along that you were going to show up one of these days and I would fall head over heels in love." He smiled sheepishly. "I was only having as much fun as I could before you got here."

"You knew I was going to show up?"

"Not you in particular. Never would I have guessed I'd be stuck with an old maid," he teased, "but I knew someone was going to knock me off my feet someday."

279

"Maybe I better reconsider my hasty acceptance of your marriage proposal." She pouted. "It doesn't sound too flattering to know you've been sitting around all these years dreading my arrival."

"I wasn't dreading it, in fact I thought you took your own sweet time getting here!" He kissed her possessively. "If you marry me, I'll keep you supplied with all the cute little bottles of beer, pickleloaf lunchmeat, and champagne you can eat and drink for the rest of your life," he tempted with a devilish twinkle in his eye.

Courtney closed her eyes and whispered sickly, "How could a girl refuse a proposal like that?"

"It would be foolish to try," he agreed, pulling her down on the blanket once more, his hand stroking her stomach suggestively. "It may have taken you long enough to get here, but I plan on keeping you for a lifetime now that you finally made it."

They dressed quickly and walked back to their cars arm in arm. The sun was just beginning to sink slowly in a large, round, orange ball in the western sky. To Miss Courtney Spenser and Dr. Graham Merrill, the world seemed a much better place today, because four people had finally come into their very own special season of love.

"Mother! I refuse to go through with this! The very idea! Why, this is sheer craziness! I simply refuse to go along with this madness!" Courtney tried to put her foot down, but Bonita dragged her out the front door and locked it securely. Waving happily at Clyde and Graham, she pulled Courtney along down the walk.

"Don't be cranky, dear." She paused and looked at her daughter suspiciously. "Are you getting enough bulk in your diet lately?"

"Mother! Good grief!" She looked quickly toward Graham to see if he had overheard her mother's crass question. What a time to ask something like that!

"Don't get upset, it was just a thought. Now, concerning our plans, what's more important? The way you get married or the marriage itself?"

"But, Mother . . ."

"No buts. You love Graham, don't you?"

Courtney's gaze fell lovingly on the man waiting patiently at the curb. "Of course I do."

"Then stop being a pest and just enjoy yourself. This is going to be a blast." Bonita scurried on ahead of her daughter and joined the elderly man standing next to Graham.

Courtney shuffled slowly down the walk, still not convinced this was the proper way to be doing things.

Graham was leaning against his cycle, his arms crossed,

affectionately watching her walk toward him. He grinned as she stopped before his cycle and he handed her a helmet. "Hi!"

"Hi," she returned glumly.

"What were you and your mom talking about?"

"About . . . this nonsense." She looked at him painfully. "Honestly, Graham. Do we have to elope on the motorcycles?"

"No. We don't have to," he said patiently. "It would make the gypsies awfully happy if we would though." He reached over and pulled her toward him. Tipping her face up, he kissed her tenderly. "I'll marry you any way you say, honey. Just so I marry you tonight."

The roar of Clyde's cycle shattered the stillness as Graham and Courtney stood kissing in the early twilight.

"Come on, you two!" Bonita shouted, hopping on behind Clyde. "We have plenty of time for that stuff later on, but right now we're going to ride like the wind!"

Graham pulled away reluctantly and looked down at her seriously. "It's your decision."

Courtney glanced over at the expectant, happy looks on the faces of Bonita and Clyde and weakened. "Oh, all right!" She plopped her helmet on her head and surveyed the cycle sitting in front of her in disgust. "Never in my wildest dreams would I have thought I would be eloping on a motorcycle!" She straddled the seat behind Graham petulantly. "Now you promise you won't drive fast and you won't dart in and out of traffic like a mad man and you'll take the corners slow. . . ."

"Yeah, yeah, I will," Graham agreed, kicking the cycle into action. He absently revved the engine a couple of times, and Courtney knew full well he wasn't paying the least bit of attention to her instructions. He reached up and tightened the strap on his helmet, then put her hand intimately between his legs.

She jerked back instantly, shooting a cautious glance

over to see if her mother had noticed his action. "What do you think you're doing?" she hissed.

"Well, I figure that's where your hands are going to end up anyway. I believe the last time you rode with me I had to take a baseball bat to protect myself!"

He let out a loud whoop as she punched him in the back. "Cad!"

"Hey, that reminds me." He turned and motioned for her to lean closer. "Now that I'm going to be your husband by the end of the evening, I want a straight answer out of you, lady." His blue eyes looked sternly at her.

"Concerning what?" she asked innocently. She knew exactly "what" but she was hoping she was wrong and he had something else on his mind.

"Don't play coy with me. You know what," he insisted. "*How* experienced were you before we met?"

Courtney heaved a long, put-upon sigh. "You said it didn't matter."

"It doesn't. But I'll admit my damn curiosity is driving me up a wall." His face turned boyishly pleading. "Come on, Courtney, tell me the truth!"

Courtney glanced around uncomfortably, then motioned for him to take off his helmet so she could whisper in his ear. The helmet came off swiftly and he leaned his blond head in closer to hers expectantly, trying to hear above the roar of the cycle.

His face held no emotion whatsoever as she whispered something in his ear, then primly tightened the strap of her helmet.

He looked at her blankly, then shoved his hands on his hips irritably. "What kind of a stupid answer is that?"

"The truth! That's what you wanted, wasn't it?"

"Well, it doesn't make any sense," he protested, slapping his helmet back on his head and revving the cycle up again. "That's like saying you were on your way to a picnic and had a flat tire!"

"Are you going to sit here and grumble all day, or are we going to get married? If you don't think I have enough experience to suit your personal tastes, then I'm confident you'll have me a real pro before the week's over," she teased, giving him an intimate pinch.

"Ouch! Watch it, Miss Spenser," he warned, reaching back to pinch her bottom in retaliation. "We may have to start those lessons sooner than you expected."

With a wicked grin, he popped the clutch and squealed away from the curb in a cloud of smoke, following the cycle that had pulled out in front of them moments earlier with a sign flapping wildly in the air reading "Just Married, Tampa or Bust!"

COMING IN AUGUST 1993
HISTORICAL ROMANCE
WILD SUMMER ROSE
Amy Elizabeth Saunders

Torn from her carefree rustic life to become a proper city lady, Victoria Larkin bristles at the hypocrisy of the arrogant French aristocrat who wants to seduce her. But Phillipe St. Sebastian is determined to have her at any cost—even the loss of his beloved ancestral home. And as the flames of revolution threaten their very lives, Victoria and Phillipe find strength in the healing power of love.

_0-505-51902-X $4.99 US/$5.99 CAN

CONTEMPORARY ROMANCE
TWO OF A KIND
Lori Copeland
Bestselling Author of *Promise Me Today*

When her lively widowed mother starts chasing around town with seventy-year-old motorcycle enthusiast Clyde Merrill, Courtney Spenser is confronted by Clyde's angry son. Sensual and overbearing, Graham Merrill quickly gets under Courtney's skin—and she's not at all displeased.

_0-505-51903-8 $3.99 US/$4.99 CAN

COMING IN SEPTEMBER 1993
TIMESWEPT ROMANCE
TIME REMEMBERED
Elizabeth Crane
Bestselling Author of *Reflections in Time*

A voodoo doll and an ancient spell whisk thoroughly modern Jody Farnell from a decaying antebellum mansion to the Old South and a true Southern gentleman who shows her the magic of love.

_0-505-51904-6 $4.99 US/$5.99 CAN

FUTURISTIC ROMANCE
A DISTANT STAR
Anne Avery

Jerrel is enchanted by the courageous messenger who saves his life. But he cannot permit anyone to turn him from the mission that has brought him to the distant world—not even the proud and passionate woman who offers him a love capable of bridging the stars.

_0-505-51905-4 $4.99 US/$5.99 CAN

COMING IN SEPTEMBER 1993
HISTORICAL ROMANCE
TEMPTATION
Jane Harrison

He broke her heart once before, but Shadoe Sinclair is a temptation that Lilly McFall cannot deny. And when he saunters back into the frontier town he left years earlier, Lilly will do whatever it takes to make the handsome rogue her own.

__0-505-51906-2   .$4.99 US/$5.99 CAN

CONTEMPORARY ROMANCE
WHIRLWIND COURTSHIP
Jayne Ann Krentz writing as Jayne Taylor
Bestselling Author of *Family Man*

When Phoebe Hampton arrives by accident on Harlan Garand's doorstep, he's convinced she's another marriage-minded female sent by his matchmaking aunt. But a sudden snowstorm traps them together for a few days and shows Harlan there's a lot more to Phoebe than meets the eye.

__0-505-51907-0 $3.99 US/$4.99 CAN

LEISURE BOOKS
ATTN: Order Department
276 5th Avenue, New York, NY 10001

Please add $1.50 for shipping and handling for the first book and $.35 for each book thereafter. PA., N.Y.S. and N.Y.C. residents, please add appropriate sales tax. No cash, stamps, or C.O.D.s. All orders shipped within 6 weeks via postal service book rate. Canadian orders require $2.00 extra postage and must be paid in U.S. dollars through a U.S. banking facility.

Name _____

Address _____

City _____ State _____ Zip _____

I have enclosed $_____in payment for the checked book(s).

Payment <u>must</u> accompany all orders.☐ Please send a free catalog.